CHAPTER ONE

There's nothing like a dead body for adding weight to a wardrobe. It wasn't in the wardrobe when I bought it, of course. There was nothing in it then but a lonely wire coat hanger and a faint smell of mothballs. I didn't want to buy the thing in the first place, but the crafty old bugger wouldn't sell me what I really wanted unless I took the wardrobe too.

I'd only met Fred Crick the day before I bought it. I'd been in Ashburton minding my own business, walking past *Keepsakes* antique shop. I had slowed down for a sneaky look in the boxes of junk arranged on the pavement outside when Ron and Sheila spotted me and beckoned me in. I had to remember to stoop slightly as I entered. I'm tall, the ceiling is low and made even lower by all the paraphernalia hanging from the beams. Glass fishing floats hang in clusters like giant Christmas tree baubles, I've tangled my hair in chandelier drops before now and I'd nearly brained myself on a copper preserving pan the last time I'd come in. Entering *Keepsakes* at all had become a hazardous experience. The sheer quantity of clutter makes it dim inside the shop, and at first it wasn't easy to distinguish Fred from the dark mahogany and dusty velvets surrounding him. He was standing by the counter looking like an antique himself in his flat cap and old corduroy suit, a mug of tea in hand. He wanted to get rid of some old furniture, Ron and Sheila told me as they introduced us. They knew I was always hunting for stock.

'This is the young lady who's taken over Old Nick's place,' Sheila told him as I shook his hand. His fingers were yellowed with nicotine and his breath was smoky.

'Juno Browne,' I said. 'Hello.'

He nodded, surveying me with narrowed eyes. 'I heard Old Nick had got himself murdered.' He cleared his throat, his voice roughened by fags. 'Left you his place in his will, I heard.'

'You heard correctly,' I told him.

He grinned, showing dingy teeth. 'Bit of luck for you, wasn't it?'

I didn't like the tone of his voice or what he implied. 'No, actually it was revenge.'

Sheila laughed uncertainly. 'You mean it was revenge against his family,' she asked me, 'Nick not leaving his shop to them?'

'No,' I answered, 'revenge against me.' I'd decided this after I'd managed to pay off the last lot of business rates. During the months I'd worked for Nick I must have upset

6

For my sister Rosie

Allison & busby Limited
11 Wardour Mews
London W1F 8AN
allisonandbusby.com

First published in Great Britain by Allison & Busby in 2021.
This paperback edition published by Allison & Busby in 2021.

A CIP catalogue record for this book is available from
the British Library.

10 9 8 7 6 5 4 3 2 1

ISBN 978-0-7490-2701-8

Typeset in 11/16 pt Sabon LT Pro by
Allison & Busby Ltd.

FSC
www.fsc.org
MIX
Paper from
responsible sources
FSC® C020471

The paper used for this Allison & Busby publication
has been produced from trees that have been legally sourced
from well-managed and credibly certified forests.

Printed and bound by
CPI Group (UK) Ltd, Croydon, CR0 4YY

him and he'd lumbered me with his antique shop to teach me a lesson. Anyway, I needed some furniture to fill up empty space and it sounded as though Fred was selling cheap. He just wanted to get rid of the stuff, he assured me, clear it out. It had been taking up room in his shed for too long. He wasn't asking much for it. So, after taking his address and getting directions to his cottage, I promised I'd drive up and look the stuff over next day.

It would be my first proper foray after stock for some time. A few months before, I'd been involved in an incident that left me with a fractured skull, a broken ankle and cracked ribs. Ironically, the most serious of my injuries, the depressed fracture of the skull, was the one which had given me the fewest problems since. Once the headaches had settled down my head was fine, the thin scar on my scalp increasingly hidden by the mad tangle of my hair. But I'd been on crutches for weeks and forced to stay with my old friends, Ricky and Morris until I could manage to walk unassisted. I'd lived downstairs in their guest bedroom, all the rooms upstairs filled with rails of costumes they hire out to theatrical companies. I'd had to attend a christening in April with one leg protected by a big Kevlar boot, which rather ruined the effect of the chic Chanel dress I'd borrowed from their stock.

Now I was safely back in my own flat, and except for my ankle aching whenever I changed gear, I was fine. It was a relief to be back in my own space, even if it meant swapping Morris's cooking for mine and the Georgian gorgeousness of Druid Lodge for a flat with a mouldy kitchen wall and dodgy boiler.

And it was a relief to be out and about again, returning to my work as a domestic goddess – dog walking, gardening, caring and cleaning for my various clients round about, the business I'd been engaged in before I'd inherited *Old Nick's*. At least my enforced stay indoors had allowed me to take stock in the shop, catch up on some polishing and read some books on antiques, a subject about which I am still deplorably ignorant. I'm studying silver hallmarks at the moment, trying to educate myself on one thing at least.

So, despite the fact I had found him vaguely obnoxious, I looked forward to my trip up to Fred's place. It wasn't far to drive, White Van trundling up the hill out of Ashburton, past Buckland and over the moor towards Widecombe. It was a pretty run with spring just turning to summer, the hedgerows frothing up with the creamy yellow heads of alexanders and here and there a touch of white may blossom. I'd missed the primroses of spring, hobbling about indoors.

According to Ron and Sheila, Fred had made a pile of money selling off his old farm, except for the worker's cottage where he now lived. I found his old place, Cold East Farm, easily enough, the farmhouse set back from the road, separated by a garden and an orchard. The current owners had invested in a new thatch. It flowed like a gold coverlet over the stone building, the edges of the newly-cut reed sharp and crisp. There was a digger hard at work as I drove past; some sort of conversion work going on in the barn. By the roadside, a freshly-painted sign advertised eggs and honey for sale. There was a sense of optimism about the place, of new replacing old, of moving forward.

The same couldn't be said of Fred's cottage a quarter of a mile further on. Here the sagging thatch was turning black with rot, heavy with moss, and urgently in need of replacement. But Fred was a skinflint, Ron and Sheila warned me, and wouldn't spend any money. *Make sure he doesn't charge you too much for that old furniture*, they said. *Don't worry*, I'd told them, *I won't. For one thing, I haven't much to spend.*

I would have loved a poke about inside that cottage, but a squint through the foggy glass of a tiny window whilst waiting for Fred to respond to my knock on his door showed me nothing more than a deep and cobwebby window sill, and was as close as I got. From his doorstep I could look down the valley towards Widecombe-in-the-Moor, the fields a quilt of different greens stitched together with dark lines of hedgerow.

Fred emerged suddenly, greeting me with a nod, a skinny roll-up pressed firmly between his lips, and pulled the door sharply behind him. I could smell whisky on his breath. 'Furniture's over here.' He gestured towards a ramshackle shed and led the way. 'Just a few bits I brought with me from the farm, but I haven't got the room for 'em.' I followed him through an overgrown garden that, like the thatch, was screaming for attention, invading brambles ramping over tumbled stone walls, wandering chickens picking their way through the long weeds. 'Your new neighbours seem to be busy,' I ventured, 'lovely new thatch.'

It seemed Fred did not approve of the people who'd bought his farm. 'Call themselves farmers? Bloody toy farmers, that's all they are, them with their fancy breeds of sheep. What's wrong with an honest Dartmoor Whiteface?' he demanded. 'They're gonna do cream teas,' he sneered 'and they're converting that stone barn into holiday cottages for bloody tourists.'

'Lots of farms around here offer holiday accommodation,' I pointed out. 'It helps pay the bills.'

Fred snorted. 'Ain't proper farming, though, is it?'

The light inside the shed was dim, sunlight falling in ragged slices through gaps in the wooden walls. It was cluttered with rusted lumps of farm machinery whose purpose I couldn't identify. There were old tools hanging from the rafters, a few vegetable crates piled in the corner, and some hulking shapes hidden beneath mouldy-smelling tarpaulins scattered with bird droppings.

'Here we are!' Fred threw back a tarpaulin with all the flourish of a magician performing his greatest trick and I coughed, trying not to inhale too much of the dusty cloud flicked up from its surface. Revealed was an ugly dark wardrobe with a speckled mirror set in its door and an old chaise longue with a lump of horsehair stuffing poking through its cracked leather seating. There were several wooden fruit boxes filled with items wrapped in newspaper, a brass warming pan and a writing table.

To be exact, it was an eighteenth-century writing table in

golden walnut, its slender legs tapering to carved ball-and-claw feet, the drawer in its bow front hung with delicate drop handles. I ran a hand over the walnut veneer. The surface should have been glossy, but this was clouded and buckled, the edges of the veneer lifting, almost certainly the result of damp. A table like this shouldn't be kept in a shed, protected by nothing but an old cloth. It would take skilful restoration to bring it back to the way it should look. I slid open the drawer, which jammed halfway. I had to wiggle it gently to get it out. I turned it over. The dovetail joints were hand-cut, suggesting an early date; later they would have been cut by machine. I looked up; Fred was watching me closely. Even in the dimness I caught the gleam in his eye. I'd shown too much interest. Genuine or not, the price of this writing table had just gone up.

I replaced the drawer and looked around me as if I was expecting something more. 'Is this all of it?' I asked, with an attempt at indifference. I pointed to the wooden fruit boxes. 'What's in those?'

He shrugged. 'Take a look.'

I unwrapped damp-smelling newspaper to find a pair of ugly vases and various mismatched components of brass oil lamps, some with their glass funnels intact, all of them missing their decorative shades. There were also some stone cider jars and old flat irons, the sort of things that make useful doorstops or look good sitting by the range of a modern country kitchen. 'So, how much for what's in the boxes and that brass warming pan?' I asked. I didn't mention the writing table; I'd get round to that.

'I'm not interested in the chaise longue or the wardrobe.'

Fred gave a ferrety grin. 'You take it all or you don't get none of it.'

I pointed to the chaise with its stuffing hanging out. 'I don't want that. It needs to be completely reupholstered. It would cost me a fortune.'

Fred scratched slyly beneath his flat cap. 'Look good when it's done up, though, won't it? Some posh second-homer will snap that up.'

'Maybe,' I conceded. I nodded at the wardrobe. 'That thing's just damn ugly.' As I took a step towards it, the door creaked open, revealing its dark and smelly interior. I tried to shut it again. There was no key in the tiny lock; that was probably lost years ago. As I stepped back the door yawned wide for a second time. 'It doesn't shut.'

'It's only cos the floor in here is uneven.'

'I don't want it.'

'But you want that little table, don't you?' he said. 'My wife used to use it for a dressing table.' Suddenly it had become an item of sentimental value. 'She used to stand a mirror on it.'

'Have you still got the mirror?' I asked.

'It got smashed.' He ran his yellowed fingers pensively over the patchy stubble on his chin. 'Tell you what, you give me a good price for that table, I'll throw in the sofa and wardrobe for free.'

'I don't want the wardrobe,' I protested, 'or the chaise. If you don't want them, why don't you take them outside and burn them?'

I'd obviously shocked him. He exploded in a long, drawn-out coughing fit, the phlegm rattling in his throat. I was getting ready to slap him on the back, but he got control of himself after some truly horrible hawking noises, as if he was bringing up a fur ball.

My eyes strayed back to the little writing table. 'How much?'

If there's one thing I really don't like about the antiques trade, it's the haggling. A fair price is a fair price. I may be short of money, but I find wrangling over every last penny embarrassing. Fred obviously loved it. He named an extortionate price. It took fifteen minutes to settle on a figure I could reasonably afford. In the end we struck a bargain that included my taking all the stuff away. The little writing desk was small enough to fit in White Van. I could have taken it with me, but Fred wasn't having that. I could only pick it up when I collected the chaise longue and wardrobe, he insisted, otherwise I might not come back for them at all.

'All right,' I agreed unhappily, 'but I can't do it today.' To shift all that lot, I'd have to hire a lorry.

He shrugged. 'The stuff's not going anywhere. You pick it up when you want. Don't matter if I'm here or not.'

Before I handed over my money, I demanded a written receipt.

He'd grinned. 'Don't you trust me?'

'No,' I told him frankly.

I then had a ten-minute wait while a grumpy Fred disappeared into his cottage to hunt for pen and paper.

He didn't invite me in. Eventually he emerged with a smoothed-out piece of kitchen roll on which he scrawled the items I was buying in black carpenter's pencil. He couldn't find a pen, apparently. He apologised for the brown stain on the paper, which he assured me was only pickle. I held out my hand for it, but Fred held it back, staring at me appraisingly.

'So why did Old Nick leave you his place, then?' he asked. 'Young creature like you?'

I shrugged. 'I wish I knew.'

He gave a jaundiced leer. 'You turned his head, I reckon – all that red hair.' He ran his eyes over me in a way that made my skin crawl. 'You're like one of them Viking women off the telly – enough to do for any bloke.'

I made no response to this, other than to wonder what on earth he'd been watching. I just eyed him balefully and held out my hand for the pickle-stained receipt. He chuckled and let me have it.

I trundled down the hill in my little white van, the boxes of small items rattling in the back. Actually, we hadn't struck a bad bargain. I just hoped I hadn't made a mistake about that writing table.

On the way back I stopped at Cold East Farm. I was not so much lured by the prospect of free-range eggs and honey as a nosy desire for a look around, but I bought some anyway.

I ignored the honesty box nailed to the fence and walked up the little track towards the farmhouse. The front door was open, and I knocked, calling out a hello.

14

A little blonde angel of about two years old scampered to the door, took one look at me and turned back whimpering, colliding with a young woman with cropped fair hair who scooped her up in her arms. 'Amy's very shy,' she explained as the little girl hid her face. She smiled at my request for change and invited me into the cheerful chaos of her kitchen for a cup of tea. Her name was Carol, she'd told me, and she'd bought the farm along with her husband a year ago.

'I saw your van go up the hill earlier,' she said. 'Have you been to see Fred?'

I told her about my purchases and she laughed. 'He's a weird old chap. He sold us the farm last year, but he doesn't really want to let it go.'

'I gathered that. I don't think he approves of change.'

She rolled her eyes. 'He doesn't approve of anything we're doing. But we've only just started.' She pointed towards the barn. 'Four self-catering cottages we're creating there, and we're building a toilet block and laundry out in the paddock for campers. You've got to diversify these days if you're going to survive.'

'You're after the holiday trade, then,' I said.

Carol nodded enthusiastically. 'I'm planning on cream teas in the garden later in the year. We'll still be farming, of course. We've got a flock of a hundred and fifty Devon Longwools.' She smiled down at her little girl. 'Amy and I were just going out to see them. Would you like to come?'

We trudged over the fields, little Amy toddling on in front, Carol in her wellies lugging a bucket containing

15

some kind of sheep nibble.

'Fred spies on us from that rock up there.'

I looked up the long sweep of grass. Set on top of the hill was a bulky outcrop of granite. This was not a named tor as far as I knew, just a big rock, rising about fifteen feet from the ground, its scarred sides cleft with seams and ridges, dark bushes of gorse and elder clustering at its foot. The top was flat like a table, an easy standing place.

'He sits up there for hours,' Carol went on. 'We've seen him watching the building work through his binoculars.' She laughed, mystified. 'I don't understand why he doesn't just come down here, ask what we're up to, pop in for a chat and a cup of tea.'

Somehow Fred didn't strike me as the popping-in sort.

At the sight of Carol's bucket, a group of stocky little ewes eagerly crowded up to the gate. I don't know how they could see her, long ringlets of wool covering their eyes, but they were pretty creatures. They were bred for both their meat and their wool, Carol informed me proudly as she dished out the treats.

On our way back we had to stop in the orchard so I could admire Amy's rabbit and feed him dandelions. The blossoms of the apple trees had been scattered by the wind and petals lay like snowflakes in the grass. 'We're hoping to press our first lot of apple juice this autumn,' Carol told me. 'You must come up and try it.'

'It's a date,' I promised.

As I turned to get back in the van, I was sure I caught

a flicker of movement on the rock up on the hill, the sun glinting on a pair of field glasses. Fred, it seemed, was still watching.

Strictly speaking, *Old Nick's* isn't just an antique shop. When I decided to try and make a go of the place, I divided it up into several units in the hope of attracting other traders who would pay me rent; an optimistic plan, which hadn't worked out so far. Only two units are occupied: one by my artist friend Sophie, who uses her part of the shop as a studio, and the other by Pat, who makes craft items to raise money for the animal sanctuary she runs with her sister and brother-in-law. They both struggle for money and I don't take rent from either of them. In return, most days, they man the shop.

My part of *Old Nick's*, the antiques bit, is in what used to be a storeroom at the back, where as well as my own quaint assortment of second-hand wares, I sell vintage clothes on commission for Ricky and Morris, who are always intending to retire from their theatrical costume hire business but never manage to get that far.

When I arrived back in the shop later that afternoon, I stood in the storeroom considering where I could put that wretched wardrobe. It wouldn't look too bad standing in the corner, I decided. It would fill up some empty space, and if nothing else I could hang some of the vintage clothes in it. As for the chaise longue, I could fling some sort of cover over it until I could afford to get it reupholstered. And whether or not either item was saleable, they would fit in with the general air of a shabby but genteel brothel created by Ricky and Morris, who had filled the room with dressing screens, mirrors, rails hung with silk underwear, net petticoats, frills, beads and feather boas.

My eye lighted on the glass display cabinet where I keep a few precious antique objects under lock and key: jewellery and hatpins, diamante dress clips, a few scent bottles, a snuff box, a silver pincushion shaped like a pig. I love these tiny things and bygones that no one uses any more, like match holders and glove stretchers, page turners, candle snuffers and vinaigrettes. The little treasures in my cabinet may not be top quality but they are the most precious things I have to sell.

Unless, of course, I was right about that writing table: which brought me back to the problem of how I was going to get it home to Ashburton. I phoned Tom Smithson, who runs an antiques business near Exeter and owns a van large enough for transporting the chaise and the wardrobe. He's a kind-hearted old chap and as soon as I told him my problem, he offered to help me out.

'I've got to deliver a sideboard to a house in Broadhempston, as it turns out,' he told me cheerily. 'I can easily pop along to Ashburton, drive us up to Fred's place and collect your stuff. In fact, Vicky will probably come along for the ride. We haven't seen you for ages. How's the ankle?'

'All better now,' I lied as I rested my socked foot on my coffee table and waited for the painkillers to kick in, and we agreed to do the job on Sunday when I wouldn't have any clients to worry about. I promised them tea when we got the stuff back to the shop.

The phone rang almost as soon as I replaced the receiver. Ricky and Morris were still checking up on me every day.

'Hello, princess!' Ricky's voice sounded raucously in my ear. 'How's it going?'

I told him about my visit to Fred Crick's, my own voice echoing because he'd put the phone on loudspeaker so that Morris could hear the conversation.

'Do you want us to come along?' he offered when I outlined the plan for Sunday, 'give a hand with loading?'

'You mustn't try and lift heavy things,' Morris called anxiously from somewhere in the background.

'I'm sure we'll manage. Tom's got a sack truck. I don't think the things are too heavy and Fred might even lend us a hand if he's around.'

'Tell you what,' Ricky said. 'We'll pop down to the shop and help with the unloading when you get back this end.'

No amount of arguing would persuade them that their help wasn't needed. They hate to miss out on whatever's going on.

'We'll get the kettle on for when you arrive,' he promised.

'And we'll bring cake,' Morris shouted.

Well, that settled the matter: cake. No further argument required.

CHAPTER TWO

My alleged admirer, Mr Daniel Thorncroft, did not ring me that evening. He hadn't phoned me for two weeks. And my pride won't let me phone him. This is the man who, after a brief but eventful stay in Ashburton, swore he wanted to get to know me better and then buggered off to work in the Scottish Highlands for six months. He is passionate about his work and also inclined to be absent-minded so it's not impossible that he has forgotten about me altogether.

I've only seen him once since the incident. He travelled by train to Bristol for a weekend conference and hired a car to drive down to Ashburton to see how I was. It was very sweet of him because he could only stay an hour before he had to drive back again. I was still convalescing with Ricky and Morris then, hobbling around on my crutches. It wasn't a good day for me; I was suffering from a blinding headache and feeling wobbly but we managed a brief encounter over tea and cakes.

We had exchanged letters when I was in hospital, but it was the first time since the incident that I had seen him face-to-face. I was still uncomfortable with the fact he'd saved my life. In the past I'd always managed to get myself out of trouble. The difficulty was I didn't know how to thank him and he didn't know how to be thanked. In the end we'd agreed never to mention the incident again. It was an awkward meeting, made more awkward for me by the suspicion that Ricky and Morris, who had graciously left us alone to give us some privacy, were in fact lurking somewhere where they could hear every word.

Oddly, there was someone missing who might have lessened the awkwardness between us – Lottie, Daniel's little whippet; but he had left her behind in Scotland, looked after by friends, because she was nervous on public transport. So we talked mostly about my recovery and a little about his work and his plans for the derelict house he'd inherited from his aunt. He hoped that he'd be coming to settle in Devon as soon as he had finished his current project in Scotland. It's just he wasn't sure how long that was going to take. He almost made himself late for catching his train and our farewell kiss was snatched in haste. That was weeks ago. And in the time since, I have often thought about how intelligent and funny he was and wondered why it had taken me so long to realise how much I fancied him.

To be honest, I'm not totally sure what he does. He

works for a company involved in re-wilding projects and calls himself an 'environmental analyst', whatever that is. He claims to be no more than a glorified number cruncher, an analyst of data, and whilst I have certainly observed him crunching numbers on his computer, I get the feeling he's a lot more hands-on than that. Apparently, he was one of the founding members of this company and says his job description is 'elastic'. He does whatever is needed. He's currently involved in a scheme to return wolves to a Scottish island, except he won't say which one. He's a bit of a mystery man, intriguing but annoying. The mobile phone signal where he's currently staying is no more reliable than the one here in Ashburton, so I suppose I shouldn't be surprised at his lack of contact. We'd be better off relying on smoke signals. Anyway, typically, he left his umbrella behind when he came to visit me, and if he ever wants to see it alive again, he'll damn well have to come and fetch it.

There was no sign of Fred Crick when I arrived at his cottage with Tom and Vicky on Sunday afternoon. His battered old car was parked in his garage, visible through the sagging wooden doors, but he didn't seem to be at home. Perhaps he'd gone to the pub. He didn't respond to our knocking on his front door or calling out his name in the garden. We wandered around the back and tried the kitchen door but there was no response there either. He had told me I could take the stuff whenever I wanted, so we decided to get on with it.

In the old shed the furniture was standing exactly as before, except that the wardrobe had been tied around with a piece of frayed rope, presumably to keep the door shut. That was helpful, at any rate, and Tom is very experienced at transporting furniture. The writing table was lightweight and he carried it easily on his own. We lifted the chaise longue between the three of us, Tom at one end with Vicky and me at the other, and carried it out to the van. For the wardrobe he deployed the sack truck, sliding it underneath the base. It was heavier than I thought it was going to be. It took some pushing and wriggling to manoeuvre the wooden carcase until it was sitting safely on the metal base of the sack truck. Then Vicky and I steadied it as Tom leant it back at an angle so that it could rest against the frame as he wheeled the thing away. As he tipped it, we heard the muffled noise of something lumpy shifting its weight, sliding about inside.

'What's that?' Tom asked. 'Nothing that's likely to get broken?'

'I've no idea.' I didn't remember having bought anything else. Fred had probably stuffed it full of old rubbish he wanted to get rid of. We'd find out when we got back to the shop.

Manoeuvring the wardrobe into the storeroom at *Old Nick's* turned out to be a lot more difficult than extricating it from Fred's shed. It was a good job Ricky and Morris had turned up to help, even though they were even more ancient than Tom and not what I would call used to heavy lifting. The chaise longue and writing table fitted easily through the shop door, but Tom thought the wardrobe might get stuck when we tried to turn left through the doorway that led into the storeroom. We'd already had to move Mavis the mannequin, who usually stands in the hall displaying a sign pointing the way to *Antiques, Collectibles and Vintage Clothes*. It would be easier, he suggested, if we wheeled the wardrobe into the alley at the side of the building and came in through the door that led to the flat above. That way, we could wheel it straight down the corridor into the storeroom without having to turn it. Provided, Ricky pointed out, we could get the bleeding thing past the bottom of the stairs.

Tom and Ricky managed it between them; there wasn't room for anyone else in the corridor to do anything but get in the way, so we left them to it. By the time they finally deposited it in an upright position in the middle of the storeroom, Morris had already brewed some tea and arrived downstairs with a laden tray. The two furniture removers collapsed on the chaise longue next to each other, declaring they were gasping for a cuppa.

Ricky attempted to bounce on the seat. 'Blimey, this thing's comfortable! It's like sitting on a tomb. Hasn't it got any springs?'

Vicky asked if she could look at the items in my display cabinet. I was only too happy to let her look, grateful for any knowledge she was willing to pass on. She picked out a couple of scent bottles. 'I like this ruby glass one,' she said, rolling the little cylinder in her fingers. 'But you should be charging more for it. This cap is nine-carat gold.'

She picked up the other one, a squat, heavy bottle that I thought was Chinese. It was made from a white, stony material, the surface cloudy and opaque. 'I found that in a car boot sale,' I told her. 'It's agate, I think.'

Vicky shook her head, closing it in her palm. 'It's jade.' She smiled at me. 'Jade is cold to the touch, just as amber is always warm.'

'I thought jade was green.'

'This is what we call mutton-fat jade. It's pale and cloudy like this. And this isn't a scent bottle.' With delicate fingers she prised off the cap and drew out a tiny spoon attached to the underside of it. 'I thought so. You see this little spatula? It's for snuff.' She glanced at the price label. 'Again, you could up the price a bit. This is an old one. On the whole,' she added, returning the bottles to their glass shelf, 'you're building up a nice little collection in there. You've got a good eye. I'm very tempted by that silver pig pincushion.'

'Birmingham silver,' I told her, showing off my newly learnt hallmark knowledge, '1893.'

We sat happily chatting over mugs of tea and the chocolate cake provided by Morris. I asked Tom what he thought of the writing table.

'It'll need a bit of spending on restoration,' he admitted, 'but it'll be worth the expenditure. It's a pretty thing, very saleable.' He asked how much I'd paid for it. 'Well done,' he added with a grin. 'But don't attempt to restore it yourself,' he warned. 'Get it done professionally.'

'Don't worry,' I mumbled through a mouthful of cake. Restoration was not something I'd even contemplate trying.

'So, what's in the wardrobe?' Vicky asked. 'Do you remember?'

'No, I don't.' I put my mug of tea down and stood up, dusting cake crumbs from my fingers, and untied the knot in the piece of rope that was keeping the door closed. It was frayed at one end and felt slightly oily, as if it might once have been used as a tow rope. As I coiled it up in my hand, the door of the wardrobe yawned slowly open and I took a step backward. Behind me I could see Morris's bald head reflected in the mirror, his little gold specs halfway down his nose, Vicky sitting next to him, poised elegantly with her mug of tea, and Ricky's louche figure lounging on the chaise next to Tom, his long legs stuck out in front of him.

Something dropped out of the wardrobe door with a soft thump and lay on the floor inches beneath. There was a moment of shocked stillness in the room, then the sharp intake of Vicky's breath.

'Good God!' murmured Tom. 'That's not—'

'Bleedin' hell!' Ricky started. He sprang forward as if he'd been poked by a cattle prod.

The something was a hand, a man's hand, lying palm upward, fingers loosely curled, and attached to an arm that disappeared behind the wardrobe door.

'There's someone in there,' Vicky breathed.

'Don't move!' Ricky commanded. 'All stay where you are! I'll look.' He peered cautiously around the wardrobe door and into its dark interior. Then he stood perfectly still for several moments, transfixed by what he was seeing inside.

'Who is it?' Morris whispered fearfully. 'Is he dead?'

'Well, if he isn't,' Ricky responded, 'I don't like the way he's staring at me.'

'Is it Fred?' Tom asked.

I didn't think it could be. The hand was too pale, too plump, the nails were clean and there was no nicotine staining on the fingers. I peered cautiously around the edge of the wardrobe door for a look.

The man slumped in the bottom of it was obviously dead, his pale eyes wide and staring, his lips drawn back in a ghastly grin as if death had come as a shock to him. He looked like a ventriloquist's dummy or a collapsed puppet with its strings cut. He was younger than Fred, with thin, crinkly brown hair receding from a round face.

'Who is he?' Ricky asked me, his gaze held by the corpse.

'I don't know.'

'Well, you had him delivered.'

'I've never seen him before.'

'We're sure he's dead, are we?' Tom came to join us by the wardrobe door. 'Oh, yes,' he added, seeing the fixed grin and staring gaze, 'so he is!'

Even so, I thought we ought to feel for a pulse. After a

moment's hesitation, I knelt down and placed my fingers on his wrist.

'Anything?' Tom asked.

I shook my head. There was not the faintest flicker. 'Nothing at all,' I withdrew my fingers, unable to resist the impulse to wipe them on my jeans. 'He is um . . . still . . . well, he's not cold. He can't have been dead very long.'

'Phone the police,' Ricky instructed Morris as he edged nervously round the door to take a peek. But Vicky had already pulled out her phone.

'You won't get a signal down here,' I told her. 'Use the landline up in the flat.'

'Right.' She headed upstairs, sensibly deciding not to look at the corpse herself.

'Tell them there's been a murder,' Ricky added.

'How do we know he's been murdered?' Morris asked, blinking nervously.

'What d'you think he's doing in there, playing hide-and-seek? Looking for Narnia?'

'No, but—'

Ricky rolled his eyes in exasperation. 'He didn't stuff himself in the wardrobe, now did he?'

I looked down at the piece of frayed rope that had kept the door tied shut. It lay on the floor in a big question mark. 'No,' I agreed grimly. 'He didn't.'

CHAPTER THREE

As he stood surveying the inside of the wardrobe, Detective Inspector Ford did not look like a happy man. 'You've done it again, Juno,' he admonished me, glowering from under his heavy brows.

'It's not my fault I keep finding bodies,' I protested. 'I don't do it deliberately. I didn't buy the wardrobe and ask Fred to chuck in a corpse for free.'

'You say Fred Crick wasn't about when you picked the wardrobe up?'

'No,' I responded, 'well, he didn't answer his door.' I wouldn't have put it past Fred to have deliberately ignored our knock so that he didn't have to come out and help move the furniture.

The inspector turned to his colleague, Detective Sergeant deVille. 'Get up to his place and find him. We need to ask Mr Crick some questions. And get Collins up there as well.'

'Sir,' she answered crisply. As she passed, she shot me a sharp look from her strange, violet-coloured eyes. Relations between Cruella and I were not exactly cordial.

'Let's clear this room, shall we?' Inspector Ford went on, 'Let the scene of crime officers do their job?' He ushered us all out before him and we trickled into the main shop. 'Constable, we will need to take statements from each of these ladies and gentlemen,' he addressed the woman in uniform who'd been hovering awkwardly in the hall like an animated version of Mavis, 'and then I would like them all to go home.' He turned to me. 'Is there another room we can use?'

I suggested the kitchen upstairs but the inspector decided it would be better if we all waited up there and he took our individual statements down in the shop. So we sat around the kitchen table waiting for our turn to be called and having a macabre conversation about the logistics of stuffing a dead body into a wardrobe, particularly if it didn't want to go. It's the kind of thing people do when they are feeling slightly hysterical.

'Were there any signs of violence on the body?' Vicky asked.

I shook my head. 'Not that I could see, but he was sort of . . . folded up, collapsed forward. I couldn't see much of him.'

'You know, the thing is,' she went on, frowning, 'while we were at Fred's place earlier, I had the oddest sensation that we were being watched.' She gazed up at me, her blue eyes serious. 'Didn't you?'

'Can't say I noticed,' I admitted. 'Perhaps Fred was lurking somewhere, peering at us through his binoculars.'

'Your imagination's getting the better of you, old girl,' Tom told her cheerfully.

'It is not,' Vicky responded, annoyed. 'I had a definite feeling we weren't alone.'

'Well, I didn't notice anything.'

'Well, you wouldn't!' she retorted. 'A herd of elephants could have hurtled through the place and you wouldn't have—'

She was interrupted by a tentative knock as the lady copper stuck her head around the door.

'I'm sorry, Miss Browne,' she said to me, 'but I'm afraid forensics is going to have to remove the wardrobe.'

'Blimey! He's not still in it, is he?' Ricky demanded. 'Can't they get the poor bugger a stretcher?'

'The body has already been removed, sir,' she reproved him, her cheeks reddening.

'Take no notice of him, miss,' Morris said to her kindly. He nudged Ricky with his elbow. 'Show a bit of respect.'

'They can take the wardrobe and burn it,' I told her. 'I never want to see that thing again.'

'Tell them they can borrow my sack truck to move it,' Tom called to her.

She nodded and made a hasty retreat. Shortly afterwards we heard a lot of banging from downstairs. It seemed the forensics team weren't finding it any easier to move the wardrobe than we did.

I don't understand why statements have to take such a long time. Frankly, there wasn't a great deal to say, but we sat in that kitchen for hours. I was left till last, of course. But instead of taking my statement, the inspector told me he was driving me up to Fred's place.

'I want you to show me this shed. I want to see exactly where this wardrobe was standing before you took it away.'

'You think whoever stuffed that poor man in there might have left traces behind?'

He grimaced as if he thought this was unlikely. 'We live in hope.'

In fact, it wasn't the inspector but the WPC who drove. As we broached the top of the hill, heading towards Widecombe, an urgent buzzing came from the inspector's phone.

'What?' he demanded loudly of the caller. 'You're joking? Oh, bloody hell!' He sighed heavily as he disconnected. 'Step on it, Constable!' he urged the driver. 'Fred Crick's cottage is on fire.'

There's a lot of smoke when a thatch catches fire. We could see it, thick and black, billowing into the soft pink of the early evening sky long before we arrived. We could smell it too, taste it, acrid and bitter even inside the car. By the time we reached Fred's cottage it was well alight, each window a blazing rectangle lit by orange flames. Two firemen perched up on ladders were battling with drag hooks to pull the thatch away, flinging aside the smouldering reeds and sending sparks flying into the air. Other crewmen worked with hoses, flooding the ground with puddles that shone golden, reflecting the flickering light of the flames.

There were three appliances in attendance, crews drawn from Buckfastleigh and Newton Abbot as well as from Ashburton and Torquay. All thatched properties were held on a fire service 'at risk' register, I learnt later from a talkative fireman, and it was standard practice to bring additional pumps and a water bowser to such a property whenever a shout came in. There was also an ambulance drawn up on the roadside. As we stopped and got out of the car, I could see Cruella and Detective Constable Dean Collins standing in the road, talking to the fire officer in charge.

'Take Miss Browne to that shed,' Inspector Ford instructed our driver, slamming the car door as he got out. 'Get her to show you exactly where she found this wardrobe. I'll be with you in a moment.' And he strode off to join his fellow officers.

It was almost dark inside the shed, the only light an orange flickering glow coming through the gaps in the walls, but I showed the constable where the wardrobe and the other furniture had been standing. She cast around, shining her torch over the earthen floor; but if there were any significant footprints, Tom, Vicky and I had probably obliterated them with all our comings and goings.

* * *

When the inspector appeared, he didn't seem much interested in footprints. 'Come with me, Constable,' he barked. 'Back in the car please, Miss Browne,' he ordered me, 'and stay there.'

'Oh, don't you want—?'

'Just do as I tell you!' he snapped. Then he drew breath and after a moment added more politely, 'Please, Juno.'

As I marched a little huffily back towards the car, I heard him murmur to the constable, 'This is a double murder we're looking at now.'

I stopped in my tracks, turning back to stare at the blazing building. The crew were playing their hoses on the roof, flames crackling upward through what was left of the thatch. I could feel the fierce blast of heat from where I stood.

'It's all over now,' a voice told me with gloomy satisfaction. I turned to see a fireman leaning against his vehicle, keeping an eye on proceedings. He beckoned me over.

'What d'you mean?' I asked.

'We can't save the place. We had two men in the loft with hoses, but we've pulled them back. We're pulling all the guys out from inside.' He jerked his head in the direction of the vehicle's radio. 'I've just heard the orders come through on comms.' He nodded at the blaze, the glowing light reflecting in his eyes. 'Whoever set this going did a good job of it.'

'It wasn't an accident, then?'

He grinned. 'That's what we're supposed to think – poor old bloke put his frying pan on the stove, sat down for a cigarette and fell asleep in his chair.'

I couldn't drag my eyes from the burning building. 'Is he still in there?' I felt sick at the thought of it.

'He was.' He gestured towards the ambulance. 'He's in the bone wagon now.' Just as he spoke, it pulled silently away from the verge and drove off, no blue lights flashing, no sirens wailing. 'No rush,' he chuckled grimly.

'We can tell, you see,' he went on in the voice of a man who enjoyed airing his knowledge. 'We can follow the path of the fire.' He'd seen me get out of the police car with the others and I wondered if he might have mistaken me for a detective. I suppose I should have told him I was just a nosy civilian, but I didn't. I let him chatter on.

'Clearly an accelerant was used. And the other thing,' he beckoned me closer, as if he were sharing a secret, 'a lot of smoke often smothers a fire before it can get started. But whoever did this left the front door and the back door open, just enough – made sure the fire had plenty of oxygen – opened the hatch to the loft as well.' He nodded in the direction of Inspector Ford and Cruella, fast approaching. 'Make sure you tell your boss.'

I scuttled back towards the car, but I was too late, I'd been spotted. 'I told you to stay *inside* the car, Miss Browne,' the inspector admonished me, holding open the door.

'Sorry.' I slid on to the back seat and repeated what

the fireman had told me. 'I think he thought I was one of you,' I added lamely as the inspector frowned at me in the rear-view mirror.

'And why would he think that?' Cruella turned around to look at me, her little face pinched with disapproval. 'You realise impersonating a police officer is a serious offence—'

'Oh, shut up, Sergeant!' The inspector silenced her as if she were a yapping terrier and her mouth shut like a trap.

'The point is,' I went on, struggling to suppress a smile, 'that when we called to collect the furniture, the cottage was locked up tight. We tried to knock Fred up, and went around to the back door but it was all locked.'

'And what time was this?'

'About three, I think.'

'And you didn't see anyone else around at that time?'

'No. Although Vicky said she felt someone was watching us.'

'Yes, so she said in her statement,' the inspector acknowledged. 'And you saw no other vehicles parked around here anywhere?'

'None.'

'Thank you, Juno.' I must have restored myself to his good opinion, I was 'Juno' again, not 'Miss Browne'. He thought for a moment, his tapping his fingers on the steering wheel. Then to my relief, he ordered Sergeant deVille to stay at the scene with him and arranged for Detective Constable Collins to drive me home. I could have cheered. I sat in the car with dire warnings from the inspector about staying put and waited.

Dean greeted me loudly as he slid his considerable bulk into the driver's seat. 'What have you been up to now?' He brought with him a smell of scorched clothing, as if he'd been standing too close to the blaze.

'I haven't been up to anything,' I protested indignantly.

'What's all this I hear about a body in a wardrobe?' He turned to look at me, his blue eyes twinkling. 'You getting them delivered these days?'

I groaned. 'Don't you start.'

He grinned as he turned his head. I studied the back of his neck, thickset, the brown hair shaved to stubble. Dean and I were mates. I was godmother to his daughter. He could be a useful source of information if I leant on him in the right way.

'So, do we know who he was, the man in my wardrobe?' I asked.

'No, *we* don't,' he responded, in his flat northern vowels. 'He wasn't carrying any kind of identification. And,' he added, trying to sound severe, 'you know I couldn't tell you if we did.'

I let him get away with that, for the moment. 'What about Fred? The fireman I talked to said the fire had been started with an accelerant.'

'Well, he was burnt to a crisp if that's what you want to know,' he answered grimly. 'Something had been poured over his body.'

I shuddered. 'That's awful.'

'It's not what killed him, though,' he said, glancing at me in the rear-view mirror, 'he was already dead. And no, I am not going to tell you how he died,' he added emphatically before I could ask. 'For a start, we won't know that for sure until after the post-mortem.'

'Do we know how the man in the wardrobe died?' I asked.

Dean shook his head. 'No. Not yet. The crucial thing is to find out how long he'd been in there.'

'Well, he seemed fairly . . . um . . . fresh,' I volunteered. 'I mean, he was still faintly warm. And there didn't seem to be any signs of violence. Do you think he was murdered by the same person who killed Fred?'

He shook his head, grinning despite himself. 'Stop asking questions you know I can't answer.'

'Perhaps Fred killed him.'

Dean braked and turned to look at me. 'I'm gonna chuck you out of this car in a minute, Juno,' he threatened, 'and make you walk home.'

He looked as if he meant it so from then on I confined my chatter to enquiries about Dean's growing family: his wife, Gemma, was expecting for a second time. But as we drove down into Ashburton and turned down the lane towards my house, I tried again.

'You will let me know what you find out?'

Dean sighed. 'Juno—' he began.

'He was in *my* wardrobe,' I argued. 'I *paid* for him to be collected.' That last bit was a lie, Tom hadn't charged me anything.

The car stopped and Dean laughed as he got out of the driver's seat. 'I expect I'll be able to tell you more in a day or two,' he said consolingly as he held open the door for me. 'In the meantime, don't go poking your nose in where it doesn't concern you.'

'As if I would,' I responded, piously.

He gave the godmother of his child a peck on the cheek. 'I've heard that before, an' all.'

The phone rang just as I was wrapping a towel around my wet body. I'd had to wash the lingering smell of smoke out of my hair, and as my bathroom lacks a shower this meant a wallow in the bath. I hurried to the phone hoping that it might be Dean. He might have decided to spill a few beans of information after all.

'Is that Miss Browne with an "e"?' a lazy voice drawled.

'It is, Mr Thorncroft,' I answered, as coolly as I could manage.

'My dear Miss B, how are you?' Daniel always speaks to me as if he's a Victorian professor. 'How's your poor head?'

'Fine, much better than my poor ankle.' I sat down so that I could hoist the aforementioned aching limb onto the coffee table and rest it, ignoring spots of water dripping onto my bare shoulders from my hair.

'You haven't been overdoing it, have you? I've been trying to get hold of you all day. What have you been up to?'

'Oh, nothing much.' Bill leapt up onto the coffee table and used my leg as a bridge to reach my lap where he curled up, purring. He seems to feel my lap is his by right, despite the fact he's not my cat and belongs to Kate and Adam downstairs.

'Is it your words or your tone of voice that makes me immediately suspicious?' Daniel asked doubtfully.

'Well, I really couldn't say.' I hesitated. Should I tell him what had happened? He'd find out eventually but there was no need to alarm him yet. I decided not to. 'Anyway, you're a fine one to talk. Where have you been for the last two weeks?'

'Ah, you missed me!'

'Well, I've been vaguely aware that something was missing,' I admitted. 'How are the wolves?'

'Wonderful! We spent last night in a cabin on the island, listening to them howling.'

'We?' I asked before I could stop myself.

'Another colleague and I,' he answered without missing a beat. 'I wish you'd been there, Miss B. It was a glorious night for stars, completely clear, and with the wolves baying in the distance—'

'Ah, the children of the night—' I began, making a rough attempt at a Transylvanian accent.

'—what music they make!' His Dracula voice was better than mine.

We both laughed. Then silence.

'So, the project's going well?' I asked, which was really my way of asking *When will it be finished? When will you be coming back here again?*

There was a pause. 'Yes, it is, but I won't be able to get down for a week or two,' he answered evasively. 'Hopefully, the project can carry on without me after that. But I've got to attend a climate change conference in Norway, so . . .'

'I shall keep your umbrella hostage until you arrive,' I warned him.

We talked a bit more nonsense before we said goodbye. I put the phone down feeling slightly heavy-hearted. I despise a jealous nature, but I couldn't help wondering about his night in the cabin and who this other colleague might have been.

CHAPTER FOUR

Dogs can be a menace up on the moor at this time of year. They're likely to scare ground-nesting skylarks from their chicks and chase spring lambs. So next day when I took the Tribe, the group of dogs I walk each morning, for their walk we kept to a shady woodland valley. It was a fine morning, sunlight filtering through leaves and glinting on a shiny brook where the dogs paddled happily and I picked my way across the rushing water over stepping stones. Amongst the mossy boulders at the water's edge the ferns were lush, but new ones, lodged in tiny crevices, were waiting to unfurl their tightly coiled fists and stretch their fronds. Summer was still waiting to happen. As if on some silent signal, the dogs stopped their paddling and snuffling about and went racing heedlessly through a misty lake of bluebells, their paws throwing up clots of earth and moss as they went.

One member of our Tribe was missing. While I'd

been in hospital, Sally the old black Labrador had broken everyone's hearts: going to sleep in her basket, never to wake again. I missed her plodding solidly beside me, never leaving my side no matter how far ahead the younger dogs raced. I missed her wise, grey-flecked face. Her owners had been devastated, swore they would never have another dog, couldn't go through that heartbreak again. But her absence had torn such a gaping hole in their hearts that they were thinking of a new puppy. I'd tried to persuade them to give a home to a rescue, one of Pat's dogs from the sanctuary at Honeysuckle Farm, but it had to be a black Lab, they said.

After our walk I had to call in to the police station and give my statement, officially, to Cruella. I am never easy in her company. But she's had to learn it's unprofessional to let her personal feelings show and I did my best to do the same, giving my account of yesterday's events as clearly and simply as I could. She asked me more than once if I was sure about the time that Tom, Vicky and I had arrived. I said I was, and ventured to ask if the time was important. But she wasn't in a mood to give out information, just gave that smug little twist of her mouth. 'It's relevant to our enquiries,' was all she'd say.

Mondays is one of my busy days with clients, and I was late arriving for my first because of my trip to the cop shop; I didn't get to *Old Nick's* until halfway through the afternoon. Sophie was minding the place, working on her latest exquisite watercolour, and full of indignation.

'You can't go back there,' she told me, jerking a thumb towards the storeroom. 'A policeman came around this morning and told me that no one was to go in there until the man from forensics had dusted the rest of that furniture you brought in yesterday for fingerprints.'

'Hell's teeth!' I cried, disgusted. 'How long's that going to take?'

'I don't know,' she responded pointedly, shoving her big red-framed specs up the bridge of her titchy nose. 'He's only just arrived. But I must have looked a complete idiot, because I didn't *know* anything about a dead body being found here in a wardrobe. And neither,' she flashed her dark eyes for additional emphasis, 'did Pat!'

'Oh, I'm sorry, Soph!' I sank down on a stool by the counter. 'I should have phoned you but yesterday got sort of busy.' I told her all about it then, her dark eyes growing rounder as I described poor old Fred Crick being murdered in his cottage.

'God, that's horrible!' she murmured. 'And no one knows who this other man was, the one in the wardrobe?'

'Dean said there was no identification on him.'

Sophie was silent a moment. 'It's never dull being around you, Juno,' she said a little primly, picking up her paintbrush.

'Well, that's one thing in my favour, I suppose.' I tiptoed into the corridor that led to the storeroom, craning my neck to peer inside. I could see the forensics person, suited-up in white-hooded overalls, bending forward to brush fingerprint powder over the surface

44

of my newly-bought writing table. I cursed softly at the thought of the dusting and polishing that I was going to have to do when he'd finished.

'Oh, one thing,' Sophie remembered as I crept back into the shop. 'A woman came in and left you this.' She waved a business card at me. 'She's coming back to see you before closing time.'

'Fizzy Izzy,' I read. The words were in zigzag script, as if the letters had been electrified, and then, in a more sedate font, 'Designs on Silk.'

'She paints on silk,' Sophie explained, just in case I hadn't got that bit, 'scarves, cushion covers and things. She brought some of her stuff; it's really lovely. I think she wants to rent a unit.'

I could have rubbed my hands with glee. I just hoped the white-suited alien in the storeroom had buggered off before she arrived.

Sophie decided to call it a day and go home, leaving me to cash up. I knocked on the door of the storeroom and asked if it was all right if I closed it. I explained I was expecting a visitor. The white-suited one stared at me through his goggles and nodded slowly. I shut the door with some relief. I didn't want a potential rent-payer being scared off by finding out about another dead body on the premises.

Then I phoned Pat, and Elizabeth, who also volunteers her help in the shop when she's not working at her part-time job at the surgery, explaining what had happened the day before and that they weren't to be surprised if there was a police presence around in the next few days. Pat received this news with awestruck cries of horror at first, fading into sighs of resignation; Elizabeth with total calm. It was as if they had learnt to expect this kind of thing.

Fizzy Izzy turned up promptly at five-thirty, a large lady with dark auburn hair scooped up in a messy bun and wearing a long, silk jacket painted with hummingbirds in brilliant, jewel-like colours. I assumed she'd painted it herself. She carried a bulging laundry bag in one hand and thrust the other out for me to shake. 'Fizzy Izzy,' she announced loudly. 'It's short for Felicity Eliza, but you can call me Fizz.' She was probably in her forties but exuded a youthful, buzzing energy.

'Juno,' I said, shaking her hand.

'Oh, I've heard all about you,' she assured me with a wide smile.

I attempted to steer the conversation away from me and anything she might have heard. 'Sophie said you might be interested in renting a unit here.'

'I've brought some samples of my work for you to see.' She reached inside her bag and began pulling out silk scarves, long sweeps of shaded colour, some delicate pastels, others in hothouse, rainforest hues; some patterned with intricate Celtic designs, others freely painted with flowers and butterflies. There were cushion covers with purple irises edged in gold, and a lampshade around which blue dolphins swam. It was beautiful work.

'Now,' she began, looking around at the shop, 'I would like some display space downstairs.' She pointed to the space behind Pat's unit. 'That wall and those white painted shelves would do perfectly.'

'No problem,' I told her, 'that space is free.'

'I understand you have rooms upstairs?'

The rooms I had for rent were once *Old Nick's* living room and bedroom, both newly decorated with polished wood floors and steel spotlights in the ceilings. I led the way up the staircase.

'Of course, I'm aware that a murder took place in one of these rooms,' Fizz dropped her voice to a whisper, 'Poor Mr Nickolai.'

'This one,' I admitted, pointing into the living room.

'I take it there haven't been any ghostly manifestations,' she went on, her brown eyes round and serious, 'only I'm very sensitive to atmosphere.'

'None at all,' I assured her. This was not quite a lie. I don't believe in ghosts and Nick had certainly not manifested in any form. But from time to time I got the sneaky feeling that he was still around, having a laugh.

Despite her reservations she strode into it briskly. 'This would do beautifully.' She began inspecting electric sockets and switching lights on and off.

'Would you be planning to work up here?' I ventured. 'Only this room is technically two units . . .'

'Oh no, no,' Fizz waved a heavily ringed hand. 'I'll need it all!' She gave me another wide smile. 'I need a lot of space. I could put my big worktable in the middle here. Silk has to be stretched on a frame, you see, before it can be painted. The frames for my scarves are six feet long and frames for the wall panels larger than that.'

I decided Fizzy Izzy was a name that suited her. I felt as if I was standing next to a firework with the blue touchpaper already lit; she might explode in colourful sparks any moment. 'I hold silk painting workshops,' she rattled on, 'and this room would be perfect for my students, especially with the kitchen next door. And there is a loo, I take it?'

'Of course.' Nick's old bathroom was on the landing.

'I would need to put in a sink over in that corner . . . at my own expense, of course,' she added hastily. 'Silk has to be rinsed several times during the painting process. I use a lot of water.'

I eyed the polished wooden flooring that I had put down at so much expense. 'Does that mean the floor would have to come up?'

'Only in that one corner,' she assured me.

I agreed to it, a bit reluctantly. We fell then to the subject of rent. The cost of hiring a double unit upstairs with further display space down in the main shop didn't seem to bother Fizz one bit. I explained that she'd be required to man the shop at least one half-day per week. No problem, she assured me. We shook hands. She wanted to start work on getting the sink put in straight away. The only slight sticky moment came when she said, 'I take it I will be able to display some of my work in the windows?'

'Well, the windows really belong to Sophie and Pat . . .'
I began.

She seemed put out. 'In all the other places where I've
sold, the window space was always communal.'

'I'm sure we can sort out something.' I assured her. 'I'll
speak to the others.' I could just imagine how well that
conversation was going to go down. But frankly, if Fizz
was prepared to pay rent for three units, I didn't want
anything to put her off. Sophie and Pat would just have
to lump it. After all, they weren't paying rent at all; a fact
I'd better warn them not to mention in front of Fizz. She
went off, highly pleased, with a promise to return with
her first month's rent money in the morning. I locked up,
switched off the lights in the shop and opened the door
to the storeroom to see if the forensics man had left yet.
He was still there, dusting away with his little brush.
I cleared my throat and he straightened up, turning to
stare at me through his goggles.

'I'd like to go now and lock up the shop,' I said,
probably louder than I needed to. 'Do you think you
could let yourself out when you've finished?' I pointed
along the corridor to the side door. 'You can get out that
way. Just drop the latch.'

He nodded silently and gave me a thumbs-up.

'Thank you.' I smiled at him. 'Goodbye.'

I stifled a laugh. In my excitement about renting the
units, I'd nearly forgotten him.

CHAPTER FIVE

Maisie is my oldest client, by age, anyway. She's ninety-five. She has an agency carer to help her bathe and dress in the mornings, and I call in on her two or three times a week, an arrangement paid for by her daughter, Our Janet, who lives up north. There are clients I've worked for longer, but Maisie is so much a part of my life that even if I could afford to give her up as a client, I don't think I could bear not to visit her.

Jacko, her all-sorts terrier, behaved disgracefully when I took him out to fetch her shopping, snarling at other dogs and burying his teeth in the tyre of a mobility scooter that tried to pass him on the pavement. He's always like this. I think he suffers from some kind of doggie dementia. He certainly talks to himself, keeps up a growly monologue all the time we are out. I took him to training classes once. The woman who ran it assured me that there were no bad dogs and that Jacko was only aggressive out of fear. At the end of the first session she begged me never to bring him back. I've tried to improve his behaviour but nothing works: not yanks on a choke-chain, clicks from a clicker, bribery with treats, threats to send him to the dogs' home, to have him shot, nothing. I could never take him walking with the Tribe. Maisie refuses to consider my buying him a muzzle and remains unimpressed by my warnings of what might befall Jacko if he ever actually bit someone. To be fair, it's usually other dogs and wheeled vehicles he objects to sharing his pavement with; but there's always a first time. Maisie won't believe he's badly behaved because, old and frail as she is, she hasn't taken him for a walk in years. Apart from the times when I take him out, he has to content himself with running around in her garden.

Safely back from town without bloodshed or impending lawsuits, Jacko returned to his favourite dozing spot on the window sill, using the back of the sofa as a step up. I unpacked Maisie's groceries and entertained her with my account of what happened on Sunday. Fred Crick was ever a bad lot, she pronounced with a shake of her head, and she wasn't surprised he'd come to a nasty end. I didn't take too much notice; she says this whenever anyone dies. I said I'd see her again on Thursday and set off to see Tom Carter.

During my convalescence, my friend Elizabeth had taken over visiting Tom, an interesting seventy-something who was counting the days to his hip replacement. Crippling arthritis was the only reason he had agreed to accept my help with cleaning his tiny cottage and doing his shopping in the first place. But now I was back at work, Elizabeth still kept up her visits, fuelling a great deal of speculation at *Old Nick's*. Call it attractive-interesting-still-sexy-seventy-something-man meets elegant-cool-charming-sixty-something-woman but it seemed likely that, Tom's hip operation allowing, they might become more than friends. Sophie, Pat and I were agog.

So, my visit to Tom that morning was as much social as because he might want my help. As it turned out, he needed some shopping fetched. But before I went to the shops, I made coffee and sat down for a chat, Tom shifting his leg to make room on his old leather footstool so I could rest my ankle. I told him about the body in the wardrobe and the fire at Fred Crick's place.

He smiled grimly. 'It was a busy day on Sunday by all accounts. Search and Rescue got called out in the evening.' Tom had been a member of a Dartmoor Search and Rescue team himself until his hip prevented him, and his frustration at not being able to go with them on a shout was plain. 'The woman who runs that guest house at Hemsworthy Gate reported one of her guests missing. He'd gone out walking on the moor in the morning and didn't come back for his evening meal.'

'Did they find him all right?'

'They didn't find him at all.'

'No?' I responded dumbly. 'But they always find everyone.'

'Not this time.'

'Do you think he might have run off, done a bunk?'

Tom scratched his balding head. 'He'd only arrived the day before, they said, so he couldn't have run up much of a bill. And he'd left money and personal possessions in his room. He must have meant to come back for them.'

I thought about this as I walked into town to get Tom's shopping. In order to call out Search and Rescue, you first have to dial 999 and tell them which service you require. So, the police would know that a man staying at the guest house had gone missing and by now, as he hadn't been found, must be investigating his disappearance. Inspector Ford and his team were probably way ahead of me, but I did wonder if the missing walker might already have turned up. In the bottom of my wardrobe.

Back in the shop, Elizabeth was reading the newspaper.

'I've just been to see Tom,' I told her as I bounced in.

'Oh yes?' Her voice betrayed not a particle of interest; she was nothing if not cool. She lowered the pages and looked at me over her reading glasses. As always, she was immaculate, her silvery-blonde hair swept up in a smooth French plait. I envy her. My curls are uncontrollable.

'Fizzy Izzy has arrived,' she informed me, her steely grey eyes glinting with amusement.

'Oh, yes? She's our new trader.'

'So I gather. She's paid her deposit, left those things,' she nodded to some folding wooden display stands and heaps of laundry bags dumped in a corner, 'and has gone off to fetch her microwave.'

'Microwave?' I repeated. 'Didn't you tell her there's already one in the kitchen?'

'This is for her studio upstairs. She uses it to fix her silk dyes, apparently.'

'She cooks them?'

'The colours have to be fixed with heat.' Elizabeth laughed. 'Fizzy Izzy! It's a good job I don't call myself Lizzy or things might become rather confusing around here.' There was a knocking noise from upstairs. 'That's her plumber.'

'Already?'

'He's investigating the pipes.'

I puffed out my cheeks in a sigh.' She doesn't waste any time, does she?'

I nipped upstairs to take a look at what was going on, and received a nod of greeting from a man in overalls who was on his hands and knees in the corner with a steel tape measure. He told me he wouldn't have to take up the new flooring; he could connect the pipes for the new sink by drilling through the wall into the kitchen. I nodded. This was the lesser of the two evils, I supposed.

Fizzy Izzy returned. I could hear her as I came downstairs, chattering loudly to Elizabeth. She had dumped her microwave on the floor, set up a display stand in the corner of her unit and was busy unpacking her laundry bags, pulling out coloured scarf after coloured scarf like an old-fashioned magician. Elizabeth held one up, fine and translucent, sweeping in colour from palest turquoise to deepest jade. 'How do you get this delicate marbled effect?' she asked, tracing it with her finger.

'Salt,' Fizz replied, without stopping. 'I fling salt crystals at the silk when the dye is wet.'

'Fascinating,' Elizabeth murmured. I saw her examine the price tag and the faintest raising of her eyebrow. Not cheap, obviously. 'Will you give us a demonstration, when you've got your studio set up?'

'Good idea,' Fizz grinned cheerfully. 'Just as well you all find out how these things are made. Customers like to know.'

Elizabeth suppressed a smile and cast me a glance. 'Well, quite.'

'And of course, I won't always be here,' she prattled on. 'I sell most of my work at art exhibitions and craft fairs. Don and I go all around the country in our camper van. We love it.'

'Don's your partner?' I asked. 'Is he an artist too?'

'He's a woodturner.' She turned to look at me. 'It's only a hobby with him, of course.

'He works in finance.' I detected a slight smugness in her tone. 'I'll probably display one or two of his pieces here, if that's all right with you?'

'Of course.' I glanced at my watch. I had another client to see before the end of the afternoon, an elderly lady in the village of Woodland. I usually see Mrs York on a Monday but she'd had visitors so I was squeezing her in the following day. I made my escape and left Fizz to her unpacking under Elizabeth's watchful eye, promising to return before closing time. But I was longer with Mrs York than I expected and by the time I got back Elizabeth had already cashed up, locked up and gone home. I let myself in and switched on the main lights. Fizzy had been busy. Her corner of the shop grabbed attention immediately, the display stands draped with scarves in gorgeous colours, plump painted cushions, bags and lampshades laid along the shelves, and hanging on the wall, a large silk panel. A myriad of brightly coloured fish flitted amongst branching coral as dolphins swam above them, patterns of rippling water reflected on the smooth surface of their backs. The effect was breathtaking.

What I'd really come back to the shop for was to clear up the mess that I knew the forensics man would have left behind. The furniture would be covered in the fine silvery powder he used. He might have confined his dusting to the writing desk and the chaise longue, but I know from experience that damned powder gets everywhere. Fortunately, Sophie had the foresight to cover over the vintage clothes rails with old sheets before he started. Even so, I was meticulous with my dusting and sponging before I felt it was safe to remove the sheeting from the clothes and go home.

On my way out I saw something I hadn't noticed on my way in. On the broad window sill in Pat's window, her stock of knitted shawls and animals and her stands of handmade earrings had been shoved unceremoniously to either side to make room for an easel displaying a large sign: *Fizzy Izzy*, it read, *Designs in Silk*.

'Oh, hell's teeth,' I muttered.

* * *

56

Detective Constable Dean Collins did not want to admit I was right about the dead body in my wardrobe. I could tell by the long sigh he exhaled down the phone.

'Bloody hell, Juno!' he complained. 'Just keep this to yourself, will you? He hasn't been formally identified yet.'

'But you're sure it's him?'

'Yes,' he conceded grudgingly. 'The constable who answered the missing person's enquiry found his driving licence in his room at the guest house. The photo is certainly of the bloke in the wardrobe. We've managed to contact his family. His brother's coming down tomorrow to do the formal ID.'

'So, who was he?' I pressed him. 'What was his name?'

'Well, you'll read about it soon enough in the *Gazette*, I suppose, but you never heard it from me, right?'

I swore I wouldn't breathe a word.

'His name is Peter Gillow and he's a teacher from Basingstoke. Or he was, just retired, according to the brother. Come down here on holiday to see Dartmoor.'

'You can't see much of it from inside that wardrobe,' I objected. 'What was he doing in there?'

'Well, we don't know, Juno,' Dean retorted, 'we can't ask him.'

'Do we know what he died of?'

'Not yet.'

'Any more news on Fred?'

'No. We're trying to find out who the last person was to see him alive – apart from the killer, obviously. It might have been you. We don't know where he went for the next couple of days. But he was a bit of a recluse from what I hear, kept himself to himself, he didn't like spending his money.'

'I can believe that.' I became aware of a faint mewling sound in the background, which gradually increased in volume to a mighty wail. 'Is that my goddaughter I can hear?'

'Yes, we're trying to get her off to sleep,' Dean muttered ungraciously. 'We'd just about managed it when you rang.'

'I'll let you get on with it, then.'

Then I phoned Elizabeth. How had she let Fizz get away with putting her sign up in Pat's window, I wanted to know. She had warned her it wouldn't be acceptable, she told me, that she should wait until I'd discussed things with Pat, but Fizz was adamant. In the end, Elizabeth had decided it wasn't her responsibility to sort these things out, but mine. Sadly, I had to agree.

I rang Fizz next. She listened in hostile silence to my telling her that I had removed her sign from Pat's window, and it would be a much better idea to add her name to the advertising board that I propped up at the corner of Shadow Lane. I promised I'd get Sophie on to it first thing in the morning. I got off the phone feeling that the best thing I could do was give Fizz her rent back and tell her to forget the whole thing but decided to hold fire. 'Why is life always so complicated?' I asked Bill.

He was sitting on my window sill gazing out into the twilit tangle of the back garden. He was spending more and more time up in my flat these days, instead of downstairs with Adam and Kate, where he belonged. The flat, and indeed the whole house, is seriously in need of refurbishment. But I'm prepared to put up with leaky pipes, whistling draughts and other annoyances in return for low rent and the leftovers I'm gifted almost daily from *Sunflowers*, the vegetarian cafe they run. Kate was pregnant and I wondered how Bill would like it when there was a screaming baby about the place. Perhaps he could already sense that change was coming, had picked up the general atmosphere of excitement as the little spare bedroom was being converted into a nursery. Perhaps when he sat on Kate's lap, he could sense the new life within her. Or perhaps it was simply as it had always been: Bill preferred my company.

The garden was rapidly fading into shadow, one diamond star hanging like a lamp over the rooftops of Ashburton. It made me think of Daniel up in the Highlands with his wolves. I really wanted to see him again, but a part of me was relieved he wasn't coming back too soon. I haven't had a man in my life for a while now, and I wasn't sure how I felt at the prospect of sharing my intimate space, let alone my intimate spaces, with anyone else, even someone as nice as he was. I stroked Bill between his ears and he turned to gaze at me with his one emerald eye. 'Did you know,' I asked him as he rubbed his cheek against my hand, 'that cats of one colour were worshipped as gods in ancient Egypt?'

The smugness of his purr told me that he did; and he knew that black cats were worshipped best of all.

CHAPTER SIX

The woman who ran Hemsworthy Gate Guest House frowned at me with suspicion.

'You're not from the *Dartmoor Gazette*, are you?' she asked, her brown eyes narrowing. 'I've already spoken to your lot twice and I don't know any more than I've told you already.'

'No, indeed I'm not,' I assured her. The local newspaper was a pestilential nuisance as far as I was concerned and had caused me considerable embarrassment in the past. I stood in her hallway next to the tiny desk with the 'reception' sign on it. She'd appeared when I'd pinged the little bell, hastily stuffing a yellow duster into the pocket of her nylon overall.

It was in fact three days since the *Gazette* had splashed the murder of Fred Crick in his burning cottage, together with the death of Peter Gillow 'in suspicious circumstances' across their front pages. Fortunately, my part in the discovery of his body had not been revealed by the police otherwise its reporters would have been pestering me for an exclusive. But I wanted to find out what was going on and Dean Collins was telling me nothing. I was gagging to know how the poor man had died but it wasn't just simple curiosity on my part.

He had arrived in the wardrobe I'd bought. I felt responsible for him; I owed it to him to find out what had happened. 'And I'm not from the police either,' I added, just to make that clear. I didn't want Cruella coming after me for impersonating a police officer. I explained my connection to Mr Gillow.

'They didn't say that in the paper,' the woman said, horrified, 'not about his body being in a wardrobe.'

'They probably don't want to make that bit public,' I explained. 'I'm just trying to find out how he ended up there.'

She invited me to sit in the residents' lounge. It had an air of being entirely unused, the spread of local magazines on the coffee table too tidy to have been touched. I selected one of a dozen empty armchairs.

The woman, who told me her name was Joan, perched on the arm of a chair herself. 'He was an inoffensive little chap, Mr Gillow,' she told me. 'He was looking forward to exploring Dartmoor, poor man. He'd just retired and was very interested in archaeology, in seeing all the Bronze Age sites. He told me all about it at breakfast. We like to chat to our guests,' she went on, 'especially when they're here on their own, like he was. He was supposed to be staying for two weeks.'

'Did he mention where he was planning to go that day?'

Joan nodded. 'He showed me on the map. I'd made him a packed lunch. He was going to start at Haytor – well, they all do, don't they?' she added, smiling. 'It's the obvious place to go from here – see the quarry and the granite railway, then walk to Hound Tor. He wanted to see the remains of the medieval village. I said to him, he could walk to Widecombe from there, finish off with a nice cream tea and still be back in time for supper.'

I frowned. 'Fred's place is a bit out of his way. He didn't mention that he might be visiting someone?'

Joan shook her head. 'He didn't say that he had any friends in the area. Perhaps he got lost.' She smiled a little sadly. 'I couldn't help noticing his walking boots, all of his gear – it looked brand new.'

'He could have just treated himself to new kit,' I said. 'But you don't think he was an experienced walker?'

'Even if he was,' she spread her hands, 'if you don't know the area around here . . .'

She didn't need to explain. Dartmoor could be a killer even for those who knew it well. But it had been a fine day, that Sunday, none of the suddenly descending mists or icy squalls that could disorientate and kill the inexperienced walker.

'Oh, one other thing,' she added after I'd thanked her and she'd accompanied me to the door.

'He checked before he set off – I remember we laughed

about it – he double-checked he had his pills with him.'

'Pills?'

'He always carried his pills, he told me,' she said sadly. 'He had a weak heart.'

'Well, he must have been a complete bleedin' plonker if he could get himself lost in broad daylight on the road between Hound Tor Down and Widecombe,' Ricky declared acidly. He and Morris were in the shop, fussing about with dresses on their vintage clothes rail while I filled them in on the latest. 'Mind you, it's a mystery to me why anyone wants to go walking about up on that moor – nothing but bog and fog!'

'Nonsense,' Morris scolded mildly. 'There's nowhere more beautiful on a sunny day.'

'When we go up on the moor, we drive about from pub to tea room,' Ricky retorted. 'Other than for refreshments, we hardly get out of the car.'

Morris gave a reluctant nod. 'True,' he admitted.

I hadn't been able to discover much more about Mr Gillow. Dean confessed eventually that the post-mortem had revealed he'd died of a heart attack, but that didn't explain how the poor man had ended up stuffed in my wardrobe. As for Fred Crick, someone had poured petrol over his body after killing him with repeated blows from something like a shovel, then set fire to his cottage. At the moment the police had no suspects for the crime and believed it was probably a burglary gone wrong.

'How's your new girl settling in?' Morris asked as

Fizz was heard loudly singing along to the radio in her studio upstairs.

I groaned. In the few days Fizz had been here she'd already caused upset, spreading her silk stuff about and repeatedly impinging on Pat's selling space. Sophie had rescued the situation, allowing her to drape silk scarves among the watercolours in her window, but Pat wasn't impressed and frankly Fizz had shown herself about as sensitive to atmosphere as a Sherman tank. I had tried to explain to her the system for entering all sales in the ledger, so that at the end of each day we'd know who had sold what and who was owed money. I wasn't sure she'd understood, and I didn't feel confident about her ability to mind the shop on her own. Not that she was stupid; she just didn't pay attention. She was really only interested in her own stuff. I wasn't much cheered either by a chat with one of the traders from Ashburton Art and Antiques Bazaar, who told me that Fizz used to rent space there, had been nothing but a load of trouble and everyone had been glad to see the back of her.

'The jury's still out,' was all I said in reply, remembering Elizabeth's calm reminder that it was early days and we should speak as we find, not be swayed by the gossip of other people. Quite.

Meanwhile, her studio was taking shape. The sink had been installed and we had all helped to drag her huge worktable upstairs. It had been quite a challenge fitting it through the door. In the end I'd had to get a screwdriver and unscrew the legs so we could slide the top through sideways. Rolls of silk kept arriving and wooden frames of various sizes. The walls were decorated with some truly stunning silk paintings. I began to wonder if she might be moving in herself when I passed her on the stairs clutching an iron and a hairdryer, but she assured me these were only needed to help fix colours and speed up the drying process. Silk *dyes* have to be steamed, she told me solemnly, hence the steamer and the microwave, but silk *paints* must be fixed with dry heat, hence the hairdryer. Fine, I thought to myself, seeing in my mind's eye the little wheel on the electricity meter whirring faster with each ping and blast of hot air.

She had also made me realise how quiet and peaceful the place used to be. Her radio was playing from the moment she arrived until she left, she tended to sing along with the music and she was heavy-footed on the stairs. A small price to pay, I reminded myself severely, for the amount of rent she would be bringing in. Even so, I was relieved when she left at about four o'clock that afternoon. Everyone else had gone and I experienced silence and a slightly astonished sense of calm.

It didn't last long. The bell on the shop door jangled as a woman came in and asked if she could look around. Of course, I told her. She wandered about for several minutes, studying everything, picking up things and putting them down again, declaring that everything was lovely. I asked her if she was looking for anything in particular.

'I'm trying to find a present for a friend,' she answered,

beaming at me. She was short and rather heavy around the hips, gold-rimmed specs hanging on a chain around her neck, her curled fair hair half-hidden under a brown felt hat. When she smiled, I noticed a gap between her two front teeth. 'I'm not sure what I'm looking for, but I'll know it when I see it.' She pointed a gloved finger in the direction of the back room. 'May I look in there?'

'Be my guest.'

She looked around the collectables and vintage clothes for so long that I'd almost forgotten about her when she came out again. 'I think I've spotted the very thing,' she smiled sweetly, 'but I'm going to go away and have a little think about it.'

'Fine,' I told her. As she left the shop my own smile vanished. I know all about people who go away for a little think: they never come back. I bet that's the last I ever see of you, I thought to myself. Unfortunately, it wasn't.

CHAPTER SEVEN

Next day I walked a new recruit for the Tribe. Dylan was not a replacement for old Sally – her owners were still making up their minds about a new puppy – but had been referred to me by Becky who runs a mobile dog grooming parlour. She's just started the business and invested a lot of money on a specially kitted-out van in which she can bathe and generally pouf-up the pooches, which she bought second-hand from someone upcountry. I passed it in White Van on my way from Ashburton to Rewlea Cross, our wing mirrors kissing fleetingly as we squeezed by each other in the narrow lane. It was still painted in the livery of the previous owners, a lurid pink, *Pretty Paws* emblazoned in curling script on the sides. We stopped and wound our windows down.

'Isn't it ghastly?' Becky demanded, wrinkling her nose in disgust. 'I've got to get rid of this dreadful pink and find something else to call it. If you think of anything clever, let me know.'

I promised I would. It was Becky's neighbour who owned Dylan and required my walking services. Dylan was not the sort of dog to be found in a grooming parlour, pink or otherwise. He was more of a wash-down-with-the-garden-hosepipe-and-a-quick-shake-afterwards sort of dog. He was a long-haired German shepherd with, according to his owner, a bit of something else thrown in. He was a beautiful dog, and he was big.

'Why do you think he's got something else thrown in?' I asked. He looked all German shepherd to me.

'His ears won't stand up properly,' his owner told me. 'One stands up and the other flops forward all the time.'

I didn't see anything wrong with that myself, I thought it was rather beguiling.

'And, not to put too fine a point on it, for a German shepherd, he's a bit thick.'

Dylan, who'd been boisterously chasing a ball around the garden, confirmed this damning opinion of his intelligence by losing it in the fish pool where it bobbed out of his reach whilst he stood whining at it.

As with all new dogs, before I introduced him to the Tribe, I took him out a few times on his own. He needed to get used to me and I wanted to see how he behaved on the lead and off, get some idea of his temperament and whether he'd fit in with the other dogs, as well as whether he would ride happily in the van. So, on Saturday afternoon I drove him up towards Widecombe-in-the-Moor and parked at Cold East Farm. I tied Dylan to the gatepost, with instructions to sit and stay, instructions he wasn't very happy with, and walked up the path in the hope of seeing Carol. She might have more news about the fire at Fred's cottage. Unfortunately, she wasn't at home. I returned to Dylan waiting anxiously by the gate.

I walked him up through fields towards the rock at the top of the hill. It was a dry day, grey-tinged clouds scudding across a wide blue sky and throwing their shadows on the land beneath; breezy enough to ruffle Dylan's fur as I let him off the lead. He bounded away up the field. I'd brought one of his favourite toys, a hank of grubby rope, which he chased after with lunatic enthusiasm when I threw it, although he didn't seem to have much of a clue when it came to bringing it back. After giving it a good shaking, he lay down chewing on it, one ear cocked, watching me from a rolling brown eye when I caught up to him, only to get up and race off with it as soon as I got within grabbing distance.

As I followed him up the grassy slope, the sun shone out from behind a cloud and something glinted in the dark green line of trees up on the summit, something like sun shining on a mirror, or on glass. Then I saw a flash of colour, light red, perhaps a jacket. There was movement, definitely someone up there under the trees. I stopped, shading my eyes to look. I thought about Fred watching the farm through his binoculars. Except that it couldn't be Fred now, could it? Because Fred was dead, battered to death and burnt inside his cottage. The flash of colour disappeared a moment later; whoever it was had gone.

Dylan decided to come back to me with his damp and grubby toy in his mouth and drop it at my feet. We enjoyed a brief tussle, a game of tug-of-war, with a lot of play-growling on Dylan's part, before I launched it up the slope for him to chase and ran after him. My ankle was aching by the time I reached the brow of the hill and I was breathing hard.

Charred beams and blackened walls were all that was left of Fred's cottage, wound around with blue and white police tape printed with the warning 'Do Not Cross'. This was still a crime scene, eerily silent, the smell of old bonfire hanging over it.

I grabbed Dylan by the scruff and slipped on his lead, worried he might go plunging about inside the broken walls, padding through the scorched and ashy debris. But he hung back, wary and uncertain, as if amongst the burnt wood, blackened stone and fractured glass he could scent the lingering smell of death. He seemed fidgety and nervous.

Who had killed Fred Crick? The police, with no sign of a motive, witness or suspect were still pursuing the line that his murder was a burglary gone wrong. After all, the only thing that anyone knew for certain about Fred was that he was a tight old bastard with a fair amount of money stashed away. Perhaps thieves had come looking for cash. The thought that upset me was that he was already dead in that cottage whilst Tom, Vicky and I were in the shed removing the furniture. Or even worse, what if he wasn't dead? Perhaps our visit had interrupted a crime in progress. What if he was inside, a helpless captive of his murderers, listening to us in the garden calling his name?

As for Peter Gillow, he had no connection to Fred: or if he did, the police hadn't found it yet. He didn't seem a likely burglar, so what was he doing there? Was he just an innocent bystander, an accidental and unfortunate witness to a crime? Dean told me that the pathologist hadn't been able to establish which had come first: the heart attack or his incarceration in the wardrobe. Had he suffered a seizure and then been bundled in the wardrobe – in which case, who had performed the bundling? Or had being stuffed in the wardrobe caused him to have heart failure? The latter seemed unlikely. There were no signs of his trying to fight his way out, no scratching with bloodied fingernails on the inside of the wardrobe door, no bruising on his knuckles as he'd tried to punch his way free. Anyway, the wardrobe was a load of junk. It wasn't well enough made for him to have suffocated: too many ill-fitting joints, too much air coming in between the shrunken panels. But someone had tied that rope around the wardrobe, the same someone, presumably, who had killed Fred Crick.

Dylan was whining softly, anxious to be away, and we moved up to the brow of the hill, to the rock. Although there was a steep drop at the front, from the back the chunky lump of granite was an easy climb; a series of smaller rocks rising up from ground level, almost as if nature had provided a stairway to reach its flat, tabletop. I peered over the edge, a drop down of about ten feet to the bushes clustered at its foot.

I could see why Fred used to come here: the view across the valley was breathtaking and it was an ideal place to watch what was going on at the farm. I could pick out Carol and little Amy coming back from a walk across the fields.

'C'mon Dylan,' I said, 'time to go.'

We returned through the line of dark trees from where I had seen someone watching us earlier. There was no one there now. Yet as we turned away, I thought I caught the flicker of a movement from the corner of my eye. It halted me mid step and I looked back; I could see nothing. But Dylan growled softly. I stood still for a moment while the wind stirred the branches, shifting the shadows on the ground beneath. But if anyone had been watching us, they were out of sight now.

Back at Cold East Farm, I put Dylan into the back of White Van and strolled to the farmhouse door to say hello. I chatted with Carol for a few minutes about Fred's murder and the dreadfulness of it all and whether theft could have been a motive. Carol admitted she was nervous. There had been a spate of burglaries at farms roundabout since she and Neil had taken over and they'd had a quadbike stolen. She was worried the same thieves might be back, that it might start happening again. I understood how she felt. From what I'd read in the local press, some of these robberies had been violent, gangs of armed thieves attacking isolated farms where they knew they'd be long gone before the police arrived. And Carol had no close neighbours, no one she could run to for help if she and Amy were alone.

I asked her if she'd seen Peter Gillow on that Sunday. The police had shown her his photograph, she told me, but she hadn't seen him. Whilst we were talking, Amy was pulling her mother's hand, trying to tell her something.

'What is it, darling?' she asked.

Amy whispered to her.

'Amy wants you to know about her rabbit,' Carol explained. 'Tell Juno what happened to him.'

'Mr Fox,' she hiccupped sadly, her little face crumpling.

'Oh no!' I cried. 'Poor rabbit!'

'But we're going to buy you a new one, aren't we?'

'Oh, don't buy one!' I told her about Honeysuckle Farm's rescued animals. 'They've got dozens of rabbits. I'll get you one.'

Promise made, I bought another half a dozen eggs and returned to the van. Dylan was sitting upright, nose pressed against the window, watching for my return with the expression of one who fears he may have been abandoned for ever. He greeted me as if I'd been gone for days.

I called in at *Old Nick's* after I'd taken Dylan home. Pat was minding the shop, some unidentifiable fuzzy animal taking shape on her knitting needles. There was no sign of Sophie or Elizabeth and the shop was silent, so I assumed Fizz wasn't around either. Pat was wearing the martyred air of someone who's had enough of knitting and of her own company.

'Quiet day?' I asked.

She responded with a grunt. 'You're going to have to watch that new one.'

'Fizz?' I asked as she rolled up her knitting and stabbed the needles through the fuzzy ball of wool. 'Has she been in today?'

She sniffed in disdain. 'No sign of her. She told Sophie she was going upcountry to one of them craft fairs she goes to. But when I come in and opened up this morning, I found she'd left all the lights on upstairs and' – she paused for dramatic effect, stabbing the air with one bony finger – 'the iron! She could've caught the whole place on fire.'

I doubted that but I lamented the wasted electricity. 'Who locked up last night?' As far as I knew, Fizz had not yet been trusted with this responsibility.

'Well, Sophie did,' Pat admitted, 'but she didn't need to go upstairs so she didn't check in the studio. Why should she?'

'I'll have a word with Fizz when I see her. In the meantime, perhaps we'd all better check upstairs before we close up.'

Pat tutted, pushing a lock of lank brown hair behind her ear. I sensed there was more to come and waited. After a few moments of silence, she muttered, 'She told Sophie she thought my knitted animals were amateurish.'

74

'How do you know this?' Sophie would never repeat anything like that to Pat.

'I heard her.' She hunched a shoulder pettishly. 'I didn't say nothing. I pretended I hadn't heard.' Pat is a woman who speaks her mind and not one to be intimidated, two things I love about her. The fact she hadn't given Fizz an earful made me wonder if she secretly felt her knitted toys were amateurish too.

'Well, she's wrong, isn't she? Your animals are quirky and funny, and people love them. You sell lots, so what does she know?'

Pat smiled weakly. 'That's what Sophie said.'

'Well, there you are, then.' I gave her a hug. She's bony and stiff, uncomfortable with affection; it was a bit like hugging an ironing board. 'Don't let Fizz get under your skin. She probably doesn't mean anything. She's just tactless, that's all. I'll lock up,' I told her. 'You go home.'

I was just counting up the day's meagre takings when who should come in but the dumpy little woman who'd been in the day before and gone away for a think. She was still wearing the little brown hat over her thick blonde curls. She must have been in her sixties and it occurred to me as I looked at her afresh that the abundant blonde curls might be a wig.

'I've decided,' she told me, smiling widely and showing the little gap between her front teeth, 'what to buy my friend.'

I followed her to the back of the shop where she

pointed to a small enamel brooch displayed in the glass cabinet. 'That one,' she told me, 'the bumblebee brooch.'

I took it out for her and back to the counter where I wrapped it up in tissue paper.

'Would you mind writing me a receipt?' she asked. 'Just in case?'

'You're still not sure she'll like it?'

My customer gave a slight, apologetic shake of her head. 'Well, she might prefer that little swallow pendant. I'll tell her about it. And if she thinks she'd rather have that, you wouldn't mind if I changed it, would you?'

'Of course not,' I assured her, grateful the word 'refund' hadn't come into the conversation.

We didn't have much call for receipts in *Old Nick's*, but when I'd set the shop up, I had bought a duplicate receipt book from the post office, the old-fashioned sort with the two copies separated by a sheet of carbon paper. Carried away by optimistic enthusiasm, I'd had a rubber stamp made with the name of the shop on it and stamped my way through the whole book. The receipts were numbered. So far, we'd only reached number four. I wrote out her purchase and at her request added 'Paid in Full' at the bottom and signed it. I tore off the top copy with a flourish and handed it to her. She gave me her funny little gap-toothed smile again and went away, happily clutching her purchase. And I had thought she wouldn't come back. Just goes to show what I know.

My fridge was so empty it echoed, a bit like my stomach, although that made more of a growl. I heaved a sigh as I stared into the brightly-lit void. I wasn't getting my usual supply of cafe leftovers from my landlords, downstairs. I don't know what was going on. I don't think it had anything to do with Kate's pregnancy, more a sign that *Sunflowers* was doing better business and there weren't so many leftovers to go around. I was happy for them if business was looking up, but not if that meant my supply of vegetable samosas and apple flapjacks was going to dry up. All I had left was eggs. I realised I hadn't seen Kate or Adam for a day or two. I'd better knock on their door, see if all was well. I closed the fridge door. I wouldn't starve in the next two days, but there was every chance I'd get egg-bound.

Adam answered the door, looking vaguely like a pirate with a large knife clutched in one hand. He was chopping onions, he told me. I could see the evidence lying on the chopping board, sliced transparently thin. I wished I could do that. I come from the chunky veg school of cookery; no knife skills at all. Kate was curled up in a chair by the kitchen fire. Her tummy didn't show much yet, just a gentle curve, but she wore the roseate glow of approaching motherhood. No one would guess she'd been hanging over the toilet every morning for the last week, barfing. She gave me the sleepy-eyed smile of someone who's just woken from a nap and stretched, dislodging Bill from her lap. Shamelessly he began to weave his body in figures of eight about my ankles. *Tart*, I accused him silently. I offered to make us all a cup of tea, brewing ordinary tea for me and Adam and some disgusting herbal concoction for Kate, whilst onions sizzled in the pan and Adam got to work dicing a sacrificial pepper. I'd have thought the last thing he would have wanted to do after cooking at *Sunflowers* all day would be to cook supper at home, but I suppose he was used to it.

I drew up a kitchen stool and sat cradling my tea. We chatted about pleasant subjects like corpses stuffed in wardrobes and old men being murdered in their own homes before we moved on to how our respective businesses were faring, the general state of disrepair in the house and what Adam was planning to do about it.

'You might as well know,' he said, changing the subject, 'Kate and I are thinking of selling the business.'

'Selling *Sunflowers*?' I was shocked. 'But I thought the place was just starting to do well.'

They had been struggling for years, but now, with the greater popularity of the veggie diet, I thought they were finally turning the corner.

'We're only thinking about it,' Kate admitted, flicking her dark plait back over one shoulder.

'Now's a good time to sell,' Adam went on, as he shredded a bunch of basil, 'while the books are looking good.'

'But what would you do?' I asked.

'Adam's been offered a job as chef.' Kate mentioned the name of a very expensive health spa up on the moor.

'They approached me about developing a gourmet plant-based menu,' he said, grinning.

I laughed. 'Whizzing up kale smoothies for rich ladies to sip in the jacuzzi?'

'Something like that.'

'Wouldn't you find that a bit restricting?'

'Not on the money they're offering.'

'And I could develop my own business from home,' Kate added, her eyes bright with enthusiasm. 'Events catering for parties and weddings and things. It would be easier working from home once the baby comes, and we wouldn't have the overheads of running the cafe.'

'It doesn't sound as if there's much to think about,' I told them. 'It sounds like a no-brainer.' But even as I spoke, I felt they were making a mistake. Closing the cafe didn't feel right to me.

Adam commenced the slaughter of some plump, juicy tomatoes. 'If you can stand a three-bean chilli,' he said, 'you're welcome to stay for supper.'

'I think I could cope,' I admitted, 'but only if you let me buy the wine.'

Whilst the cooking progressed, I slipped down to North Street to get a bottle of red – organic, of course. Would I ever be like Kate and Adam, I wondered, cheerfully domesticated? I couldn't see it somehow, doubted I could ever settle down with anyone. Would I want to, with Daniel for instance? With him I'd be lucky if I got the opportunity. Apart from his physical absence, there was another potential barrier to our forming a lasting relationship in the form of the first Mrs Thorncroft, deceased. Claire had died tragically and there was still a part of Daniel that was not comfortable with the idea of moving on. He'd had one woman in his life since her death: Meredith. But just as we didn't talk about the incident, Daniel and I never talked about Meredith.

There was still some warmth in the evening sun as I strolled through Ashburton. A few folk were sitting at picnic tables on the green by the river, nursing glasses from the Victoria pub down the road, enjoying the last of the rays. I continued down North Street, past the little grey stone town hall with its belltower, towards the shops.

Where the pavement widened, a group of youths huddled together clutching skateboards. I skirted around them to get into the shop and almost collided with the burly figure of Detective Constable Dean Collins. He stopped in the doorway, a couple of pasties, packets of crisps and bars of chocolate balanced against his manly chest, and a takeaway coffee clutched in one hand. His jaw dropped when he saw me. 'Oh, bloody hell,' he muttered.

'Anyone would think you weren't pleased to see me,' I responded sunnily.

For a moment his attention was taken by the malingering youths. 'On our way to the skatepark, are we, lads?' he called out to them. He might not have been dressed in uniform, but Dean is so obviously a copper he might as well wear a blue light on his head. The boys took the hint and loped off in the general direction of the recreation ground, grumbling.

I pointed at the goodies he was clutching. 'On a diet?'

'Working supper,' he responded glumly.

'Working on what?'

'Police business.' He set his jaw firmly as if he wasn't going to say any more. 'Now, excuse me, Juno—'

I stayed in the doorway. He couldn't get past me without risking serious damage to his pasties. 'Any progress on Fred Crick's murder?'

He sighed, giving in to the inevitable. 'We're stuck for a motive, beyond the possibility of robbery. We've been trying to find his family.'

'I didn't realise he had one.' Stupid of me, really, it was unlikely Fred had farmed Cold East Farm for all those years single-handed.

'Had a wife – she ran off and left him years ago – and there was a son, but we can't find any trace of him either.'

'Maisie said that Fred Crick was a bad lot and she wasn't surprised he'd come to a sticky end.'

Dean frowned. 'Did she say why?'

'No,' I admitted, 'but Maisie says that about a lot of people.'

'Well, ask her, will you?'

I grinned. 'Do I get Brownie points if I find out anything?'

He grunted. 'You might get a few black marks knocked off.'

'Charming!' I stood aside to let him pass. 'By the way,' I called out as he crossed the road to his car, 'did you find Peter Gillow's rucksack?'

He placed his coffee cup on the roof of the car as he reached for his keys. His brows knitted together and I nipped across the road to join him. 'Rucksack?' he repeated.

'The landlady at the guest house made sandwiches for him. He must have been carrying them in something, and he had a map.'

'No, we haven't found a rucksack,' he replied, 'and what were you doing talking to the owner of the guest house?'

'It's a free country.'

Dean shook his head. 'Watch it, Juno,' he advised, then got into his car and slammed the door. I knocked on the window, picking up the coffee cup from the roof and waggled it at him. He lowered the window and took it from me, placed it carefully on the seat next to him and started up the engine without another word.

'Love to Gemma and Alice,' I mouthed, waving. I could see him muttering fiercely as he drove off. I turned back across the road into the shop to apply myself to the business of buying wine. That three-bean chilli would be ready by now.

CHAPTER EIGHT

Sunday lunch was a bag of cheesy chips bought from the Hound of the Basket Meals, a catering van that has set itself up in a discreet corner of the lay-by near Hound Tor and become an accepted part of the landscape; a place of refreshment for walkers and drivers alike. As I had nothing better to do, I decided I'd trace the route Peter Gillow had taken from Hound Tor and try to discover how he'd ended up at Crick's cottage.

I'd started earlier at Haytor, the rocks busy with hikers and climbers on a sunny Sunday morning, and followed the track of the old granite tramway used in times gone by to transport rock from the quarry to the coast. Then I branched off downhill towards the tumble of stones that marked the remains of an ancient settlement, the valley floor speckled with clumps of yellow gorse that shifted in the breeze. 'When gorse ain't in flower, then kissing's out of fashion,' Maisie always says.

A lark rose suddenly from the ground, hanging in the air like a tiny feathery star and singing out a warning. I must have strayed too near her nest, somewhere on the ground close by, and I changed direction. The long ridge of Greator Rocks jutted ahead of me like the bony spine of a buried dinosaur breaking through the ground; beyond them Hound Tor thrust against the sky, the ruined towers of a castle carved by rain and wind. On a sunny morning the tor looked impressive enough; but it needed to be seen at sunset, in mist or moonlight, or with great storm clouds lowering over it, to understand why it inspired myth, why it had become a place of legend.

I poked around the rocks and ruins for a bit, stepping carefully among the lumps of fallen granite, as I am sure the historian Peter Gillow would have done. He must have found it fascinating, seeing all this for the first time. My problem was that from the medieval village, I wasn't sure which route he'd taken. He could have followed the minor road that led directly down to Widecombe. If I was going to do the same, I might as well get in the van and drive, save the wear and tear on my ankle, but I decided to cut across to Honeybag Tor and drop down on to the road from there, even though it would require a hike back up the road to rescue the van from the car park later.

This meant I approached Crick's cottage across country, from the back, rather than arriving at his front gate from the roadside. I came up over the hill behind Cold East Farm and climbed the rock, looking down on the farmhouse with its golden thatch, the orchard, pretty with bluebells. I could pick out the roof of the henhouse, the beehives and the paddock behind the farmhouse. The deep trench dug for the foundations of the new campsite shower block was a straight muddy scar in the grass, the digger, small as a toy from here, sitting idle at one end. In the more distant fields, sheep stood out white against the green grass, like tiny woolly clouds.

I made my way through the copse of dark firs towards Fred's cottage. From the edge of the trees its burnt and blackened walls stood out clearly, the empty doorway garlanded with tape. I could smell the carbonised wood, the ash. As I made to step out from the flickering shade, a movement snagged my attention and I held back. Someone was treading through the long grass in Fred's garden, someone not deterred by the tape around the gate forbidding entry. Whoever it was, he disappeared into the shed. I crept forward as close as I dared, sheltering behind a tangle of stunted elder bushes and raised my binoculars, training them on the shed door and waited for him to come out.

It was several minutes before he did. He must have had a good look around in there. If he was a policeman, I didn't recognise him. He was no member of the local detective team and he wasn't in uniform but dressed in dark jeans and a leather jacket. He was tall and fit-looking, tanned, his light brown hair cut short. He turned his head towards me suddenly, as if he could sense my presence, then came stepping through the long grass towards the tangle of bushes, seemingly staring straight through me. My heart gave a nervous flutter. As he came closer. I could see piercing blue-green eyes. Then he stopped, silent and alert, sweeping his gaze around, listening for any sound. I held my breath.

I didn't want him to discover me. If I'd been walking along the road, I could have stopped by the gate quite naturally and engaged him in conversation, found out what he was doing there. But it would be difficult to explain what I was up to lurking behind a bush spying on him, especially if it turned out he was a policeman after all.

A crow cawed, sudden and raucous. The man watched it flap away towards the dark trees, then he turned his back. He left the garden, putting a hand on the gatepost and vaulting over the gate in one smooth movement. I picked my way around behind the bushes. I could see the road, a silver-grey Peugeot parked on the opposite verge. He climbed into it and started up the engine, but from where I crouched, peering intently through the branches, I couldn't get a view of the number plate as he drove away.

Silver-grey Peugeots seemed to be everywhere in Ashburton the next day. At least, that's the way it seemed as I was in town fetching Maisie's prescriptions. Not that I had any way of identifying the one belonging to the man in Fred Crick's garden, even supposing it was parked in Ashburton at all. But I couldn't stop noticing them. I wanted to know what the man had been up to. Perhaps, like me, he was just a nosy individual who'd come across the burnt-out cottage and decided to have a snoop around. And perhaps it was that fit body, tanned face and those astonishing turquoise eyes that I found myself remembering, that made me clock every silver-grey vehicle I saw parked at the roadside.

Maisie had not been very helpful regarding Fred Crick. It wasn't that she didn't have plenty to say, it just didn't amount to much in the way of information.

'Drunk,' she pronounced scathingly when I'd asked her what she knew about him. 'Every Saturday night, used to get chucked out of the First and Last, regular. Course, I'm talking about years ago.'

'How do you know?' I asked.

'My nephew Lambert,' she said. 'He liked a drink, did Lambert – *not*,' she assured me, solemnly holding up a finger, 'that our Lambert ever got drunk. He could hold his liquor. But many's the time he helped carry Fred Crick home.'

'Is he still around, Lambert?' If he was Maisie's nephew he was probably about Fred's age, and Fred was seventy if he was a day.

'No,' she told me sadly, 'dreadful accident with a tractor years ago. Shame, he was a lovely lad.'

'I'm sorry.'

'He had a wife, Fred did.' She screwed up her eyes, struggling to remember her name. 'Vivian. She ran off . . . oh, years back. Not long after the boy had gone.' She gave a little chuckle. 'Some people said she'd run off with her fancy man.'

'Boy?' I repeated. 'You mean their son?'

'He ran away when he was just a boy.' She tutted and shook her head. 'He and his father didn't get on. Talk was, he'd run off to join the navy or the army or something. I don't remember.' She leant forward conspiratorially and lowered her voice, although the only one to overhear us would be Jacko snoozing on the window sill. 'Lambert used to say that when Fred was in his cups, he would swear the lad wasn't no son of his. And Vivian Crick turned up in church on Sunday with a black eye more than once.'

'No wonder she ran off.'

Maisie grunted. 'Had enough of Fred, I reckon.' She laughed. 'She shouldn't have stood for his nonsense. Walloped him with her rolling pin, that's what she should have done, showed him who was boss.'

'Someone walloped him with something,' I told her, 'before they set fire to his cottage. Do you know if he ever got mixed up in anything nasty? Was he ever in trouble with the law?'

'I don't know no more than what Lambert used to tell me,' Maisie said. 'And he's been dead a long time. He used to say Fred turned nasty when he'd had too much to drink.'

'So, he might have made enemies, then?'

Maisie chuckled again. 'Looks like it, don't it?'

'Yes,' I agreed. 'It do.'

I called in at the shop later, to find Fizz regaling Sophie with tales of all the stuff she'd sold at the craft fair she'd attended. She was doing her first solo shift manning the shop next afternoon and I wanted to make sure she was clear about everything. I'd come in at closing time, I promised her, to lock up. She assured me that there would be absolutely no problems.

'Well, there shouldn't be,' Sophie lowered her voice as Fizz sailed up the stairs to her studio, 'it's simple enough.' She rolled her big dark eyes. 'She'll be lucky if she gets any customers, anyway.'

'Have we had any today?' I asked, expecting the answer no.

'Well, no, except' – she giggled – 'this gorgeous-looking bloke came in. He had fantastic eyes, sort of greenish-blue, almost turquoise.'

I stared at her. 'Short brown hair?' I asked. 'Really fit-looking?'

'Oh yes, very.'

'Was he wearing a leather jacket?'

'Um . . . yes I think he was. D'you know him?' she asked excitedly.

'No, but I think I know who you mean. He didn't buy anything?'

She shook her head. 'He spent a long time looking around your stuff out at the back. I asked if he was looking for anything, if I could help him in any way . . .'

I bet. Her black eyelashes would have been batting away like butterfly wings.

'He asked where the furniture had come from. I said he'd have to talk to you—' She took in a shocked little breath as if she'd just realised the significance of what she was about to say.

'What?' I asked.

She gazed at me, her dark eyes wide. 'He said he was looking for a wardrobe.'

Dean Collins refused to be impressed. 'There's no point in getting excited,' he told me over the phone. 'Unless we can find him and you can both positively identify him, we can't be sure you and Sophie are even talking about the same bloke.'

'Of course we are!' I responded in disgust. 'It was the same man snooping around in Fred's shed and then in the shop, asking about a wardrobe.' Sophie and I had described him in great detail to each other – the lean, tanned cheeks, the strong jaw, the fit body. To be frank, there weren't any other men around here who were that drop-dead gorgeous.

'Could be coincidence,' he argued with what I considered a serious lack of imagination. Did it not occur to him that this man, snooping around the remains of Fred's burnt-out cottage, could be the murderer returning to the scene of the crime? Didn't he think that the same man, asking about a wardrobe, could be significant?

'Possibly,' he conceded as if he was determined to be obtuse. 'More to the point,' he went on, 'what were *you* doing snooping about there?'

'Where?' I asked innocently.

His voice suggested that he was running out of patience. 'Stay away from Crick's place, Juno. It's a crime scene.'

I snorted. 'There doesn't seem to be a lot of investigating going on.'

'You're wrong there. We've just had a report back from forensics on Peter Gillow's clothes. There were bloody fingerprints on his jacket, and the blood wasn't his.'

'Fred's?' I asked.

'That's right.'

'So, Peter Gillow was involved in his murder?'

'No, we don't think so. These prints were under his arms.'

'Just where they would be if someone had lifted his body,' I said after a moment,' if they were lifting him—'

'—into the wardrobe.' We both spoke together.

'There's also a trace of blood on that piece of rope.'

'So, whoever killed Fred put Peter's body in the wardrobe and tied the door.'

'Well, we were pretty sure of that before,' Dean pointed out, 'but this would seem to confirm it. And there's more.'

He made me wait. 'Well?' I prompted.

'Among all the debris, fire investigators have found buckles from what they believe was a rucksack.'

'In Fred's house?' I frowned. 'So Gillow went in there?'

'Not necessarily. Whoever disposed of his body in the wardrobe, might have decided to chuck the rucksack in the fire.'

'Oh, by the way,' I remembered. 'I talked to Maisie . . .'

'And?'

I repeated the things that Maisie told me about Fred's drunkenness and his wife and son. But the police had heard all that already, Dean told me smugly, from making their own enquiries.

'You haven't found either of them yet?'

'Not so far. We're going back twenty years, remember. They could have changed their names, moved anywhere. It could take a long time to track them down, and even then, we've no reason to suppose that they're implicated in Crick's murder. Robbery still seems the most likely motive.'

Poor old Fred, I thought as I put the phone down. It occurred to me that if he had been robbed, the money I had paid him would have been nicked as well; and if it hadn't, then my hard-earned cash had simply gone up in smoke. And all I'd got out of it were a few brass bits and bobs and some damaged furniture that could cost me more than it was worth to get restored. I sighed deeply. The receipt I'd made him write me was a fat lot of good now.

Next day was my proper day for looking after Maisie, my regular slot for cleaning her cottage, hanging her laundry, doing her shopping and walking her dog. This particular morning was enlivened by a visit from Pam the chiropodist who, at no small risk of personal injury, clipped her way bravely through Maisie's horny toenails. All the time she was watched suspiciously by Jacko who, from the safety of Maisie's lap, growled at her throughout the entire procedure. Perhaps it was the flying chips of toenail that unsettled him but occasional slaps on the snout from Maisie and orders to hold his noise had no effect at all.

She told Pam the same story she tells her every time she visits, about what beautiful feet she'd had as a young woman, and how she always varnished her toenails in a shade of peachy pink. It was sad, seeing her veined old feet now, to think of them in peep-toe sandals. Peachy pink was the shade that Maisie now reserved for colouring her hair.

It was as I was leaving, all jobs done, that she said suddenly, 'I remembered something . . . it came to me in the night . . . something about Vivian Crick.' She scowled, holding a crooked finger to her lips. 'It was something Connie told me.'

I paused in the act of shrugging on my coat. 'Who's Connie?'

'Lambert's widow.' She tutted impatiently as if I ought to know that already. 'She was friends with her . . . I remember!' She nodded, pleased with herself. 'She said that Vivian never had no fancy man.'

'When she left Fred, you mean?'

'Right,' Maisie wagged her head with certainty, 'Connie didn't like what people were saying about Vivian, that she'd run off with some man. It came to me

93

of a sudden. She said that Vivian Crick was a respectable married woman. She didn't have any bloke on the side.'

'Do you think she was right?' I smiled. 'Perhaps Vivian was better at keeping secrets than Connie knew.'

She frowned, pursing her lips. 'She and Connie were pretty close.'

'Well, I don't suppose it matters. Whether Vivian had a boyfriend or not, she'd obviously had enough of Fred.'

In the afternoon I had to drive to Newton Abbot for one of my clients, Chloe Berkeley-Smythe. She'd deposited an expensive suit with the dry cleaner before she'd gone on her latest cruise and forgotten to collect it. She'd rung me from Tenerife in a panic that they might sell or dispose of uncollected garments, and as it was to be several more weeks before she came home, would I be an angel and go and collect it for her? This meant letting myself into her cottage with the spare key I kept so that I could search for the relevant ticket. Of course, I couldn't find it. It was probably in Tenerife, lurking in the depths of Chloe's luggage.

But when I explained my dilemma to the lady behind the counter in the dry-cleaner's she was quick to reassure me. Some people's garments had been waiting for collection for over two years, she informed me. It was the reason they asked people to pay for their dry-cleaning upfront. And she was well acquainted with Mrs Berkeley-Smythe. Would I care to take the other garments that were waiting as well as her suit, garments she had obviously forgotten?

I came out staggering under the weight of the suit, a winter overcoat, a long blue cocktail dress and several beaded sweaters, all hung on thin wire hangers and sheathed in slithery plastic bags. Who on earth buys sweaters that need dry-cleaning? People with more money than sense, obviously: enough said.

Whilst I was in town, I bought some new valve caps for the tyres on White Van. Someone keeps pinching mine, at least the posh metal ones. It happens all the time; as soon as I replace them, they're gone again. It's either kids doing it out of mischief or there is some obsessive valve cap collector somewhere with a house full of them. This time I just bought the cheap plastic jobs. Whoever it is leaves those alone.

Newton Abbot is a busy market town, and at the wrong times of day, full of traffic.

I was in White Van, waiting in a long queue of vehicles creeping towards the traffic lights near the supermarket when my mobile phone burst into life. As I'd already given up on making any immediate progress and had put the handbrake on, I decided to risk slipping it out of my bag and holding it to my ear. 'Hello?'

'Oh, Juno!' a voice wailed loudly in my ear. 'Can you come to the shop?' it pleaded tearfully. 'Can you come right away?'

It took me a moment to recognise the voice. 'Fizz? Whatever's the matter?'

'Oh, Juno,' she snivelled. 'I'm so sorry. Can you come? I think I've done something dreadful!'

CHAPTER NINE

It took me another half an hour to reach *Old Nick's*. Fizz must have phoned Sophie and Elizabeth as well because they were standing in the shop listening to her tale of woe as I walked in.

'Well, she gave me the receipt, you see,' she was explaining in a voice close to tears, 'and it said it was all paid for, so I didn't bother to check . . . I just let her have it all . . .'

'What's up?' As the shop bell jangled the three of them turned to look at me. Fizz had plainly been snivelling, mascara in ragged black rings under her eyes and her nose glowing red. Sophie's little face was troubled and she bit her lip when she saw me.

'You'd better sit down,' Elizabeth advised me calmly. 'It looks as if you've been robbed.'

'Robbed?' I echoed. 'Robbed of what?'

She handed me the receipt she held. I'd written it myself: number four. At the top I had written 'bumblebee brooch' and the price. Beneath it was a long list, in a reasonable forgery of my handwriting, of other items: a ruby glass scent bottle with gold cap, silver pig-shaped pincushion, Chinese snuff bottle, a pair of diamante dress clips, silver hatpins – various – a Victorian silver cake slice with mother-of-pearl handle . . . As I read through it I began to feel sick. It was almost my entire stock of small valuable items, those I kept locked in the display cabinet, and at the bottom, next to my signature, the words 'Paid in Full'.

'I'm so sorry,' Fizz whispered, struggling to find her voice. 'She said she'd paid for everything when she bought the little brooch . . . she gave me the receipt, you see . . .' She lapsed into tears and carried on blubbering. I stared at the receipt in a state of shock. 'It wasn't until she'd left the shop,' she managed at last, 'I bothered to look at the ledger. I was going to make a note that the things had been collected . . . and then, when I saw they hadn't been entered in the ledger at all, I checked the receipt book . . . and I saw that none of those things were written on the copy . . . only the brooch . . .'

'I don't think I'd have bothered to check either,' Sophie added hastily, 'to be fair.'

I stared down at the forged handwriting, at my signature, at 'Paid in Full'. 'No,' I sighed, depressed. 'Why would you?'

'What reason did this woman give,' Elizabeth asked, 'for coming back to collect what she'd already bought? Did she say why she didn't take it all on the day she claimed she'd paid for it, why she only took the brooch?'

Fizz gulped. 'Yes. She said that on the day she'd bought the things from Juno she'd been going to a friend's birthday party and she'd wanted to take the brooch because it was a present . . . but she didn't want to carry all the other stuff around in her handbag because there would be a lot of people there she didn't know and' – she threatened to dissolve into tears again – 'she said you can't be too careful. She said you'd promised to hold on to it all for her till she came back.'

'And you didn't wonder why Juno had just left these things in the cabinet?' Elizabeth asked with an edge to her voice. 'Or why she hadn't marked the items as sold?'

'Not until it was too late,' she admitted miserably. 'I'm so sorry, Juno.'

'Did she say why she'd bought so many things?' Sophie asked.

Fizz shook her head. 'I assumed she was a collector . . . or another trader.'

I asked her to describe the woman, although I knew exactly what she was going to say: mid-sixties, short, slightly dumpy, blonde curls, felt hat.

'And a space between her front teeth,' I added.

'Oh yes! Yes, she did have this little space! The thing was, she was so pleasant and polite, and she had the receipt, you see—'

'It's not your fault.' Anyone could be taken in by that sweet, grandmotherly air.

'I'm going to go upstairs and make us some tea,' Sophie announced suddenly. 'I think we all need one.'

'Good thinking,' Elizabeth agreed, 'although what we really need is gin.'

She gestured at the receipt that I still held limply. 'I don't think our little con artist intended to leave that behind her.'

Fizz blinked suddenly as if struck by a bright light. 'She did bustle off rather quickly when another customer came in. I think you're right. I picked it up from the floor after she'd gone. She must have dropped it on her way out.'

Elizabeth directed one of her steely glances in my direction. 'Time to call the police, I think, don't you?'

Detective Sergeant Cruella deVille could hardly keep the smirk off her nasty little face.

'This is a well-known scam, I'm afraid.' She tried to sound solicitous as she slipped the receipt into a plastic evidence bag. 'There have been similar cases in the last few weeks in Topsham and in Exmouth.'

I watched the evidence bag disappear into her briefcase. I didn't need it any more. I'd already totalled the value of the stock I'd lost. Little things add up. I'd been robbed of a thousand pounds I couldn't afford to lose. 'But we're not usually lucky enough to get hold of the receipt,' Cruella added. She favoured Fizz with her strange little tug of a smile. 'Well done!'

The rest of us exchanged glances; frankly, Fizz was the last person we felt deserved congratulation.

'They usually pick on places like this,' she went on, 'where a number of people look after the shop at different times. That way they are never served twice by the same person, by the person who wrote the original receipt.'

'They?' I repeated.

'It's a pair doing this,' Cruella explained, 'a man and an older woman, possibly mother and son, although descriptions vary slightly.' She consulted the statements she'd taken. 'You both describe this woman as having blonde curly hair. In Topsham it seems she was a brunette.' Again, she gave her odd smile. 'Same space between the front teeth, though.'

'What about the man?' I asked. 'Does he go round in disguise as well?'

'He seems to be someone witnesses have difficulty remembering. They describe him as ordinary, undistinguished, non-descript.'

Sophie frowned. 'So how much chance does Juno stand of getting her stuff back?'

Cruella shook her head in what was supposed to be a sad gesture. 'Very little, I'm afraid.' I could tell she was enjoying every minute of this conversation. 'I don't suppose you have photographs of the items in question?' she asked, turning her violet eyes on me.

Feeling like an idiot, I shook my head.

She sighed sorrowfully and spread her hands in a helpless gesture. 'Well, in that case, the best you can do is to write us a detailed description of all the stolen items. We'll send an officer around the local antique shops—'

'They wouldn't have the nerve to try and sell Juno's stuff in Ashburton, surely?' Sophie asked indignantly.

'Nerve is something that confidence tricksters have a

great deal of,' Cruella told her smugly. 'But it's more likely they'll dispose of it further afield. Unfortunately, we don't have the manpower to send officers to antiques fairs or car boot sales.' She flashed the violet gaze at me again. 'I'm afraid you'll have to do that yourself. But unless your stuff is invisibly marked or you've got photographs, then you've got little proof it's yours, even if you do find it.'

With that she tidied her papers and shut her briefcase with a snap. She headed for the door and then turned once more, her gaze at first encompassing us all, then drilling in on me. 'The trouble is antique dealers are an unscrupulous lot.' She smirked. 'There's very little honour among thieves.'

'Well!' Fizz breathed as Cruella departed with a jingling of the shop bell. 'How rude!'

The interesting thing was that for the fraudsters to know who was serving in the shop at any particular time, they would have to have studied what went on at *Old Nick's*. Sophie, Elizabeth and I discussed this long after Fizz had escaped, fleeing guilty and ashamed after several more gushing apologies. This meant that they must have made repeated forays into the shop – and none of us could remember noticing the woman with the space between her teeth before – unless they had been observing the comings and goings in the shop from somewhere else. But there was no obvious place that they could observe from – across the road, for instance – because apart from the undertakers and the launderette, there were no other businesses in Shadow Lane; and *Old Nick's* windows faced a blank stone wall, the back of an ancient house that was now flats.

The launderette was a place where someone could sit for a long time without being noticed, but that was further down the lane on the same side, it offered no view. But it was somewhere that you could keep popping in and out, we decided, walking past the shop to see who was behind the counter; so that must be what they had done.

Elizabeth invited me to supper. Olly would be glad to see me, she said. I hadn't seen him since before Fred's murder and he was eager to hear all the grisly details. I didn't relish the idea of an evening with only Bill for company. Just the sight of the empty shelves in the glass cabinet depressed me. I accepted her offer with gratitude.

But before we left the shop, I phoned Vicky and Tom. They ran a similar business to *Old Nick's* except on a much larger scale, with dozens of traders under one roof. I warned them to beware of unremarkable men and dumpy women with spaces between their front teeth. They promised they would keep an eye out, especially if anyone tried to sell them anything. Vicky was pretty certain she would recognise the Chinese snuff bottle or the pig-shaped pincushion if they came her way. As for being scammed, they'd suffered themselves many times over the years. It seems there is nothing new in the antiques business.

Elizabeth moved in with Olly last year. She poses as his aunt, although they are not actually related. She was homeless at the time and Olly, then just fourteen, had been secretly living alone since the death of his great-grandmother over a year before. My getting them together was an arrangement that suited them both. Elizabeth had somewhere to live and Olly had a responsible adult looking after him and was no longer in danger of being taken into care by social services.

He was fifteen now, and although he had shot up a few inches since I first met him, he could still pass for a twelve-year-old. The raging hormones of adolescence had not yet kicked in, no sprouting hair or unsightly blemishes to mar the maiden smoothness of his cheek. He grinned when he saw me and closed the lid of his laptop on the homework he'd been doing. I was a welcome distraction. 'I'll help with supper,' he volunteered, putting the laptop into his schoolbag.

'There's no need,' Elizabeth told him crisply as she laid out onions and a packet of mince from her shopping bag onto the counter. 'It's only spaghetti bolognese. I'm sure we can manage without your help. You carry on with your homework.'

'Nah,' he responded, snatching up a bulb of garlic, tossing it with one hand and catching it with the other, 'that would be inhospitable to our guest.'

Elizabeth shot him a sideways look.

'I'll finish it later,' he promised. 'It's only writing up a physics experiment. And it didn't work anyway.' His eyes lit up with excitement as they rested on me. 'Tell me about the fire and this dead bloke in the wardrobe.'

That wasn't all I had to tell him about. Whilst Elizabeth chopped onions and browned mince and Olly skinned tomatoes to make a sauce – his cooking skills put mine to shame – I sat with a glass of red wine at my elbow and told him all he wanted to know about the unfortunate Peter Gillow, the more unfortunate Fred Crick, finishing with a description of what had happened in the shop today to the equally unfortunate me. Though, to be correct, I wasn't as unfortunate as the other two: at least I was alive.

'This Fizzy Izzy woman sounds a right idiot. I think you should sack her.'

'Well, I don't actually employ her,' I pointed out as I set the kitchen table, 'and anyway, I need her rent.'

Elizabeth looked up from the stirring, releasing garlicky, tomato-laden aromas from the steaming sauce. 'She's already cost you more than this month's rent.'

'True,' I sighed, 'but it wasn't really her fault.'

She gave a dry smile. 'I just can't wait to hear what Pat's going to say about it.'

In spite of myself I laughed. 'I notice she didn't send out a distress call to *her* this afternoon.'

'She was probably wise.'

Olly looked up from grating parmesan cheese into a bowl. 'Do you think the police will catch her, this woman?'

'Who knows?' I responded gloomily. 'From what Cruella says it sounds unlikely.'

He narrowed his pale blue eyes. 'I might become a detective.'

Elizabeth raised her brows. 'Oh? What happened to

your desire to become a jazz musician?'

'Jazz musician?' I hadn't heard this latest in the long line of Olly's career aspirations. Chef, scientist and vet were obviously things of the past. 'I didn't know you could play jazz on a bassoon.'

'The bassoon's rubbish,' he said dismissively. 'I want to play the saxophone.'

I glanced at Elizabeth whose lips compressed firmly. She'd recently bought Olly a new bassoon because at the time it was his passion, and he was desperate for a better instrument than the one he loaned from the youth orchestra. It had cost her a lot of money. There was a moment's uneasy silence. Then she declared the Bolognese was ready, and we set to draining pasta and tossing salad and taking the warming garlic bread from the oven and the subject wasn't mentioned again.

Once we were at the table, I told them about Becky and her new mobile dog-grooming enterprise, and how she was looking for a name to replace the awful *Pretty Paws*.

'Shampoodle!' Olly suggested, waving a hunk of garlic bread, and then after munching thoughtfully for a few more moments, 'Wagger Washer!'

He carried on like this for the rest of the meal. When we'd finished, I volunteered to wash the dishes so that he could get back to his homework. But he'd barely opened the laptop when he suddenly held up a finger, struck by sudden inspiration. 'I've got it!' he cried.

Elizabeth and I both turned to look at him. 'Got what?'

'LaundroMutt,' he answered.

When he'd finished his homework, he announced he was going up to his room.

'Oh yes?' Elizabeth enquired mildly.

'Yeah,' he grinned. 'I'm gonna smoke drugs and watch porn.'

'Before you commence this evening of debauchery, I suggest an hour's bassoon practice, seeing that you have your grade eight exam next week.'

He rolled his eyes and sighed but didn't argue. He seemed content for Elizabeth to order him around, even though they weren't related and she was living in his house. But he'd grown up ruled by his great-grandmother, the indomitable Dolly. By all accounts she was a force to be reckoned with. Elizabeth's theory was that he liked her ordering him around because it gave him the feeling of security he'd lacked when he was living alone. A few moments later we heard the instrument's sad song coming from the living room.

'What's all this about a saxophone?' I asked.

Elizabeth shook her head. 'He's been to a few jazz concerts at the arts centre recently and has been bitten by the bug.'

'But you spent so much on buying him that bassoon,' I protested.

She shrugged elegantly. 'I don't mind that. I've told him, he can experiment with as many instruments as he likes, but if he wants to buy a saxophone, he'll have to pay for it himself. And I don't want him to give up the bassoon, not when he's doing so well.' She had been a music teacher herself once. For a moment we listened to the melancholy music drifting across the hall. She flashed me a smile. 'The brat's got talent.'

'Now then,' she went on, pouring me another glass of red wine, 'tell me about this fellow that Sophie got excited about the other day, the man who enquired about the wardrobe. She tells me you saw him at the scene of the crime.'

I shrugged. 'There's not much to tell, except that it's an odd coincidence, his poking around at Fred Crick's place where the wardrobe had come from.'

'You know, he might be completely innocent,' she suggested. 'He might genuinely be looking for a wardrobe and had heard that Fred had one to sell. He turned up, hoping to buy it, and discovered he'd come too late.'

'Then why did he come to the shop?'

'Well, it's a fairly logical place to look if he really is trying to find a wardrobe. He might have toured all of the antique shops in Ashburton, for all we know.' She eyed me shrewdly. 'But you don't think so. You think he might be Fred's murderer?'

I remembered him standing in Fred's garden, alert, eyes narrowed, listening to every sound. I remembered his smooth leap over the gate. He moved like a hunter. Some seeker of second-hand wardrobes just didn't fit the image.

At that moment an elderly cat, long and slender-limbed, leapt on the kitchen window sill and yowled through the glass to be let in. Elizabeth got up to open the window and he flowed down over the sill like poured milk, mewing a greeting.

'What did Sophie say to this man,' she asked, scratching Toby behind the ear, 'when he enquired about the wardrobe?'

'Only that we didn't have any wardrobes at the moment. I don't think he hung around for a chat,' I laughed, 'although she would have liked him to.'

'If he was as handsome as the two of you describe, I'm sorry I missed him.' Her grey eyes twinkled. 'But his coming into the shop was probably just a coincidence, you know.'

'Probably,' I agreed, knowing perfectly well that she didn't believe that any more than I did.

Sometimes you don't need to know very much about a person to trust them. Instinct, I suppose; it's not how much you know, but whether the little you do know feels right. I don't know much about Elizabeth, there are large parts of her past she doesn't talk about. She's something of an enigma but I'd trust her with my life. 'Do you mind if I ask you something?'

'Ask away.'

'What happened to your gun?'

'My father's old Luger?'

'That's the one.' For months she'd carried it about in her handbag.

'If you're asking to borrow it, the answer is absolutely not.'

I smiled. 'No, I wasn't asking that. I just wondered if you still carried it around.'

'It is safely locked away,' she assured me, lowering her voice, 'somewhere where Olly will never find it.' She leant towards me across the table. 'And he doesn't know it exists, in case you're wondering about that too.'

'No, I wasn't. But it reminds me, you promised to teach me a few moves.'

Olly had long been a victim of bullying at school. Elizabeth's arrival put a stop to that. First, she had talked to his teachers in the strongest possible terms; secondly, she had made Olly go into training, making him run with her every morning; and finally teaching him what she referred to as 'a few useful moves'. It had done the trick; he wasn't bullied again. He might be a little weed, but he was a tough, tenacious little weed and the school bullies had learnt not to mess with him. At some time, during one of those periods that Elizabeth didn't talk about, I suspect she had served in the military. And we had both decided that as I had what she called a talent for getting into trouble, I should learn some of these useful moves too.

'No time like the present,' she said.

'Just after supper?' I asked weakly. 'Is that a good idea?'

She raised an eyebrow. 'You think you'll never meet an assailant just after supper? Surely the whole point is that assault is unpredictable. You never know when an attacker might strike, or where or how.' Then she laughed. 'You're right, it is getting a little late. We'll choose a dry afternoon when we can use the garden. I can demonstrate on Olly. He'll love it.'

'Hopefully, this will just be a case of closing the stable door after the horse has bolted.'

She gave me dry look. 'Hopefully. I can teach you some

moves that might be helpful, but self-defence is really more about a state of mind, of being ready, reading signals, seeing the trouble before it starts and *hopefully*' – she picked up her wine glass – 'running away.'

'Running away?'

'Believe me,' she said, taking a sip, 'running away is always the best policy.'

'And if you can't?'

'Then you must fight,' she told me, her grey eyes serious. 'You have to assume he's going to kill you unless you disable him. You have to fight to win. And for a lot of women, that involves doing things that are counter-intuitive.'

'Like?'

'Like letting your attacker get as close to you as he can.'

'So, how do you fight to win?' I asked.

Olly came in at that moment, to help himself to an apple from the bowl on the kitchen table.

Elizabeth smiled up at him. 'Olly, how do you fight to win?' she asked.

He looked surprised for a moment and then grinned. 'Go mental,' he recommended.

CHAPTER TEN

Next day, I made it my business to visit all of Ashburton's antique traders. I gave each of them a description of the woman with the gap between her teeth and told them exactly how she'd conned me and Fizzy Izzy. I also mentioned the non-descript son. I handed out a list of the items that had been stolen from me. Every time I repeated what had happened, I felt more angry. By the end of the day, I was ready to make an even bigger space between the old girl's teeth. I had got over my shock. Now I wanted revenge.

The local tourist information centre publishes an 'Ashburton Antiques Trail', a leaflet for visitors listing the antique shops in town. I had visions of the old girl with a copy in her hand visiting them all, ticking them all off, making up her mind which one to con. Why had she singled out *Old Nick's* for this honour? Most antique shops in town were run by owners who were on the premises all the time, so I suppose they made more difficult targets. The place that was most like *Old Nick's* with several dealers under the same roof, was the Art and Antiques Bazaar. But it was larger and more open, easier to watch what was going on, to overhear what was passing between trader and a customer; harder for Old Gappy to return and claim she'd paid for things she hadn't.

I hadn't been into *Keepsakes* since the day I'd met Fred in there and agreed to look at the furniture he had for sale. I felt bad. I should really have gone to talk to Ron and Sheila before. After all, I'd no idea whether he was just an acquaintance or a real friend of theirs. They'd told me he was tight-fisted but that didn't mean they didn't care about him and I should have gone to see them after his murder and offer them my condolences. I must have looked a bit shamefaced when I stepped in through the shop door. I apologised for not calling before.

'Don't be silly, Juno,' Sheila said with a smile. 'You've nothing to apologise for. But isn't it a terrible thing,' she went on, 'poor Fred murdered like that? Are the police getting anywhere with finding the culprits?'

I repeated the usual litany about a robbery gone wrong. 'Did you know Fred well?' I asked.

'No, not well, did we?' She turned to Ron who was trying to find a square inch of clear room on a flat surface to put down a pile of old records. I moved a teddy bear from a low nursery chair so he could put them down on the seat. There was nowhere to put the bear, so I handed it to Sheila.

'I went to school with him,' Ron said, straightening up with a sigh. 'But he was never a friend of mine.'

'Do you know if he was ever in trouble with the law?' I asked.

Ron puffed out his cheeks, considering. 'I think he might have got arrested for being drunk and disorderly once or twice. Why do you ask?'

'Oh, I don't know,' I admitted. 'I just had an idea that maybe he'd got involved in something he shouldn't and that's what got him killed.'

Ron grunted. 'Well, I wouldn't put it past Fred to have got involved in something dodgy. Tell you what, I'll ask Sam Weston. He used to farm land not far from Fred's place and they used to drink together. I see him now and again in the Silent Whistle. Next time, I'll ask him.'

Sheila looked anxious. 'I don't think you can go round asking people about things like that.'

'Don't worry, I'll be discreet,' he told her. 'I haven't seen him for a while. Fred's murder is bound to come into the conversation.'

'Look, Fred isn't the reason I came in.' I went through the story of the gap-toothed fraudster again.

Ricky and Morris popped into the shop whilst I was out pounding the antiques trail, heard about the fraud from Sophie and phoned me on my mobile. They expressed various degrees of shock and horror and insisted on my coming to Druid Lodge for supper that evening to tell them all about it. I didn't turn them down. If nothing else, at least this was an event I could dine out on.

There was a dead man staring at me. I opened my mouth to scream. The corpse from the wardrobe, Peter Gillow, was standing in the shop doorway, his pale eyes fixed on me in a soulless gaze. This meant that I was either hallucinating or he was a zombie: either way, screaming seemed like a good idea.

His eyes widened in horror as my mouth opened. 'No! No!' he cried, flapping his hands in agitation. 'I'm Henry! Henry Gillow, Peter's brother. Please don't scream!'

My mouth hung open. 'Henry?' I breathed.

'Peter's twin brother,' he explained hastily as he took a nervous step into the shop.

I gaped at him, brain reeling. 'Identical twin brother,' I managed to gasp at last.

'You must be Miss Browne,' he said awkwardly. 'Didn't the police mention that I would be coming to see you?'

No, they did not. They had mentioned that Peter Gillow had a brother who lived upcountry somewhere, who had identified his body. They neglected to mention that he was an identical twin who would be coming back to Ashburton any time soon to scare the living crap out of me. I could hear the laughter all the way from the police station. 'No, no they didn't.'

Henry's round, red face crumpled like a baby's. 'I'm

so sorry. I didn't mean to frighten you.'

I was still finding it difficult to take him in. My view of his brother had only been brief, and he wasn't wearing the same ghastly grin, but as far as I could tell, the two men were identical with the same cherubic, round face and receding crinkly hair. Perhaps Henry was a little fatter but I couldn't swear to it. He was also quite ruddy-cheeked, which Peter had not been; most likely because he was dead.

He hovered nervously for a few moments and pointed to Sophie's empty chair. 'May I sit down?'

'Oh, please.' I tried to gather my scattered wits and half rose, but he already had his hand on the back of the chair and was dragging it to the counter where I was sitting.

It was the end of a long day. When I came back from my tour of Ashburton's antique shops, I'd had to repeat everything that had happened the day before to Pat and listen to her outraged expressions of horror and scathing opinions of Fizz's gullibility. I was glad when she went home. I was enjoying a few minutes alone in the shop, quietly cashing up, looking forward to supper with Ricky and Morris. Now I'd been confronted by a ghost. I felt decidedly wobbly.

'I hope you don't mind my coming to see you,' Henry began anxiously, 'I'm sure you can understand, I would like to know more about the circumstances of my brother's death.' He fixed me with an earnest gaze. 'What was he doing in that wardrobe?'

I hesitated. 'You're asking me?'

He nodded vigorously.

'Well, I don't know, Mr Gillow.'

'Henry, please.'

'I don't know, Henry. All I can tell you is that he wasn't in there when I bought it a few days before.'

He was still staring, expecting me to provide him with answers.

'Don't you know what he was doing there . . . I mean, at Fred Crick's cottage?' I asked. 'Did he know Fred?'

'Not to my knowledge,' he admitted helplessly. 'As far as I'm aware, Peter wasn't acquainted with anyone in this part of the country. This was his first visit.'

'I'm sorry it ended so tragically.'

He sighed. 'And in such distressing circumstances.'

I tried to recount, as tactfully and sympathetically as I could, how we had found his brother's body, but I could hardly describe the way he had been doubled up in the wardrobe like a puppet with its strings cut, or the ghastly grin on his face. I didn't really know what he expected me to tell him. I'd worked out that if the pathologist was right about time of death, taking into account the time it took us to load the furniture, drive to *Old Nick's* and unload it again, that Peter could only have been dead in that wardrobe for a very short time before Tom, Vicky and I had arrived at Fred's, maybe less than an hour.

'You and your brother were close?' I ventured. 'Being twins?'

'As boys, yes,' he said. 'Later . . .' he wagged his head,

116

considering, '. . . yes and no.' He leant forward across the counter and lowered his voice. 'Miss Browne,' he said sadly, 'there are many people who would not have considered my brother a nice man.'

I dropped my voice to match his. 'Oh?'

'Nothing was ever proved, you understand,' he went on. 'It was one pupil's word against his . . . but the headmaster offered Peter early retirement as an alternative to . . . erm . . . prosecution . . . and he decided to take it.'

'This was at a private school, was it?' I couldn't believe such an arrangement would have been on offer at a state school.

He nodded. 'All boys,' he whispered, his cheeks reddening.

'I see.'

'I fear you do. My brother had been in trouble before, many years ago . . . in fact, for a long time, my wife had discouraged his visits to our home.'

Well, that was one question I didn't need to ask. It seemed Henry and Peter were not identical in every way.

'I have always felt that Marjorie's attitude lacked compassion,' he added, his eyes trained on the wedding ring he was twisting nervously.

'Henry, are you saying that Peter might have had enemies?' I asked.

'Enemies?' he repeated, shocked.

'Do you think someone had a reason for killing him?'

'No, no, no!' he assured me in a rush. 'Peter was

someone to be pitied rather than—'

'Yes, but forgive me, you're his brother. Not everyone may have felt the same. You yourself said some people would not consider him a nice man.'

'No but—' His shoulders slumped in reluctant acceptance. 'I suppose it might be possible. But it doesn't explain what happened here . . . I mean . . . he didn't know anyone *here*. No one knew him. Not here.'

'Thousands of people come here on holiday. Perhaps he bumped into someone he knew, someone from his past, someone with a grudge against him.'

Henry was shaking his head. 'No, I can't believe it.'

'Someone shoved him in that wardrobe,' I pointed out.

His eyes welled up and he groped soundlessly for a handkerchief. I felt dreadful. I offered the poor man a cup of tea, but he declined, blowing his nose noisily.

'Did the police talk to you about Fred Crick's murder?' I asked.

'They think that perhaps poor Peter got mixed up in it, although I can't see how. He certainly hadn't gone there to take part in a robbery.'

'Perhaps he was just in the wrong place at the wrong time.'

'Which leads us back to the mystery of what he was doing there at all,' Henry sighed hopelessly. 'I just keep going round in circles. That was why I was hoping you might be able to shed light on things, Miss Browne.'

'I can't help, I'm afraid. You've spoken to Joan, who

runs the guest house where he was staying?'

'Yes. She was very kind.'

'Well, if your brother had been heading from Hound Tor to Widecombe, as Joan seemed to think, then Fred's cottage was a little out of his way. I suppose he could have got lost. Was he an experienced walker?'

'No, not really,' Henry admitted. 'He was very keen on archaeology, had been involved in a number of digs. He'd always been interested in Bronze Age settlements and saw his retirement as an opportunity to broaden his knowledge.'

'Well, he couldn't have picked a better place. Dartmoor has more Bronze Age sites than the rest of Western Europe.' I'd read that bit in a guidebook.

'Is that so?' Henry raised his eyebrows. 'He was a lonely soul, my brother,' he added sorrowfully.

'I wish there was something I could tell you.'

He pulled himself together and smiled. 'It was very kind of you to talk to me.'

'If I think of anything . . .' I promised vaguely.

He looked at his watch. 'It's time I was going. I have to catch a bus. I'm staying in Exeter until tomorrow. This is just a flying visit.'

'Are you a teacher too?' I asked.

He shook his head. 'My wife and I run a sweet shop. We sell old-fashioned sweets . . . in jars.'

'Mint humbugs and pineapple rock?' I asked, smiling. 'Coconut mushrooms?'

'That sort of thing,' he nodded. He reached into the

bag he carried and for a moment I hoped he might be carrying some samples, but what he drew out was a pencil, pink, with a rubber at one end and *Ye Olde Sweet Shoppe* stamped on it in gold. 'You can keep that,' he told me, generously.

I was overwhelmed. 'Thanks.'

'Marjorie finds it difficult on her own, standing all day, you know, so I must get back.'

I had a vision of his wife then, Marjorie the Uncompassionate, standing all day on legs swollen with varicose veins, her face as sour as an acid drop.

'Besides, I have a match on tomorrow night, so I must—'

'Match?' He didn't strike me as the sporty type.

'We're champions of our local league,' he told me proudly. He almost simpered.

'Football?' I asked. I must have been wrong about the sporty bit.

'No, no.' He gave a hiccupping little laugh. 'Darts.'

I suppose it wasn't surprising, considering the sort of day I'd had, that although I fell into bed exhausted, I couldn't get to sleep. Ricky says I think too much. Maybe it was all the wine and good food he and Morris had plied me with. I was at their place for ages, telling them first about the con at the shop and then Henry Gillow's unexpected appearance, filling them in between mouthfuls of chicken and mushroom pie and a very good Rioja. Over the last few days, I have been invited out to supper three times. If

I keep on having crises I might never have to cook again.

I don't know about thinking too much. It was difficult not to think about the dead body in the wardrobe. I have a wardrobe in my bedroom. Like most of the furniture it had come with the flat, which means it's really old stuff that Adam and Kate had inherited along with the house. When they had decided to let out the upper floor, Kate had tried to make the bedroom look less dark and gloomy by painting the wardrobe and matching chest of drawers a pale eggshell blue, picking out the mouldings in white. And it did look pretty; but it was still a wardrobe, and I couldn't look at it without remembering Peter Gillow folded up in the bottom of the one I'd bought from Fred Crick. When I closed my eyes, I saw a collage of drifting faces: Fred, the Gillow twins, the stranger with the blue-green eyes. When they all smiled at me and showed spaces between their front teeth, I knew I was dreaming.

Then the bloody phone rang. I jerked awake, blinking blearily at the green numerals of my bedside clock. Cursing, I hauled myself out of bed, dislodging a grumbling Bill who'd been curled up next to my tummy, and stumbled into the living room to pick up the phone. 'Hello?' I mumbled.

At first I thought there was a lunatic at the end of the line and then realised it was Daniel greeting me in Norwegian, practising for his conference in Oslo.

'Do you know what bloody time it is?' I demanded.

'Yes, it's . . . Oh, this watch has stopped! What time is it?'

'It's a quarter to one—'

'Oh shit!'

'—in the morning,' I added unnecessarily.

'I'm so sorry, Miss B, did I wake you?'

'Guess!' I pushed the hair out of my eyes and thanked god we weren't doing FaceTime.

'Sorry. I just wanted to hear your voice.'

I ignored the little fizzle of pleasure this gave me. If he wanted to hear my voice, he was damn well going to hear it; after all, he was paying for the call. I told him everything, starting with the corpse in the wardrobe, Fred's murder, the burning cottage, the elderly lady fraudster with the space between her teeth and finally being scared shitless by an apparent visit from the undead in the form of the corpse's identical twin brother. He listened in awestruck silence.

'Wow!' he breathed when I eventually drew to a halt. 'You've been having quite a time of it, haven't you, Miss B?'

This struck me as such a ridiculous thing to say, I laughed.

'And the police haven't got any idea who's behind these deaths?'

'Not so far.'

Daniel went very quiet. He does this on the phone. He thinks. He thinks for so long I have to break the silence just to make sure he's still there.

'I suppose you're going to tell me to leave everything to them and not get involved,' I said accusingly.

'No.'

I wasn't sure I'd heard right. 'No?'

'If you didn't do what you do, Miss Browne with an "e", you wouldn't be you, would you?' he answered simply.

'No.' I felt myself smiling. 'Don't suppose I would.'

'Just be careful,' he added, more solemnly.

I promised. And after I'd put the phone down, I realised I didn't tell the whole story. I hadn't told Daniel about the good-looking stranger with the blue-green eyes. I'd left him out. Now, why had I done that? I wondered.

CHAPTER ELEVEN

The following Sunday I took myself back to Newton Abbot. A grand antiques fair was being held at the racecourse. This was in addition to the usual car boot sale, which I visit there regularly and is held outside. The antiques fair took place inside the hospitality suite, the precious items under cover, the stallholders having paid much more for their tables than the rag-bag assortment of traders-in-tat outside. They paid for shelter, for light and heat; they paid to be near the bar, the restaurant and the loos. I usually wander fairs looking for something interesting and affordable to buy. Today I was hunting for my stolen stock.

This involved a lot of peering closely at things, which led to inevitable enquiries from hopeful dealers about what I was looking for. I told my story to each of them and handed out my list of stolen items. I was met with expressions of sympathy and shakes of the head. No one had tried to sell them any ruby glass scent bottles or Chinese snuff bottles in mutton-fat jade.

I couldn't help wondering if what Cruella had said was true. If they had bought any of my stolen items, would they admit it? But she thought all antiques dealers were the same, all like Old Nick. And Nick had gone to prison for receiving stolen goods more than once.

I had to replace the items that had been stolen but I couldn't afford much. I stood at a table considering a dainty art deco powder compact in pale blue enamel and told the dealer my story.

'You know, that sounds like what happened to a friend of mine,' he said. 'A man came into her shop and bought something, asked for a receipt, and then came back again a few days later. There was only my friend's assistant in the shop at the time and he told her he'd come to collect items he'd already paid for. They were all written on the receipt, so the poor girl handed them over.'

'When was this?' I asked.

'A couple of months back now. It was jewellery that was taken. I think Ann lost a couple of thousand.'

'And this friend . . . Ann . . . she's not here today?'

He shook his head. 'Her shop is in Okehampton – *Ann's Antiques and Curios*, she's called. I don't think I've got her number on me, but it'll be in the phone book if you wanted to look her up. I'm sure she'd be happy to talk to you.'

'That's very kind, thank you.'

I felt obliged to buy the compact then, but I came

away smiling. Sympathy for my plight made him knock off thirty per cent.

Ricky was on the phone as soon as I got home. 'Got any time this week, Princess?' he asked. 'We could do with a hand.'

'Costumes for a new show?'

'The DOs are doing *The Mikado*. They were so pleased with the job we did for 'em on *Iolanthe*, they've come to us again.'

The DOs, or Dartmoor Operatic Society as they should be known, are a much-loved but elderly society that performs the works of Gilbert and Sullivan. They usually go to a specialist company in London for their costumes. But last year they were sent fairy costumes inappropriate for the ladies in the chorus and Ricky and Morris helped them out.

'I think they're feeling the pinch a bit,' he went on, 'trying to cut costs. I know the price of hiring the theatre for the week has gone up a lot this year. At least if they get their costumes from us, they'll save themselves the costs of carriage.'

'Yes, of course I'll come and help, but I don't know when,' I warned him, 'I'll have to look in the diary.'

'We'll be making kimonos for all we're worth.' He began to sing, 'Three little maids from school are we', then cackled with laughter. 'Bet you there won't be one of 'em who's not got her bus pass.'

'I'll come up as soon as I've got a day free,' I promised.

'But I'll probably have to swap shifts with one of the girls in the shop. I'll let you know.'

'Well, whenever you can, my love,' he responded happily, and rang off.

I didn't get a chance to tell him what I'd learnt about *Ann's Antiques and Curios*. Instead, I dug out an old copy of the phone book and looked up her number.

Fizz had obviously got over any sense of responsibility she might have felt about my being defrauded of a thousand pounds' worth of stock. When she next breezed into the shop, and she'd stayed away for several days, it was as if the whole thing had never happened. I didn't want her to go on feeling wretched with guilt forever, but some small sign of contrition might have been nice, or at least an enquiry about whether the police were getting anywhere with tracing my stuff. But after a cheery hello she bounced on up the stairs, announcing that she was planning on holding a silk painting workshop in her studio on the last Saturday of the month and she hoped that would be all right with everyone. Sophie reminded her that she'd promised us a silk painting demonstration and Fizz told her that she couldn't spare the time but we were welcome to go up and watch her work whenever we liked. A few seconds later, her radio blared into life. On top of a pulsating rhythm someone was yelling at us to get down and boogie. For a woman of her age, she has very juvenile taste in music. Sophie slanted me a dark look, put down her paintbrush and went to the foot of the stairs.

'Would you mind either turning that down or closing the door?' she yelled. For Sophie, that was confrontational.

'Sorreee!' Fizz's voice cooed back and a moment later the getting down and boogying was muffled by the shutting of her studio door.

'I don't know how she can stand it,' Sophie muttered.

'Can't she use an iPod or something?' I asked. I don't know much about these devices. I refuse to pay out for fancy Wi-Fi equipment that relies on Ashburton's unreliable signal.

Sophie raised her eyes to heaven. 'She says the leads for the bits you stuff in your ears get in the way of her painting. They do, actually,' she admitted. 'I tried working with one once.'

'We could always put the radio on down here,' I suggested, 'drown her out with something more pleasant. The customers might like it.'

Sophie looked around her at the empty shop and raised her dark eyebrows. 'The who?' I pulled a face at her.

'Have you noticed that, by the way?' she asked, pointing with her thumb back over her shoulder at a new sign that was attached to the bannister rails above Mavis's head.

Silk painting Studio Upstairs, it read, with an arrow pointing the way.

I hadn't noticed it. 'How long's that been there?'

'She put it up there. It's a good idea, actually,' she added hastily, 'but I told her she should've asked you first.'

'Well, she should,' I sighed. 'But as it's a good idea, I won't bother to mention it.'

I had other things to think about. I dug out my diary and between the two of us we worked out that if I swapped one of my afternoons with one of her mornings, I could have a free day to help Ricky and Morris with *The Mikado* costumes. After my phone call of the previous evening, I also wanted to blag a free day for a trip to Okehampton.

'You do realise that Fizz is going to be here on her own this afternoon?' Sophie asked.

'Hell's teeth, no I didn't!' I responded, horrified. 'No Pat?'

Sophie shook her head. 'Not until tomorrow.'

I sighed. 'Well, I don't suppose that we're likely to get another lot of fraudsters through the door.' But the idea that Fizz would be in charge of *Old Nick's* again was one I didn't relish. I had hours of gardening to do that afternoon and wouldn't be able to get back before closing time.

'Perhaps Elizabeth could help,' Sophie suggested.

I shook my head. Elizabeth would be on reception at the doctor's surgery. 'Fizz will just have to manage. She won't make the same mistake again, that's for sure.' But I popped up to see her, just to make sure she understood she was going to be in charge.

She was in the process of stretching a plain silk scarf onto a frame ready for painting, her brows knit, the tip of her tongue peeping from her lips in concentration as she secured the fabric. She did this with sharp little hooks like animal claws, attached to thick rubber bands which in turn were tied to the wooden frame. Each rubber band had to be stretched from the frame and the claws hooked into the scarf, just under the rolled hem, at intervals of a few inches all the way around, so that the whole thing was suspended, rather like the skin of a trampoline on its springs. It made me tense just watching her. As each set of claws gripped the delicate fabric, stretching the next became more difficult, the rubber band in more danger of snapping, the hooks of biting her finger. One wrong move and the silk could be ripped. But she knew what she was doing. When the final hooks were in place, the surface of the silk was taut as a drum.

'When the silk is wet it mustn't touch the table underneath, you see,' she told me earnestly, 'otherwise it could be ruined. That's why it has to be suspended.'

I picked up a three-clawed hook, tested one of the points with my finger and winced. 'Will the people at your silk painting workshop have to use these nasty hooks?' I had visions of blood everywhere.

'They're called stenter pins,' she informed me, taking it back. 'And no, they won't. The workshop is for beginners only, you see, so they'll each be tackling a simple picture, not attempting a scarf. For pictures we use these three-point pins.' She picked up a box of what looked like drawing pins and rattled it. 'But they leave holes in the silk, so we can't use them on scarves. But with a picture, the edges will be hidden under a frame or a mount, so the holes won't show.'

'You know you'll be manning the shop this afternoon?' I asked. 'You're OK with that?'

'Oh, yes of course,' she responded airily. 'No problem.'

I thought I'd better press the point. 'You're not nervous,' I asked, 'after what happened last time?'

She trilled with laughter as if this was hugely funny, 'No, of course not.'

I failed to see the joke myself. 'Right then, I'll be back before closing time. You can get me on my mobile, if you need me . . . actually, no, you can't,' I remembered, 'there's practically no signal where I'll be going, but you can always phone Sophie or Pat if you get any problems. They won't mind.'

She didn't answer. She was humming along to the radio, staring at her blank piece of silk, already seeing colours and shapes that no one else could see. I gave up and left her to it.

When I got back to *Old Nick's* later it was deserted. No customers and no sign of Fizz.

No visible sign. I could hear her all right, thumping about upstairs, radio blaring. Meanwhile, anyone could have come into the shop and helped themselves to the cash in the till or anything else they wanted.

I marched up the stairs and flung open the studio

131

door. Fizz didn't hear me coming because she was singing along to the music as she bent over her silk scarf, drying the paint with a hairdryer.

'Fizz!' I yelled and she jumped.

'You startled me!' she cried, straightening up as she switched the dryer off. 'You shouldn't do that. If I'd had the paintbrush in my hand this could have been ruined!'

I ran an eye over the nearly completed scarf. Blood-red poppies outlined in gold danced against a cream background scattered with stalks of corn. It looked stunning but I wasn't in the mood to appreciate it. 'Fizz, you're supposed to be looking after the shop.'

She blinked at me, baffled by my anger. 'I can the hear shop bell from up here.'

'With this racket going on?' I strode over to the radio and switched it off. 'You didn't hear me until I walked into this room and then I had to yell at you.'

She opened her mouth to speak, but then closed it again, her lips tightly compressed.

'Looking after the shop means being downstairs,' I went on, 'ready for customers.'

'Well, I was for a while,' she answered pettishly, 'after Sophie left. But it was so quiet, I thought it wouldn't hurt if I crept up here for a bit.'

'It doesn't matter how quiet it is.'

She pouted and her brown eyes became shiny with tears. 'I think you're punishing me for what happened the other day.'

I took in a deep breath. 'I'm not *punishing* you at

all. But I am cross that you come up here and leave the shop unattended. And I would have thought, frankly, after what happened the other day, you would have been more careful.'

A man's voice drifted up from the shop below. 'Hello? Anybody about?'

He proved my point. 'You see? We didn't hear him come in, did we?' I jerked an arm towards the studio door. 'Now, would you mind going downstairs and seeing what he wants?'

Wordlessly, Fizz stomped past me and down the stairs. There was no apology. She obviously saw herself as the injured party.

I knew who the man was, I'd recognised his voice. 'Ah!' I heard him say as Fizz appeared in the shop. 'You're new! Is the lovely Juno about?'

'I know you.' Fizz's voice rose squeakily with excitement. 'You were on television!'

'Digby Jerkin,' came the suave reply. 'Hello.'

I smiled as I trotted down the stairs. I hadn't seen Digby for ages.

'You were in that series with your wife,' Fizz went on. 'Oh, I'm hopeless with names . . . um . . .'

'Amanda,' he told her. 'Amanda Waft.'

'Oh yes!' Fizz cooed. 'You were marvellous! What was it called now?'

'*There's Only Room for Two*,' Digby answered, laughing.

God, it sounded dire.

'It was a long time ago now,' he chortled. 'You must have been quite a little girl.'

'Not that little,' she simpered.

It was before I was born.

As I walked into the shop, Digby turned to give me a hug and kissed me on both cheeks. I had to stoop slightly; he's shorter than me and stocky, his black hair turning a becoming silver, strangely in all the right places. He would have been considered handsome in his youth, although his thick neck and slightly protruding eyes always make me think of a frog. He's a dear fellow, though, unfailingly chipper and courteous. 'There you are!' he cried. 'I was just passing and thought I'd pop in and see how you are. How's your head?'

'Better, thanks,' I assured him. I glanced around but there was no sign of Amanda.

'She's in the estate agents,' Digby told me, pulling down the corners of his mouth. 'Haunts the place,' he added mournfully.

'Still no luck?' He and Amanda had retired from the acting business, come to settle in Ashburton and had been renting a cottage while they looked for a property to buy.

He sighed. 'No, we're still searching for our perfect for ever home.' Then he smiled at Fizz. 'I see you've got a new recruit.'

'This is Fizz, and this is all her lovely silk painting here.' Dutifully I pointed at the display of her work, where Fizz had already taken up her position, ready for a sale.

Digby, bless him, knew a cue when he heard one and made lots of admiring noises. 'I'd better keep Mandy out of here, she'll love all this. Just look at those beautiful scarves!'

'Perhaps you'd like to buy her one as a gift?' Fizz suggested coyly, holding up a blue one painted with dragonflies and then a pink edged with roses.

'No, no, noo!' Digby sucked in his breath as he shook his head. 'I'll only pick the wrong one, m'dear. Much better if I bring her in and let her choose her own. I will, I promise!' he added as he made his escape. 'You must have tea with me and Amanda,' he told me. 'She'll be delighted to see you.'

Yes, I must, I agreed, although I doubted if Amanda, who floated in her own little bubble of reality, a bit like Fizz, would remember who I was.

'Give my love to that pair of old queens if you see 'em,' he added jovially.

'I'm helping them with costumes for *The Mikado*.'

'*Mikado*, eh? Jolly good! I played Nanki-Poo once.' He waved and the shop door jangled cheerfully as he let himself out.

It trembled into silence and I turned to look at Fizz, who was consulting her watch.

'Would you like me to take you through the cashing-up procedure again before you go?' I asked. My temper had been improved by Digby's visit, reduced to a gentle simmer.

'I can't,' she told me stiffly, her winsome bubbliness

evaporating with Digby's departure, 'I've got an appointment.' With that she turned and clumped up the stairs to her studio.

I heard her banging about up there for the next few minutes, the hairdryer blasting briefly. Presumably she was tidying up her stuff. She came down again, and with the air of someone deeply offended, wished me a curt goodnight and left. I puffed out my cheeks in a sigh. I was beginning to wonder if she might not be worth her rent money after all.

I locked the shop, plodded up to the kitchen and made myself a cup of tea. Whilst I waited for the kettle to boil, I wandered into Fizz's studio and looked around. The scarf was now completely dry, released from the tension of the frame and pegged to a clothes line. It was delicate, almost sheer, the blood-red poppies and golden stalks of corn glowing on its iridescent surface. Fizz was so talented. It was a pity she was such a pain in the arse.

I wandered downstairs with my tea and cashed up. This didn't take long. The ledger showed we'd had two sales during the day: a pair of earrings for Pat, and, irritatingly, a silk-painted cushion for Fizz. I mooched along the corridor to the storeroom, my heart sinking at the shelves in my display cabinet, bare except for one small powder compact. I'd wandered around the boot sale after I'd purchased it, trawling the stalls outside and come away with a brass photo frame and a small copper tray embossed with art nouveau twining foliage, both waiting for a polish; as were all the bits of brass

I'd bought from Fred Crick. The boxes of newspaper-shrouded objects rebuked me silently. I ought to take them home and spend an evening with the brass polish.

I also ought to do something about the furniture I'd bought, at least find out what it was going to cost me to get the chaise reupholstered and the writing table restored. I'd never have spent the money on the damned stuff if I'd known I was going to lose all that stock. I ran a hand over the table's clouded surface.

I don't know to this day what made me open the drawer. I pulled it out and studied it. There was something about it that wasn't right. I placed it on the tabletop, lining up the front edge with the front edge of the table. The drawer was short by about four inches. I hunkered down and squinted into the space it had come out of. I couldn't see much so I slid my hand in as far as it would go, hoping I wasn't going to get my arm jammed. My fingertips brushed against wood at the back of the space and there was a slight movement.

I pushed harder and felt wood flap inwards. 'Aha!' I said aloud, a secret compartment. I pushed once more, the wood flapped inwards again and my fingers touched something inside the space behind it. But I couldn't quite reach. I needed something to hold the flap open whilst my fingers teased out whatever it was.

I looked around but couldn't see anything suitable. I fetched a broom and tried fishing about with the handle, but the weight of the brush at the other end made it awkward and difficult to manage. Back in the shop I investigated Sophie's pot of paintbrushes, but although some of them had long handles, none of them would reach. Then I popped up to Fizz's studio. The frames she used for stretching silk were made of four pieces of notched wood that came apart so that they could be adjusted to create different sizes. I picked up one piece and took it downstairs, slid it carefully into the drawer space and pushed. The flap clicked open. I slid in my hand, touched what felt like paper, gripped it carefully between my fingers and drew it out. There were three sheets of writing paper, rolled into a cylinder after being confined in a narrow space for such a long time.

I opened them out. It was cheap lined paper, ragged down one edge as if ripped from a book and written on in what looked like biro. Not an eighteenth-century love letter inscribed on parchment, then – shame.

I flattened the pages out and placed them under a dish, delaying the pleasure of reading them until I had fitted the drawer back in place and returned the piece of Fizz's frame to the studio. She'd never know I'd borrowed it.

CHAPTER TWELVE

It's only common sense that pieces of paper hidden in a false compartment have something interesting written on them, something secret and forbidden. I decided to delay reading the pages until I got home. I slid them into my bag, loaded up White Van with the boxes of brass bits and drove back to the flat.

I delayed my reading further still by not getting the papers out of my bag until I'd had my supper. I ate scrambled eggs on toast, made a coffee, grabbed an apple and a couple of biscuits and settled down on the sofa my legs drawn under me, ready for a read. Bill leapt up on to the cushions. He loves a good story and listened attentively as I read out loud.

The pages were from a letter. It had no date and was untidily written, the handwriting large and ill-formed, not always sitting on the line. Consequently, there weren't too many words to a page. *My darling Jay*, it started.

I am sorry you have not heard from me in such a long time. He found the last letter I was writing to you and burnt it. He burnt all my paper and pens too. I tore these pages from an old book I use to write down recipes, but for many days I had no pen. I had to steal one from the post office when I went into town. They keep it on the counter for customers to write with. I felt like a criminal, although I've heard the man laugh and say people are always taking pens. They put them in their pockets by mistake, he says, so perhaps it's not so bad. I miss you so much, my darling.

Of course, he started on his nonsense soon as he found my last letter. I knew he would. But he was too much falling over drunk to hit me. The time before when he broke my wrist, I think that frightened him. He said he didn't mean to do it, said it was my fault. But then in his eyes it's always my fault. They asked questions at the hospital and I could tell they didn't believe his story about me falling down. They asked me on the quiet if I wanted to call the police and gave me the phone number of a place for battered wives. I told them I was all right. This time he didn't dare go too far. But he is always watching me, spying on what I'm doing, asking questions and accusing me of things. He tries to make my life hell, but I don't care. He can do what he likes. One day I shall run away and go where he can never touch me again. I have nearly got the money together. I just pray that he never finds where I am hiding it.

I shall come to you, my darling. I pray for you every

day, for God to keep you safe.

You must not try to write. It was finding your first letter to me that started off all his rages. But if you move on again, my love, you must let me know. You can give me word of your new lodgings if you send to—

I shuffled the pages I was holding. Where was the rest of the letter? But that was the last page. This was the point at which the writer must have been forced to stop, to hide her letter away, to cram it in the secret compartment. And she never got back to finishing it.

I let out a breath I hadn't realised I'd been holding. I hope she managed to get away in the end, to join her beloved Jay, whoever he was. How long had that letter been lying in that drawer? Twenty years? Thirty? And who had written it? Fred said he'd brought the writing desk with him from the farm, but had he always owned it? Was this a family heirloom, or something he had bought himself at some time? He didn't know about the secret compartment and its contents, that's for sure. The writer must be Vivian Crick, who'd turned up in church with a black eye, who'd run off and left her husband and never been seen again, her husband Fred, always coming home drunk.

Well, bloody good for her! Three cheers for Vivian! Maisie's friend Connie, who was close to her, swore she didn't have a fancy man. She was wrong. Vivian had Jay. And she was better at keeping secrets than anyone knew.

Dylan the German shepherd was not so stupid, it turned out. He'd learnt how to open the kitchen waste bin, for one thing. It was one of those fancy ones that you don't have to risk contamination by touching with fingers. You just wave a hand over it and a movement sensor opens the lid automatically. Dylan had worked out that if he waved his snout over the lid it would have the same effect, allowing him access to all the goodies inside. His owner told me he came down that morning to find the contents all over the kitchen floor, all scraps eaten and every single food wrapper licked clean.

He was also bright enough to work out his place in the pecking order when I introduced him to the Tribe – after a brief tutorial in 'Who's Boss?' by Nookie the Siberian husky. Perhaps he was just being cautious on his first day, like a new kid at school, nervous and a little shy, but he seemed to settle into the group and was soon romping around chasing balls with the rest of them.

After I'd delivered the dogs back to their homes, I called in on Maisie. It wasn't my regular day to visit but it was just as well I turned up, because she'd tottered out into her back garden to put some crusts on the bird table and fallen over. She wasn't hurt, beyond bruising her dignity and scraping her elbow on the stones of the path, but she was shaken. Fortunately, she doesn't weigh more than a sparrow, so I was able to pull her upright and get her back inside, despite the best efforts of a yapping Jacko to get under our feet.

'What were you doing, going out there without your walking frame?' I asked her. 'Let alone in your slippers?'

'Don't you start nagging,' she grumbled as I lowered

her into her chair by the window. 'You're as bad as Our Janet.'

I ignored this reference to Maisie's long-suffering daughter and fetched some cotton wool and a bottle of TCP from the bathroom, flipping the switch on the kettle as I passed. I found the walking frame in the bedroom. 'It's doing a fat lot of good in here, isn't it,' I chided her, wheeling it in and parking it next to her chair.

She muttered something under her breath but allowed me to bathe her elbow and put a plaster on it. 'I wanted to feed the starlings,' she told me. 'They're silly birds but I like 'em.'

We could see them from the window. They had descended on the table in a squabbling mob, a gang of disorderly teenagers wrangling and bickering over the scraps, throwing as much on the floor as they could stuff in their greedy beaks; food that would later be tidied up by ponderous wood pigeons.

'Starlings are the last birds to get up in the mornings,' Maisie told me, chuckling, 'and the first to go to bed.'

I laughed. 'Is that right, Maisie?' I shook a few doggie treats into Jacko's bowl just to stop him pestering and made her a mug of tea. I set it down on the little table by her and propped a cushion behind her back. 'You were lucky you didn't break any bones.'

'Jacko tripped me up,' she admitted, lowering her voice.

'If you'd had your frame with you,' I responded, lowering my own to a confidential whisper, 'he couldn't

143

have got under your feet.'

'He doesn't like the little wheels on it,' she told me. 'He bites at 'em.'

'Oh, Jacko, for God's sake!' I scolded him. He paused briefly from his scrunching, looked about him questioningly, then lowered his snout back into his bowl.

'You know we were talking about Vivian Crick the other day,' I reminded her. 'You don't remember her breaking her wrist?'

Maisie thought for a moment and then shook her head. 'No, I don't. You want to ask Connie.'

'I would if I could.'

'Well, why don't you?'

I stared at her. 'Is Connie still alive?' I'd assumed she'd passed on, like Lambert.

'Course!' She jerked her head. 'She's in Oakdene.'

'Ah!' That might make things difficult. Oakdene was a care home for residents suffering from dementia.

'But she's not one of the doolally ones!' Maisie insisted. 'She's still got all her marbles.'

Better and better, I thought. 'D'you think she'd mind if I visited her?'

'Why should she mind?' Maisie grunted. 'She gets precious few visitors these days.'

'Right, I will, then. You don't remember what her son's name was?'

She scowled. 'Connie hasn't got no son.'

'No, I meant Vivian's son, the one who ran off.'

'No, I don't know.' She narrowed her beady little eyes

suspiciously. 'What d'you wanna know all that for?'

I shrugged. 'I'm just curious.' I told her. 'I haven't really got a reason.'

She snorted in disbelief. 'And I ain't doolally neither,' she told me.

Okehampton is a fascinating little town on the northern edge of Dartmoor. According to legend, the ghost of Lady Howard, who murdered four husbands, is doomed to visit its ruined castle after dark and pick a single blade of grass from the mound it stands on. She must repeat this chore every night until the end of time. Not only that, to get there she has to take the form of a black dog and run alongside a carriage made from her dead husbands' bones. These days, she'd be out in twenty years, less for good behaviour. Anyway, despite this fascinating story, and the fact there are few things I find more alluring than the ruins of a haunted castle, I couldn't make time to visit it on my brief trip. After all, I was on a mission.

Finding *Ann's Antiques and Curios* was not difficult; she'd given me excellent directions when I'd phoned. But I was surprised by what a tiny shop it was, pretty and bow-windowed and not as I'd been led to expect, like *Old Nick's*, housing different sellers under one roof. All of the stock belonged to Ann herself and she ran the shop with the help of a friend who looked after it on Wednesdays so that she could take a day off.

She explained all this as we sat in the shop drinking tea. I'd told her my story on the phone and we'd established the similarities in our experience. 'Poor Jane, I don't think she'll ever get over the fact that she let this man get away with it.' Ann was a large, pleasant woman with a mass of fuzzy blonde hair and a deep, smoky laugh; and she was philosophical about her losses.

'Do you think he called deliberately on a Wednesday,' I asked, 'that he knew Jane would be running the shop by herself?'

She shrugged. 'I suppose so.'

'That suggests he knew the routine here. But you say he wasn't a familiar customer.'

She shook her head. 'Well, if he had been in here before, I didn't recognise him. I wrote him the receipt. He bought an amethyst bar brooch, Victorian – not worth a great deal.' She gave a grim laugh. 'Not compared with what he got away with the day after. Jane didn't recognise him either, said she'd never seen him before.'

'So, how do you think he knew when to come in?'

She nodded her head in the direction of the shop window. 'See that little cafe across the street? The police think he may have been watching the place from there.'

I asked her to describe him and she puffed out her cheeks in a sigh. 'You know, I'm not sure I'd know him again if he came in, even now. He was middle-aged, average height, average build, light-brownish colouring, nothing remarkable about him at all.'

'Did he wear spectacles?'

'He might.' She shrugged. 'I can't remember. Neither can Jane. I think he's the sort of fella who would make a good spy, you know, blend into a crowd.'

'Voice?'

She shrugged again. 'Nothing distinctive.'

'He didn't have a space between his front teeth, did he?'

She laughed. 'I don't think so. Why d'you ask?'

I described the woman who had robbed me and told her the police's theory that the two fraudsters might be mother and son. 'Well, if he is her son, I don't think that's a feature he's inherited.' She gave a smoky chuckle. 'Pity really, we could put out a wanted poster for the Gappy Gang.'

'Do you mind if I ask, did you lose a lot?'

'About four thousand pounds.' She pulled out her phone and handed it to me. 'Here, have a look.'

I scrolled through six pictures, all items of Victorian jewellery, each one more expensive than any object I had lost. 'You don't have the receipt?'

'Only the carbon copy of the original,' she told me ruefully, 'with just the bar-brooch written on it, not the one he'd conned Jane with, listing all that stuff. He'd forged my handwriting very well, that's what convinced her that his receipt was genuine.'

'Well, either he forged it or his mother did.' It would be interesting to know which one of them wielded the pen. 'And Jane had no other means of checking, you don't keep a daily record of sales?'

'Well, no,' she admitted. 'With just me here most of the time there doesn't seem much point. All sales are rung up on the till, so I know how much money's been taken at the end of the day. The till roll keeps my accountant happy. But as far the stock's concerned' – she tapped her temple with a heavily ringed finger – 'I *know* what I've sold. I know my stock. I could tell you every item on these shelves right now.'

I looked around me. The shelves and cabinets were packed, but I didn't doubt her claim for a moment. Antiques dealers need an encyclopedic knowledge, a retentive memory. Like London taxi drivers, they need the knowledge; one reason I was convinced I'd never make the grade as a dealer myself.

I handed her a copy of my pathetic list. She said she might come down to Ashburton one day and shop around. She'd come to see me if she did. I promised her a drink. Apart from commiserating with one another there wasn't much more we could say.

I took the letter with me to Oakdene that evening. I was hoping that if Connie had been a close friend, she might be able to identify the handwriting, tell me if it was Vivian's or not. I was out of luck, as it turned out. Glaucoma had robbed Connie of her sight at the comparatively young age of seventy-three. And it was for this reason, as well as arthritis, that she had become a resident in Oakdene. I found out about Connie's blindness from one of the carers on the way down the corridor to her room, so I decided not to mention the letter at first. I introduced myself as a friend of Maisie's and sent greetings from her.

'Ah, Maisie!' Connie smiled. 'Is she as incorrigible as ever?' She was sitting in an armchair by the window. The hands resting on a cushion in her lap were cruelly twisted, the fingers bent and knotted.

'Completely incorrigible!' I responded.

Despite her infirmities, Connie seemed a cheerful lady, very quietly spoken and neat in a twinset and trousers. Her hair was permed into tight little curls, a style that made her face look older than it needed. She couldn't see the effect, but I wondered if she would have minded if she knew.

'She has a daughter,' she went on, 'living up north somewhere.'

'Janet.'

'Yes, Janet.' She smiled. 'A nice girl.'

'Janet's a grandmother now.'

Connie laughed softly to herself. 'Time flies. Now, what can I do for you, Juno? You're not here just to bring me greetings from Maisie.'

I confessed I had an ulterior motive and asked her if she'd heard about the death of Fred Crick.

'Oh, yes. I always get someone here to read me the *Dartmoor Gazette* each week, just the interesting bits. It was terrible.'

'Did you know Fred?'

'Not really,' she answered, 'Lambert knew him better than me.' Then, after a moment's reflection she added, 'I knew his wife, Vivian.'

'The police are trying to trace her,' I said, 'and her son.'

'Ah. Well, the boy left long ago.'

'Do you remember his name?'

'Yes, of course. He was called Tony. Anthony, I suppose.'

'And Vivian? Maisie says she ran off too.'

Connie was silent a moment. The windows of her room overlooked the garden, and beyond the trees the sky was marbled with golden clouds, a pretty sunset that she could not see although she gazed in that direction. 'Viv disappeared,' she said at last. 'I know that people say she ran off with a man, but I never believed it.'

'You think something happened to her?'

'We were close friends, although after she married Fred, I didn't see very much of her. But I can't believe that, even if she'd been forced to leave suddenly, she wouldn't have got in touch.'

'But you've never heard from her?'

'Not a word,' she responded, sighing. 'Not in twenty years.'

'And you've no idea where she might have gone?'

'None.'

'Do you remember her breaking her wrist?'

She nodded. 'Yes, yes, she did. In a fall, that's what she told everyone. I always thought that husband of hers had something to do with it. So did Lambert. He went round to the farm, I remember, dared Fred to touch her again, threatened to sort him out if he did.'

'And how long after she broke her wrist did Viv disappear?' I asked.

'Not long,' Connie answered thoughtfully, 'some time the following year, I think.'

'We can't really blame her for running away if Fred was hitting her about.'

Connie smiled sadly. 'Oh, I don't blame her.'

'Did you ever hear her mention anyone called Jay?'

'Jay?' she repeated. 'No.'

'You're sure?'

'Yes, I'm sure. Why?' She frowned. 'Why are you so interested in Vivian?'

It was time to come clean. I took the letter from my bag and explained where I had found it. Connie listened in silence as I read it through.

When I reached its sudden end, she heaved a sad sigh. 'That's Vivian talking. I recognise her voice.'

'But you don't know who she was writing to?'

'No idea,' she admitted. 'I don't know who Jay was. But there were things that Viv didn't talk about,' she went on slowly, 'about the way Fred treated her, and why Tony left. If she had someone else in her life, I'm glad. She deserved someone decent to look after her.'

'He never received this letter,' I pointed out.

'No, she must have been forced to abandon it,' Connie conceded. 'But we don't know that that was the last one that she wrote, do we? I'd like to think she found happiness with someone new. I've always hoped that.' She smiled. 'That way I can forgive her for never getting in touch.' She reached out a hand in my direction. I took it and she grasped it warmly. 'I've heard about you,

Juno. I've heard about you from the *Gazette*—'

I let out a groan.

'No, listen!' She hushed me and there was an urgency in her voice, surprising strength in her knotted fingers. 'If something bad has happened to my friend Viv, I want to know. If you find out anything, Juno, you promise to tell me.'

'I promise.'

She smiled and squeezed my fingers before she let them go. 'I hear you're a fine-looking girl.'

'Who told you that rubbish?'

'Oh, I have my sources of information. Wonderful red hair, they tell me.'

I grunted. 'That's a matter of opinion.'

'I always wanted red hair.'

'May I come again?' I asked. 'I could bring Maisie.'

She smiled, a little wryly. 'Now that would be fun.'

CHAPTER THIRTEEN

The trouble with Ricky and Morris is that they're too generous for their own good. Remind them that they're trying to retire from the theatrical costume hire company they've been running from their house at Druid Lodge for the past thirty years and they will agree, in all seriousness, that yes, they are. Point out that they are supposed to be getting rid of the many thousands of costumes that occupy their upstairs rooms and they will agree with that too. To be fair, they managed to sell off some military uniforms not long ago, and they are selling vintage originals through *Old Nick's* – dresses that can't be hired out for plays because the fabric is too delicate or they're too small to fit the modern wearer. As Ricky puts it, 'All you tarts are much bigger these days.' But apart from that, they really haven't made a lot of progress in the selling-off and shutting-up-shop department. And the last thing they need, frankly, is to be making a set of fifty costumes for *The Mikado* to add to their stock. The trouble is, they can't ignore a cry for help, and they can't resist a challenge.

'Haven't you already got some Japanese costumes,' I asked, 'from that play we did before?'

'*The Teahouse of the August Moon*,' Ricky informed me loftily, 'is about poor Japanese villagers, not the court of the bleedin' Mikado.'

I realise that a Mikado is some kind of Japanese big-cheese so I shut up. To suggest to him or Morris that DO, a small rural amateur operatic society, could make do with something a bit less authentic on a 'their-audience-will-never-know' basis, would be to insult their professional integrity. It doesn't matter if they're making costumes for the DO or the D'Oyly Carte, the care and attention to detail will be the same.

When I trundled White Van down the drive at Druid Lodge, it was clear that costume-making was already in progress. Vast pieces of fabric were laid out on the front lawn, wide lengths of dull red satin.

Ricky hailed me as I got out and strolled over the grass.

'What's all this?' I asked.

'Auntie's curtains,' he explained. 'She had these hanging all over the house.'

'You've kept them all this time?' Auntie had been dead since before I was born, and the long Georgian windows had been dressed in something lighter and less depressing for years.

'I knew they'd come in useful one day.' He pointed at one of the curtains with a pair of dressmaker's shears. It already had shapes cut out of it. 'There's enough fabric here to make kimonos for all the courtiers in the men's chorus. It'll be good they'll all be in the same colour, make 'em look official. We'll trim them all with a contrast, of course. Point is, this material is nice and heavy, so it will hang right. And this dull sheen will look fantastic under the lights.'

'So, how come you're the one out here doing the cutting?' I asked. It was Morris who had the tailoring background, who did the cutting, by eye, with no need for a pattern.

Kimonos, Ricky explained were dead easy to cut, just composed of rectangles. This released Morris to get on with the sewing. 'It's not like they've really got to fit, not like a bodice or a doublet. They just wrap around the body and are held in place by a sash.'

'An obi,' I said.

He raised his brows at me and grinned. 'You've been mugging up.' He handed me a pile of rectangles he'd already cut, making sure I knew which ones were fronts and backs, and which ones were sleeves, with orders to carry them up to Morris in the workroom.

'His sewing machine will be on fire by now,' he cracked.

But Morris was not whizzing away on the sewing machine when I got upstairs. He was on the phone. 'No, no,' he was saying, 'all we're asking cast members to

provide is a pair of white tights and a pair of flip-flops . . .
Yes, well, those Japanese thong sandals look exactly like
. . . flip-flops . . . They'll look fine if they're all painted
black . . .' He spotted me as I laid down my rectangles
and gave me a little waggle of his fingers in greeting.
'No, no, you're very kind to offer,' he went on, 'but we
don't want anyone wearing their dressing gown, thank
you. Yes, I know they might think it looks Japanese but
. . . no, that's perfectly all right . . . No, we don't know
what we're going to do about wigs yet. Yes, we'll let you
know. Bye.'

He put the phone down and puffed out his cheeks in
a sigh.

'Trouble?' I asked.

He shook his head, pausing to polish his little gold
specs on the edge of his jumper. 'That was the DOs
agitating . . . well, their wardrobe mistress anyway, poor
woman.' He stood on tiptoe to kiss my cheek. 'How's
Edward Scissorhands getting on out there, Juno? He
hasn't accidentally stabbed himself yet?'

'No, he's doing fine. What do you want me to do?'

'Well, I've run up the side seams and back seams on
all these kimonos here,' he explained, holding one up.
'If you could just press the seams flat for me, I can set in
the sleeves.'

'Press as you go' is Morris's mantra so I got busy
with the steam iron while he put together the pieces I'd
just brought up from downstairs. We soon had a little
production line going. By the time Ricky came upstairs

with the last of the cut pieces, we had three basic kimonos already put together, draped on hangers.

'Of course, the hems need doing and the collars need putting in,' Morris told me. 'I think we'll face them with black to make them look smart. It'll go with the black and gold satin we've got for their sashes. Then that'll be the gents' chorus done.'

'Are there many characters in *The Mikado*?' I asked when we'd stopped for coffee. I'd never seen the show. Victorian operetta is not my thing.

Morris began to count them off on his fingers. 'Well, there's the ladies' chorus —'

'Too many of them,' Ricky put in grimly.

'And there's the Mikado, he has to be very grand. Then there's Yum-Yum, the young heroine, and the other two little maids. I can't think of their names for the minute – they all need to look really pretty—'

Ricky lit one of his menthol cigarettes. 'They're supposed to be just out of school,' he muttered.

'Oooh!' Morris flapped an arm excitedly. 'I was just hearing about that on the phone! They've got a youngster playing Yum-Yum. She's only in her twenties.'

'Who?'

'I don't remember her name. She's from Tavistock. She was in *Oklahoma!* there last year. Lovely voice . . . Mind you,' he added confidentially, 'she's a bit voluptuous.'

'Is that a polite way of saying she's fat?' I asked.

'Well, she's plump,' Morris conceded, 'but very pretty.'

Ricky cracked a laugh. 'She's been going yum-yum a bit too much, by the sound of it.'

'I don't see anything wrong with a plump Yum-Yum,' Morris said.

Ricky rolled his eyes. 'Plump and delicious!'

I laughed. 'This conversation is veering towards the obscene.'

'Never mind how plump she is!' Ricky blew out minty smoke. 'At least she hasn't been through the menopause.'

Morris blushed. 'Take no notice of him, Juno.'

Morris could be remarkably prim considering the downright filthy songs he and Ricky sang when they performed together as comic-double act, Sauce and Slander.

'Digby says he appeared in *The Mikado* years ago,' I remembered. 'Nanki-someone.'

'Blimey! That must have been years ago!' Ricky muttered. 'Nanki-Poo is the young hero.'

I brought them up to date on Fizz's latest antics, my visit to Okehampton, finding the letter in the writing desk and finally my conversation with Connie.

'I don't suppose that you knew Vivian?' I asked them hopefully.

'No, darling, never came across her.' Ricky answered.

'Never knew Fred, really,' Morris added mournfully. 'Well, only by sight.'

'Police getting anywhere,' Ricky asked, 'with tracking down his murderer?'

'I don't think so. They're still trying to trace Vivian

and her son, but they're convinced the murder was a robbery gone wrong.'

'And what about our friend in the wardrobe?' he added. 'Still no idea how he got there?'

I shook my head, 'None.' I told them about the bloody fingerprints on Peter Gillow's jacket.

'It's all very peculiar.'

'What if your friend Connie is right?' Morris reflected. 'What if there was something odd about Vivian going off like that?'

'Well, I don't suppose we'll ever know now.' Ricky stubbed out his cigarette in a saucer.

'Now, come on, back to work. This won't get the baby a new bonnet, will it?'

CHAPTER FOURTEEN

I hadn't forgotten Amy's rabbit. I selected Bluebell from among the many contestants at Honeysuckle Farm for the role of replacement, only to be informed by Pat that she was inseparable from her sister Primrose; so it was with two rabbits in a borrowed travelling basket that I arrived at Cold East Farm that evening after supper. I wanted to deliver the bunnies before Amy was put to bed. I just made it. She was in her pyjamas when I arrived but soon put her little red wellies on so that we could all make the trip out to the hutch to install Bluebell and Primrose in their new home. Then I read her a bedtime story while Carol and husband Neil put all the hens away for the night. This is not an easy task during the lengthening summer evenings; chickens don't want to go to bed before darkness falls and it takes persuasion and guile to get them locked up safely inside their henhouse.

But by the time I came down from reading Amy a

story, Neil and Carol were sitting at the kitchen table with a glass of wine poured ready for me. Neil is a robust young farmer, hunky-shouldered with a ready grin. Carol's background is in marketing and she seems to be the driving force behind the changes taking place at the farm. It was fun to sit and listen to their plans for the future. Their enthusiasm was endearing. I wished I felt half as enthusiastic about *Old Nick's*.

Darkness had almost fallen when I realised the time and made my excuses to leave. We all needed to get up early. Even though it was still twilight, the sky a soft indigo and not yet fully dark, Neil insisted on walking me down the track with a torch in his hand. He didn't want me tripping over in the gloom, he said. Carol stood watching from the doorway, ready to wave when I set off.

We had almost reached White Van when Neil looked back over his shoulder, frowning. 'Those sheep are making a lot of noise.' I was aware of distant bleating and turned to look back. The flock of Devon Longwools was spread out over three fields, the white shapes of ewes and lambs showing faintly in the gloom. In the far field they were not grazing peacefully but running around together in a frightened huddle. Something was wrong. We turned our steps and began to walk back up the track.

'A bloody dog's got in with them,' Neil cried, pointing. 'Look!'

I could see it then, a low shape, sleek and wolfish, circling the panicking sheep in a crouching run.

'That's not your dog?' But we'd left Kipper the sheepdog asleep in the kitchen.

'No, it's not!' Neil had quickened his stride and whistled between his teeth.

A moment later Kipper appeared in the doorway, slid around Carol's legs and raced on ahead of us, streaking up the track and through the orchard, a black and white arrow in the gloom.

Carol called out, 'What's the matter?'

Neil didn't answer, just quickened his stride, breaking into a run. I hurried after him.

Torches flashed in the field ahead, lighting up a cluster of dark figures. Kipper was barking madly, sending out a warning, a territorial threat. I could make out a lorry, a hulking black shape, lurking at the edge of the field.

'Shit!' Neil swore. 'They're stealing the sheep!'

'What is it?' Carol shouted anxiously. 'What's the matter?'

'Rustlers!' he yelled back to her as he raced on ahead. 'Call the police!'

'Neil, don't!' Carol cried, her voice rising with fright as she ran after him. 'Don't try to confront them.' She grabbed his arm. 'Please, Neil! It's not worth it.'

'Stay inside with Amy!' he ordered, shaking her off. 'You too, Juno.'

Carol clutched at my arm. 'He shouldn't try to tackle them, not on his own.'

'Go inside. Ring the police,' I told her. 'I'll go with him.'

'No, Juno!'

'Police,' I told her firmly and pulled away.

I ran across the field, stumbling, cursing the ankle that slowed me down. Neil was way ahead, yelling and waving his torch, sending a wavering beam of light into the deepening dark. A gunshot rang out; echoed in the still air. I froze. Neil cursed and the torch wavered. For a terrified moment I thought he had been shot, but the gun had been fired over our heads, a warning to keep us away. He whistled to Kipper who dropped like a stone into the grass at his command and crouched. We could see the gunman, a solitary figure, dark and hooded, standing in the field. He began walking towards us, the barrels of the shotgun levelled at Neil's chest. 'Stay where you are!' his voice was muffled by the mask that covered the lower part of his face.

Neil was breathing hard, his chest heaving, cursing under his breath, chafing in fury at being forced to stand there, helpless, whilst his precious sheep were being stolen from under his nose. But at least he had the sense to stay still, not to try anything stupid.

We heard a tailgate rattle shut. Doors slammed. An engine started. The headlights of the lorry blared out, lighting up the grass. The gunman turned away. I crouched and ran forward, stumbling as I caught up with Neil, the breath raw in my throat. Keeping low, we edged forward as far as the fence and peered over. Neil shone the torch. The gunman swung around. Above his mask his eyes gleamed briefly in the shaft of light and he narrowed them, raising the weapon. 'Kill that light,' he ordered gruffly.

Neil did as he was told, but we could still make out the dark figure backing towards the lorry, sweeping the barrel of the shotgun this way and that until he reached the cab and climbed inside. A hiss of airbrakes and the lorry pulled away. The thieves had got what they wanted.

Neil clambered over the fence and began running across the field, but the lorry had pulled out through the gate and turned onto the road, its red tail lights disappearing from sight, long before he reached it. I was beginning to limp, my ankle aching like a bastard. Walking was one thing, running quite another. By the time I caught up with him he was bending to pick up the two halves of the padlocked chain that used to secure the gate.

'They've taken a bolt-cutter to this,' he told me in disgust, flinging the halves down again. He noticed my limp.

'You all right, Juno?'

'Fine,' I said breathlessly, but accepted the arm he offered as we began our trudge back across the fields. Kipper barked to us, letting us know he was still on guard in the place Neil had left him. He yelled, calling him to heel.

'Look!' he shone the torch over four hurdles abandoned on the grass. 'They used these to form a pen. Once their dog had herded the sheep into this it was easy to drive them up the ramp into the lorry.'

We heard Carol's voice then, screaming our names into the gathering dark.

'Over here!' he cried, waving the torch as we walked towards her.

She ran to greet us, almost hysterical by the time we reached each other, and threw her arms around Neil's neck, sobbing. 'Oh God!' she cried, 'I heard that gunshot and I didn't know . . . I thought you'd been killed.'

'All safe,' he comforted her, folding her in a big hug.

'I didn't know what to do!' she wept. 'Amy's asleep. I didn't want to leave her alone in the house. I didn't dare bring her in case . . . I didn't know what to do!'

'Have you phoned the police?' He spoke slowly, trying to calm her down.

She nodded, wiping her face with her hands, struggling to pull herself together. 'I did. I'd just put the phone down when I heard the gunshot—'

'The police don't know about the gun?'

She shook her head.

'Pity!' he grunted. 'They'd get here a damn sight quicker if they did.'

I don't know how long it was before the police arrived, but it was long enough for the thieves to be well away. The officers hadn't come from Ashburton. They were part of a team dedicated to livestock and farm theft led by an Inspector Pitt, a small man with a big moustache. They could not have reached us any quicker, he informed us, because they'd been over in Princetown investigating the theft of a very valuable piece of farm machinery worth considerably more, his tone seemed to imply, than a few of Neil's sheep.

'Have you any idea how many you've lost, sir?' he asked.

'About thirty, I think,' Neil told him. 'I'll do a proper count when it's daylight.'

'And are your animals microchipped?'

There was a pause before Neil answered. He cast a brief glance at the corner where Carol and I sat. 'No,' he told him between gritted teeth, 'no, they're not.'

The inspector shook his head and smiled. He reminded me of Cruella when I told her I hadn't photographed my stolen antiques, that same smug, condescending look that tells you that you should abandon all hope of ever getting your stuff back, because you don't deserve to, you complete imbecile.

'That's a pity, sir. There've been about a hundred cases like this in Devon and Cornwall in the last couple of years. All you need to steal sheep is a vehicle, a few men and a dog.'

'And a shotgun,' I added. I'd had enough of his smugness; I wanted to wipe it from his face.

'A what, miss?'

'Juno and I were threatened with a shotgun,' Neil told him. 'They fired a warning shot.'

'They fired?' he repeated, visibly shocked. 'Are you certain?'

'It's not something you can be uncertain about,' I told him.

From then on, everything ramped up, became urgent, hurried; it was slightly unreal, like watching some television cop show. There were muttered conversations into radios about suspicious vehicles and roadblocks on the county roads. The words 'armed' and 'dangerous' seemed to keep creeping in. The police hurried away, car doors slamming, blue lights flashing. Someone would come tomorrow, the inspector informed us, to take our written statements, and abruptly took his leave.

'Do you know what really gets to me about all this?' Neil demanded. We'd been sitting in shocked silence after the police departed, listening to the ticking of the kitchen clock. 'It's not just the loss of the sheep, though that's bad enough, it's knowing there must be another farmer behind all this. You've got to know about handling sheep, you can't just herd them into a vehicle without knowing what you're doing.' He shook his head. 'How can farmers do it to each other?'

'I don't think being a bastard is confined to any particular profession,' I told him, 'certainly not to antique dealers.'

Neil laughed but his face was grim. 'Somewhere along the line there's a farmer who knows how to handle stock and how to get it to a slaughterhouse. And I bet there are plenty of those places, especially in the cities, where they don't ask too many questions about where animals have come from.'

'I'm sorry, my love,' Carol said suddenly. She turned to look at me. 'It's my fault the sheep weren't microchipped,' she explained. 'I thought it was an unnecessary expense. After all, they can be identified by their ear-tags.'

'Which can be taken off,' Neil muttered. Then he shrugged. 'Don't beat yourself up about it, love. I don't suppose it will make any difference. The police are never going to find them again anyway.'

I refused Carol's invitation to stay the night, although it was after midnight when I eventually left Cold East Farm. I had to get up early to walk the Tribe, and anyway, I wanted to be at home. My heart had started thumping like a jackhammer the moment I heard that gunshot and it didn't really settle down until was I driving down the hill towards Ashburton. I got back to the quiet, lamplit streets and breathed in a sense of safe and normal.

Then I lay under the duvet, wide awake, thinking about what might have happened if things had worked out differently, for example with Neil or me ending up dead.

Daylight came as a blessed relief, bringing with it early sunshine and the promise of an ordinary day. As I walked the dogs the sky began to cloud over and as we ambled through the woods it began to rain, just a gentle shower. I stood beneath the trees and listened to the whisper of the rain, each drop sounding different as it brushed against fern and flower, pattered on twig and bark and sang in the long grass. I stood and breathed in the smell. Rain is so often something I hurried through, head down. For once I found it soothing and wanted it to last.

As it turned out, it was one of my mornings for minding the shop. The rest of the day was more or less free. I'd been intending to give Ricky and Morris some more time with *The Mikado* costumes, but knew I'd have to go back to Cold East Farm to give my statement in the afternoon; if I didn't get a call from Carol telling me the police had arrived before.

It wasn't long after I'd opened up that *Old Nick's* got its first customers. Fizz had already arrived and gone clumping up the stairs to her studio, giving me her usually breezy greeting. I don't know if she'd forgiven me for telling her off the other day, or simply forgotten it had happened. I suspected the latter. I was sitting at the counter, reassembling the brass oil lamps I had polished. Three lamps were complete with glass funnels, the other two were just a collection of odd bits. I put these bits in a box with the other odd things that I place on a stool outside of the shop door, marked 'All items fifty pence'. Then I arranged the brass lamps on tables in my unit, with a note to self to look out for decorative glass shades for each of them, together with the brass picture frame and copper tray I had also polished.

The bell jangled, and I went back into the shop to find Digby and Amanda admiring Fizz's silk goods, Amanda cooing over the scarves in her deep, dulcet, theatrical tones. She was taller than her husband, glamorous, and slightly less than sober ninety per cent of the time, although she carried this so well that a casual observer might never have noticed.

'Morning, Juno!' Digby gave me a military salute. 'Reporting as promised.'

'Juno, darling!' Amanda echoed my name, having just been given the clue by Digby as to who I was.

I called up the stairs to Fizz. If Amanda had come to purchase some of her work, then she could have the pleasure of serving her. She didn't hear me, of course, and I had to fetch her. By the time we both came downstairs again Amanda had pulled several scarves from the display, wound one around her long neck and was calling for a mirror. Fizz was momentarily at a loss until I fetched her one of Ricky and Morris's from my unit in the storeroom.

Several minutes were spent with Fizz telling Amanda what an adoring fan of their old television series she was and Amanda protesting modestly that it was all too long ago for anyone to remember. There followed a very long debate about which scarf Amanda should choose, Digby being called upon for his opinion which was consistently ignored.

I left them to it. The counter became awash with colour as more and more scarves were tried and discarded upon it. Amanda decided that a pair of silk cushions, hand-painted by Fizz, would look stunning sitting on her bed, and there was another long discussion then about design and colour. Amanda was really very clever. The talk about the cushions was an ideal distraction. From where I was sitting, I could see the open weave shopping basket she had brought in with her and placed by her feet. Fizz could not. The pale apricot scarf nestling in it might just have slid from the counter accidentally and dropped down to rest there unobserved. But the green which floated into it next came after a definite flick of Amanda's fingers, the slightest whisking movement that ensured the scarf ended up where she wanted it. She allowed Digby to pay for one scarf in azure, which perfectly complemented her linen suit, and insisted on wearing it, asking Fizz to cut off the price label so she could keep it on. She also commissioned a pair of cushions in a design of palest apricot and gold, which Fizz assured her would look stunning and would be ready within the week. Then she placed her clutch bag on top of the scarves in the shopping basket and floated out, her faithful swain Digby, oblivious of her thievery, in her wake. Fizz rushed to open the door for them and practically genuflected as they passed.

'Well!' she gushed as she came back to her counter, all smiles. 'Fancy that, fancy Amanda Waft buying one of my scarves!'

I said nothing. I just let her get on with tidying the rejected scarves and putting them back on the display stands. And I waited. When she got to the last one, realisation dawned. She cast a glance around the floor at her feet, and then leant over the counter, for a look at the floor on that side. 'That's funny,' she mumbled, her brows drawing together in a frown.

'Lost something?' I asked casually.

'Um, yes . . . yes, um, there was an apricot scarf with

a honeysuckle motif, and a green one . . . I think. Yes, a green one with trailing ivy . . . I wonder where . . .' She gaped at me in sudden horror. 'You don't think . . . ?'

'I think I know what may have happened,' I assured her, smiling. 'I'll give Digby a call.'

I went upstairs to phone him on his mobile. To be honest, if Amanda got caught shoplifting and suffered the consequences, then the sozzled old trout had it coming, but I wanted to spare Digby humiliation he didn't deserve. He and Amanda had not got far; they were having coffee in Taylor's.

I told him that Fizz was missing two scarves. Could it just be possible, I suggested gently, that they had accidentally dropped into Amanda's shopping basket? He promised they would look, and within a few minutes he came scurrying into the shop clutching them. The poor man's face was scarlet.

'Mandy is mortified,' he told us earnestly, 'absolutely mortified! You see, she must have put her bag on top of the scarves without looking, so naturally she didn't realise they had dropped into her basket. They must have floated down.'

'Well, I'm not so sure that—' Fizz began.

'Naturally,' I cut her off, taking the scarves from Digby and thrusting them at her.

'Mandy is so embarrassed,' he continued, begging us with huge eyes to believe him. 'She has never done anything like this before.'

'Accidents happen,' I said, staring meaningfully at Fizz.

'Yes,' she conceded, with slightly pursed lips.

His chest heaved as he let out his pent-up breath in relief. 'She's really terribly sorry.'

Not sorry enough to come back and apologise herself, I noticed, but said nothing. I gave Digby's arm a comforting squeeze as I walked him to the shop door.

'Don't worry about it,' I murmured.

He cast me a look of undying gratitude. He might say that Mandy had never done this before. But he didn't know that I knew she had previous.

I have to hand it to Fizz. She was highly suspicious about what had happened, but she decided not to pursue it. She could see how distressed Digby was and she was prepared to let it go. After all, she'd got her scarves back. As for me, I wondered afterwards why I had let Amanda leave the shop in the first place, why I'd said nothing. I could easily have pointed out that the scarves had accidentally fallen into her basket and we would probably all have laughed about it. Was it because I wanted to spare Digby the embarrassment of discovering his darling Amanda was at her petty thievery again in front of Fizz? Or was it because I wanted Fizz to experience, just for a few moments, that sickening feeling you get when you realise you've been robbed? But I wouldn't have done it if I hadn't known I could get her scarves back. Would I?

CHAPTER FIFTEEN

When I rolled up at Cold East Farm later that day Neil was already at work on new defences, making his land inaccessible to vehicles from the lane that ran by the back of their property. Carol and Amy took me over the fields to see what he was up to. He'd borrowed a tractor with a front-end loader from a friend and transported two giant granite boulders from nearby moorland. As we arrived, they had lowered the bucket to ground level and were using it to nudge the rocks into position just inside the gate. Each chunk of granite was roughly the size of an armchair. Even a giant truck would come off worse in a collision and only something as small as a quadbike could drive between them.

'And I'm going to dig a trench.' He pointed to the far end of the field where only a sparse line of hedge separated his land from open moor. 'A truck could easily break through the hedge there. But they won't get very far if there's a deep ditch on the other side, a ditch and an earth bank.'

'It's going to look awful,' Carol complained, 'like the ramparts of some Iron Age fortress.'

'Never mind what it looks like if it keeps those bastards off our land.' Neil jerked his thumb at his companion who grinned at us and nodded from inside the tractor cab. 'Tim here has been telling me about a friend of his who farms near Bideford. A gang came onto his land at night and slaughtered his sheep, butchered them right there in the field, just took away the carcases. And he's not the only one. Anyway,' he added, seeing our horrified faces, 'we can plant the bank up after, put some hawthorn on the top. In a few years it'll look like any other hedge bank.'

We left them to their boulder-nudging and wandered back to the farmhouse, taking in a visit to the new rabbits on the way. Then we sat on a stone bench in a spot sheltered from the wind, our backs against the sun-warmed stones of the house and watched Amy playing. Hens fussed and pecked in the long grass, a cockerel strutted, bees buzzed drowsily amongst wild foxgloves. We turned our faces to the sun and closed our eyes.

'It's not often we get moments like this,' Carol confided, 'usually there's too much to do.'

Tell me about it. 'No building work going on this week?' I asked.

'No, our builder's on another job,' she sighed. 'Of course, we're doing a lot of the work ourselves. But I don't think much is going to get done on the shower block for a day or two. Neil's planning on using the digger for this new trench of his.'

'I think he's got the right idea,' I told her. 'Perhaps you should get some geese. They make brilliant guard dogs, raise a hell of a racket.'

'Not much defence against a shotgun though, are they?' she said bitterly, and I had to admit that no, they weren't.

'You know you said that Fred used to watch this place from the rock up on the hill,' I reminded her after a moment. 'You're sure it was Fred?'

Carol turned to look at me, frowning. 'We could see that it was him. Sometimes he'd be out in the open, on the top of the rock. Sometimes he'd be lurking in those trees at the back of his cottage.'

'And you could swear it was Fred, even from this far away? It couldn't have been someone else?'

'Well, I suppose we might have just assumed it was him,' she admitted. 'But why would it be anyone else?'

'Because I saw someone watching this place with binoculars from the top of the rock on the day I brought Dylan here, and that was after Fred had been murdered.'

Carol was silent a moment, thoughtful. 'Are you sure?'

'Yes. Look, the men who stole your sheep must have known what stock you'd got and the easiest way to get at them. And the best spot to see the layout of the whole farm is from up there,' I pointed, 'on top of the rock, from Fred's place.'

'You don't mean you think Fred had something to do with it?'

'No, I'm not saying that.' But it was what I was thinking.

'Well, if it was someone else spying on us from up there,' Carol said slowly, 'it's too late to worry about them now. They've already done their worst.'

Let's hope so, I said to myself. And then a police car drew up outside the farm gate, with an officer to take our statements. The time for enjoying the sunshine was over.

'I've got a theory,' I told Detective Constable Dean Collins on the phone later that evening.

I told him about the sheep rustling at Cold East Farm. 'Do you know an Inspector Pitt?'

He obviously did because he muttered something that sounded vaguely obscene. I didn't pursue it. The idea that Fred might have had something to do with a rustling operation had taken root in my brain. 'Well, something got him killed, didn't it?' I said, after I'd voiced this idea to Dean. 'And he was always spying on the place. What if he got involved with one of these rustling gangs, something went wrong and they turned nasty?'

'This isn't a theory, it's just a wild flight of imagination,' Dean complained. 'What evidence is there that Fred was involved in any kind of illegal activity?'

'Getting beaten to death and burnt to a crisp?'

'The poor bugger was robbed! The only criminals involved were the people that robbed him. Anyway,' he went on, clearing his throat, 'why would Fred assist a gang of rustlers to raid his own farm?'

'For money, obviously!' Dean was being more than usually dim-witted. 'And it wasn't his farm any longer. He didn't like what Neil and Carol are doing, the changes they'd made. He resented them. They've only been there a year, but they've been robbed twice. First a quadbike was stolen, then the sheep.'

'They've been unlucky.'

'Perhaps they've been targeted.'

Dean grunted, unconvinced.

'Neil thinks there must be a farmer involved in this somewhere along the line. He says only a farmer would know how to handle the stock and sell it on.'

'Well, he's right about that,' he agreed. 'One reason these gangs manage to dodge getting caught is because they don't take the stolen animals far before they change vehicles. They need a safe place to unload them and load 'em up again, and they need people who are used to handling them. Organised crime, is this, big bucks involved.'

'Does any of this stolen livestock ever get recovered?'

'Occasionally,' he admitted. 'Sometimes the criminals are forced to hang on to the animals longer than they want, or for some reason it's too dangerous to shift them. If they feel they're in danger of getting caught in possession they'll drop the poor things like hot rocks, just abandon them. A wagon load of cattle was found abandoned in Cornwall last year. They'd been stolen the week before. They hadn't been fed or watered and some of them weren't in good nick. I believe a few had to be destroyed. The farmer got most of them back, but he was lucky. It doesn't happen often.'

I sighed. 'Once upon a time I used to think organised crime just went on in big cities.'

Dean chuckled. 'Welcome to the Badlands,' he said.

Next morning, I drove Maisie to visit a friend in Moretonhampstead. They hadn't seen each other for years and I knew they'd be ages chatting over coffee; so once I'd seen her safely into her friend's house, I left them to it and went to while away an hour in an antiques centre on the edge of the town. It was set in an old chapel, with lots of different stalls and a cafe at one end where I had a coffee of my own, and sampled a slice of fruit loaf. Suitably refreshed, I got up for a serious wander around.

I had the place pretty much to myself to begin with and became very aware of the clump of my shoes on the stone-flagged floor, the echo of my voice in the lofty space above me, of the speculative gaze of stallholders as I went by. Then other people began to drift in; most, I noticed, heading straight for the cafe.

I was immediately attracted by a Torquay pottery vase in terracotta, also a marcasite leaf brooch, but decided to hang on to my pennies until I'd looked around a bit. There were more dealers upstairs in the old chapel gallery, reached by a steep and winding staircase. I made my way up the uncarpeted stairs, passing some truly horrible paintings on the walls, and stepping carefully around a vintage child's pram full of dollies, perched perilously on the top step. The gallery was long and narrow, stretching around three walls of the chapel. Once it would have been the best place for watching the congregation below, although I wouldn't have fancied sitting on one of the hard benches during a long sermon. The shape of the gallery meant that the stalls were set out in a single line, and I had to pass each one to get to the next. I mooched about, picking up bits of brass and jewellery and squinting, inspecting pottery for hairline cracks. I found a pretty green lustre preserve pot with silver lid and handle, and pulled Nick's old jewellery loupe from my pocket for a squint at the hallmarks. The little castle told me that this was Exeter silver. I was puzzling over the date mark when a man's voice floated up from the chapel floor below.

'Would you mind writing me a receipt for that, just in case my friend doesn't like it?'

There was a murmur of assent from the stallholder.

I froze, my hand on the lid of the little preserve pot. 'Excuse me, just a moment,' I said quietly to the lady I was buying it from and put it down. I looked over the rail of the balcony and found myself staring at a parting in the light brown hair of the man standing below me.

'That's very kind of you,' he was saying in a quietly refined voice, 'I'm sure you wouldn't mind if she exchanged it for something else, would you?'

'Excuse me,' I called loudly, and he looked up. Had I

ever seen his face before? Maybe not, maybe I had seen him a thousand times, this plain, unremarkable man of middle height and middle age, wearing a pair of glasses.

I might not have recognised him, but he recognised me. It's the hair I suppose, I'm easily recognisable. He blenched visibly, muttered some excuse to the stallholder and hurried away, heading for the chapel door, keeping his head down. 'Excuse me!' I called again as I scrambled my way around the gallery, hoping to cut him off, cursing the standard lamps, footstools and other obstacles that seemed to have been placed deliberately in my way.

'Stop!' I yelled, 'I want to talk to you.' I clattered on down the wooden stairs, hearing the pram full of dollies bumping down each step behind me as I went.

By the time I reached the ground floor and raced out of the porch, I was just in time to see him disappearing around a corner. I stepped off the kerb and a transit van blared its horn at me to stop me from getting mown down. By the time I'd jumped back and recovered my footing I had lost valuable seconds. The man was way ahead of me, jogging heavily, as if he wasn't very fit. I reckoned I could easily catch him up, but then a turning must have opened to his right because he suddenly disappeared. By the time I reached the same corner he was out of sight. I heard a car start up somewhere nearby and followed the road down to a small car park. There was no sign of the car by then, just the sound of it driving away. Cursing my bad luck and my aching ankle, I limped back to the chapel.

'Do you mind telling me what that was about?' the woman who'd been serving him demanded when I got back inside. She was obviously unhappy at being baulked of her customer.

I explained what had happened at *Old Nick's* and at *Ann's* in Okehampton.

'But he might have been a genuine customer,' she objected. 'People do ask for receipts, you know. You don't know it was the same man.'

'Why did he go running off, then?' I asked. 'Look, does anyone run this stall for you when you're not here?'

'We cover for each other,' another stallholder told me. They had all gathered around by now, and the ones upstairs were hanging over the balcony, listening.

'Just make sure everyone knows about this pair.' I gave them a description of the man's little gap-toothed mama.

'I don't think that fella will be back here, trying it on,' one of them told me, laughing. 'I reckon you scared him off.'

'For the moment,' I agreed, 'but he may be back, or the woman might. You might want to spread the word, tell the police here about them.' I handed out copies of my list of stolen items too. The stallholder eventually accepted that she'd had a narrow escape and I left, popping back upstairs to pay for my little jam pot, restoring the flung dollies to their overturned pram and placing it at the top of the stairs on the way.

* * *

Sophie and Pat are usually an appreciative audience and they didn't let me down when I got back to *Old Nick's* at lunchtime and told them what had just happened in Moretonhampstead.

'You're sure it was him,' Sophie asked me, round-eyed, 'that woman's accomplice?'

'Well, he was working off exactly the same script,' I told her, 'word for word.'

'And he wouldn't have run off if he wasn't up to no good, would he?' Pat paused stuffing a knitted dog. 'Have you reported it to Cruella?'

'What's the point?' The man got away, it was too late for the police to do anything. 'But at least the folks in Moretonhampstead are aware of the scam now.'

Sophie was watching what Pat was doing curiously. 'What sort of dog is that?' she asked.

'Pug,' Pat pronounced roundly. 'Or he will be when he's finished.'

There was no noise coming from upstairs, so I guessed Fizz wasn't around. The girls said they hadn't seen her but thought she might be giving a silk painting demonstration somewhere. A tiny knot of tension loosened up inside me. The sad truth was we all felt more relaxed when Fizz wasn't around.

'Could you ask her if she could price her painting materials?' Sophie asked. 'Pat and I have both tried but she keeps forgetting.'

'Painting materials?' I repeated. 'Does she sell those?'

'She's got it all up in the studio – silk paints and special brushes and nibs and stuff. Well, we don't mind selling them for her, but she needs to get everything priced.'

'We had a woman come in to buy some special silk painting book and we couldn't sell it to her because there was no price on it,' Pat complained. 'I went up there to try and find the price but nothing up there is marked.'

'Then she came back a couple of days later and Fizz wasn't here again, and she still hadn't priced it. The lady was not happy.' Sophie frowned. 'It makes us look unprofessional.'

'I'll tell her,' I promised. For all the good it would do.

We decided it was time for lunch. Sophie made cups of tea whilst I nipped to the deli and treated us to some sandwiches.

On the way I passed Pretty Paws parked by the roadside. It was locked up and there was no sign of Becky, so I scribbled a note with Olly's suggestions for new names on a piece of paper and slid it under her windscreen wiper.

I got back to *Old Nick's* loaded up with sandwiches and cakes and over lunch told Sophie and Pat about what had happened at Cold East Farm.

'I told Carol they need to get a few geese,' I said, 'they're really good at raising the alarm.'

'Or guinea fowl,' Sophie suggested, 'they make a horrible noise.'

'No.' Pat was shaking her head with great certainty as she stuffed more into the swelling sides of the poor pug. 'If you want to protect a flock of sheep, then what you need is a llama.'

CHAPTER SIXTEEN

'And she just happens to have one?' Carol asked uncertainly the following afternoon. 'A llama?'

'It's amazing what people will abandon at your gate when you run an animal sanctuary,' I told her. 'Loopy the llama, she's very good with sheep.'

Carol looked fraught. She'd been working on her laptop when I arrived, busy with her accounts, papers spread all over the kitchen table. I'd arrived unannounced and I had the feeling that she was still adding up money with half of her brain. She was too polite to tell me to go away. For one thing it had been raining heavily all day and showed no sign of letting up. And for another, little Amy thought the accounts were for crayoning on and needed entertaining. I think she could see there might be an advantage in keeping me around for an hour. Dutifully, I pulled a blank sheet of paper and her pot of crayons towards me. 'What shall we draw?' I whispered to her, although as my drawing's hopeless, it didn't really matter what she said.

I was only telling the truth. Llamas live very happily alongside sheep. Although they are usually docile, Pat told me, they become aggressive if threatened and will place themselves between the flock and dogs, foxes or other intruders. Their long-necked height makes them intimidating; Loopy reminds me of a dowager duchess peering down her long nose. And if staring an intruder down doesn't work, llamas will chase, kick and spit. I don't believe dowager duchesses usually go that far, but llamas have also got a truly ear-splitting alarm call. 'She's halter-trained,' I added, in an attempt to make her sound more enticing, 'and she's very pretty.'

Carol was still in maths mode. 'How much do they want for her?'

'Nothing,' I said. 'A donation to Honeysuckle Farm would be appreciated, but basically you'd be doing them a favour. The cost of looking after all these strays is crippling. They're always grateful to find an animal a good home.'

She sighed, considering. 'Well, there'd be no harm in taking a look at her, I suppose.'

'Pat could bring her over in the trailer. She'd want to see this place, anyway.' I grinned at her. 'She'd want to make sure you were suitable owners.'

Carol flipped the lid of the laptop. She'd had enough of accounts. 'Oh, for God's sake, let's make a cup of tea! We'll take one out to poor Daddy, shall we, Amy,' she asked, smiling down at her daughter, 'and ask him what he thinks?'

'Is Neil out there in this downpour?' I turned to glance out of the window but all I could see were raindrops running down the foggy glass. 'I know farmers have to work in all weathers but—'

'He's trying to fix the digger.' She shook her head at his folly. 'He wanted to drive it over the field today to start work digging his ramparts, but the thing won't go. I told him to get the tractor and tow it under cover, but he wouldn't listen. It would only take a minute to fix, he said.' She looked at her watch. 'That was over an hour ago.'

When the tea had brewed, I offered to take one out to him. There was no point in three of us getting wet; Carol and Amy would have to put all their weatherproof clobber on, and I was still wearing my raincoat. Carol poured the tea into a thermos cup whilst I slid my feet into the wellies I'd left by the door and bundled my curls up inside my Sou'wester. 'He'll think the lifeboat's coming to rescue him.'

For a moment I stood in the shelter of the porch, staring out at the dismal weather. Rain poured down the corrugated roof of a shed opposite, turning it slick and shiny, gushed from the end of a downpipe and drowned the ground beneath in a muddy puddle. Summer was stopping before it had begun. Then I plunged out into the downpour.

I knew where I'd find the digger, standing at the end of

the trench that had been excavated for the foundations of the new campsite block. I tramped across the paddock through wet grass and slithered over muddy patches, my way ahead obscured by drips from the brim of my sou'wester.

I arrived at the digger. At first, I didn't think Neil was there. I couldn't see him and there were no sounds of tinkering, swearing, or beating of metal on metal. I called his name, but he didn't answer.

Then I saw him, standing in the trench, motionless, rain dripping from his nose and chin, his hair plastered to his skull with wetness.

'Are you all right?' I yelled through the rain. He didn't respond, remained utterly still. 'Neil?'

He seemed to be in a state of shock. He raised his head slowly like someone coming out of a trance. 'Juno?'

'Yes, it's me. Are you OK?' Around his boots the rain had filled the trench with liquid mud. 'You should come out of there.' I reached out a hand to help him up. 'You're soaked.'

He still seemed to be in a daze. 'I found something,' he muttered.

I came around to his side of the trench so that I could look over his shoulder and see what he was staring at. Rain had washed away part of the trench wall on one side and clods of earth had fallen into the liquid mud beneath. Where it had fallen away, I could see four small white roots protruding through the mud wall. As I stared, I realised that they weren't roots.

They were fingers, skeleton white, a gold wedding ring hanging on one, loosely around the bone.

It was Vivian, of course. I knew the moment I saw that hand, knew with a sinking sense of horror and sadness. It took the police experts two days to reach the same conclusion. Skeletal remains, female, was all they'd say at first. But it didn't take a forensic pathologist to know that Neil hadn't stumbled on an ancient burial site: the synthetic material of Vivian's clothes had lasted longer than her flesh, and showed her body had been in the ground for twenty years at most. Her estimated age was between thirty-five and forty years, give or take. There was no sign of trauma on the skull, but a healed fracture of the wrist. The only indication as to the manner of death was the fracture of the delicate hyoid bone in the throat, which suggested manual strangulation. I gave her letter to Inspector Ford. The mention of her broken wrist was further evidence of the body's identity, he told me, although she was officially identified from her dental records, there being no living family member from whom a DNA match could be obtained. The son who had run away as a young lad could not be found. 'I just hope we're not going to come across his bones one day,' Inspector Ford said gloomily, 'find he never ran away either.'

Poor Vivian. She was never reunited with her beloved Jay. I wondered how long he had waited for her, how long he'd gone on expecting that she would appear. I went to tell Connie, as I promised I would, and she wept.

As to who killed her, there was really only one suspect, her drunken violent husband. No wonder he'd been watching what was going on at Cold East Farm through his binoculars. When they'd started digging in the very place where Fred had buried his murdered wife, he must have known it would only be a matter of time before they found her. None of which helped solve the mystery of who killed him, or why, or who had incarcerated the corpse of Peter Gillow in my wardrobe.

'So, we'll never know why he killed her?' Ricky muttered, trying to talk and keep pins between his lips at the same time.

Morris looked up from the sewing machine. 'He must have been in one of his drunken rages.'

Ricky wisely removed the pins. 'We know from what Juno says was in the letter that Fred hit Vivian about when he was drunk. If he'd killed her accidentally because he'd hit her too hard – but strangling? He meant to kill her.'

'Perhaps he found out about this Jay.'

'But he already knew about Jay,' I objected, 'he'd already burnt letters she'd written to him. And from what Maisie told me, Fred suspected that Tony wasn't his son.'

'Perhaps he found out she was hiding money, then,' Morris suggested. 'Perhaps she wouldn't tell him where it was.'

'That sounds more than likely.' It seemed that Fred had never reported his wife's disappearance to the police, which seemed suspicious in retrospect, but not at the time. Anyone who knew Fred would have been willing to accept the fact that Vivian had left him.

We paused in our deliberations about poor Vivian. Ricky had been studying old Japanese woodcuts and found pictures of noblemen wearing hats that looked like a small parcel balanced on the head, tied under the chin with thin black ribbons. He'd designed a prototype and he and I were now putting together one for each of the men in the chorus of *The Mikado*. Morris, meanwhile, was busy sewing Yum-Yum's adorable pink kimono.

But I couldn't help brooding about poor Viv, lying under that cold sodden earth year after year while her friends thought she'd done a flit and was enjoying a new life. I didn't know what I thought about Jay. She'd been writing to him, telling him how Fred was abusing her: why didn't he come back to do something about it? Why didn't he rescue her or at least send her the money so that she could free herself? Perhaps he didn't really want her. He was married and Vivian was just his bit on the side. Perhaps she'd been naive, thinking he wanted love when all he was after was her body. And she talked in her letter about Jay having to move on; what did that mean? Was he a business rep, some sort of travelling salesman?

'So, was this Jay the father of Vivian's boy, do we think?' Morris asked, raising his voice above the whirring of his sewing machine.

'If he was,' I said, 'Vivian must have been carrying on this clandestine affair – by letter – for years.'

Ricky sucked in his breath. 'Passion lasts a lot longer when it's unrequited.' He gave me a sly nudge with his elbow. 'Talking of which, how's that man of yours?'

'Fine, thank you,' I answered with as much dignity as I could muster. 'Still stuck in Scotland.'

Daniel had rung a few nights before and I'd updated him with what was going on. But sheep rustling and the discovery of a long-dead body didn't seem to bother him as much as the possibility that Adam and Kate might sell *Sunflowers*.

'They can't do that! It's the only place where I can get free Wi-Fi, decent coffee and is quiet enough not to spook Lottie. Where am I going to work?'

'*Sunflowers* isn't so quiet these days. Business is looking up, it's getting busier.'

He groaned. 'What if they sell it to people who don't allow dogs?'

'In Ashburton?' I asked, incredulous. 'Don't be daft!'

'You'll have to stop them, Miss B, persuade them they would be making a grave error.'

'What you need to do,' I told him, 'is get that house of yours organised. It's just sitting there.' He'd inherited a farmhouse up on Halshanger Common, a fine stone building crumbling into dereliction.

'My darling Miss B, it needs a new roof, new windows and rewiring. It's got no damp course and no plumbing,' he reminded me. 'It's a long way from superfast broadband and a decent coffee machine.'

I reminded him that everywhere on Dartmoor is a long way from superfast broadband.

He ignored this. 'I'm thinking about buying a caravan so Lottie and I have somewhere warm and dry to live while the work is being done.'

'Starting soon, is it?' I asked, injecting my voice with a note of cynicism.

'Soon, Miss B,' he answered, as he put the phone down, 'have faith.'

He is the most irritating man alive. I'd begun to think that Vivian was living in a fantasy world. Maybe I was too.

When Fizz took over her studio upstairs, I decided to move Nick's old phone down into the shop. It made sense, having it handy; it also relieved my nasty mind of the suspicion that she might be making long phone calls at my expense. So, when it rang in the shop next morning I only had to run as far as the counter to pick it up. But I didn't recognise the man who spoke until he gave me his name.

'It's Henry, Henry Gillow,' he explained. 'I hope you don't mind me phoning you.' His voice was hushed, almost a whisper. I wondered if Marjorie the Uncompassionate might be lurking behind the jars of liquorice comfits, trying to listen in.

'Of course not, Henry. What can I do for you?'

'I just heard about the discovery of the woman's body at Cold East Farm,' he told me.

'How did you hear that?' As far as I knew, finding

Vivian's body hadn't made the national news.

'Joan at the guest house phoned me. She promised, if anything came up that might be connected with Peter's murder, she'd let me know.'

'You're wondering, if Fred Crick murdered his wife, he might have murdered Peter too?'

'Well, yes. What do you think?'

'It's possible,' I admitted, 'but why? Fred himself was murdered that same afternoon. There has to have been someone else involved. Did Joan mention sheep-rustling at all?'

'Sheep rustling?' he echoed, horrified. 'Peter would never have had anything to do with sheep rustling.'

I tried not to laugh. 'No, I'm sure he wouldn't.' I explained to him the chain of events that had led to the discovery of Vivian's body, and also that someone had been watching the farm from Fred's property.

'You think that this sheep rustling gang may have been the men at Mr Crick's property when Peter accidentally stumbled on them?'

'Something like that.'

Music from Fizz's radio suddenly blared into a pounding rhythm upstairs. I thought of her rent money and counted to ten. 'But I don't suppose we'll ever know for sure,' I said, raising my voice slightly, 'unless these men get caught.'

Henry hesitated. 'Miss Browne, I have to tell you, that on Joan's advice, I looked online at the *Dartmoor Gazette* website.'

The words 'Dartmoor Gazette' always fill me with foreboding. 'Oh yes?' I tried to sound casual.

'Well, I started looking at a few back copies and I had absolutely no idea about—'

'About what?'

'About *you*, about Juno Browne,' he answered, 'how often you've been in the headlines, your previous involvement in murder cases.'

'I wouldn't call it involvement exactly.' I silently cursed the *Dartmoor Gazette* and everyone who sailed in her. 'It's true,' I admitted, 'I have managed to get myself sort of . . . muddled up . . . in murder investigations in the past, usually because it's me that discovers the body—'

'You seem to have a talent for that,' he observed, as if it was enviable trait.

'It's one I could live without.'

'Oh no, please don't say that! You see, I was wondering if I should come down to Devon and stay in Ashburton . . .'

'What for?'

'. . . so that you and I could solve Peter's murder together.'

Oh my God, I mouthed silently. 'No!' I spluttered, 'I don't think—'

'I am determined to discover who killed him. I don't care how long it takes.'

'Yes, but—' floundering around for a reason to keep him at bay I said desperately, 'What about *Ye Olde Sweet Shoppe*? What about Marjorie?'

'Her sister will come and help her,' he responded airily.

'Marjorie has a sister?'

'Eunice.'

'Eunice,' I repeated, Marjorie and Eunice, they sounded a ghastly combination. 'They're not twins, are they?'

He sounded baffled. 'No.'

'No? Well, the thing is, Henry,' I began, my brain beginning to thaw after its moment of frozen panic, 'that we don't have anything to go on. We have no suspects, with the possible exception of Fred, and he's dead. We have no clues, nothing to follow. So, I think you coming down here would be a waste of time.'

'You think so?' he asked, obviously disappointed.

'Oh, I'm sure of it.'

He heaved a sigh like a deflating balloon. 'I suppose you're right.'

'But if I should turn up any information,' I went on, my fingers mentally crossed, 'then of course I'll inform you immediately.'

'I'd be down on the next train,' he promised fervently.

'Excellent,' I lied.

'Now, you do promise?' he went on. 'If you get any information at all?'

'Cross my heart,' I told him, damning myself to several more years in purgatory, if not somewhere worse. 'The merest scrap.'

'Thank you, Miss Browne, I knew I could rely on you.'

I put down the phone. 'Hell's teeth,' I muttered.

CHAPTER SEVENTEEN

There is nothing inherently suspicious about a silver-coloured Peugeot being parked in a country lane, except that this particular country lane bordered what was left of Fred Crick's cottage. It was a narrow track leading off the road, shaded by overhanging trees, always muddy underfoot. If I hadn't casually glanced in its direction as I stopped to let a pheasant stalk across the road, I'd have missed the car altogether, tucked almost out of sight as it was.

I was only passing the place because I'd finally got around to taking the writing desk I'd bought to Steve the restorer, to get some idea of what it would cost me to have it repolished and renovated to a saleable condition.

He'd been recommended to me by several dealers as someone who could do the job well for a fair price. His workshop was on the other side of Widecombe, in an old barn behind his house. Outside his door was a lean-to piled high with odd pieces of injured furniture, their broken limbs and frayed cane seating waiting for treatment. Some of them looked like very old patients indeed.

I pushed open the workshop door; the dry smell of stored wood, mingled with glue and beeswax, made me breathe in deep, made me think of Old Nick. He'd been an expert at restoration, small items mostly. The smell conjured up a vision of him working at his table in his saggy grey cardigan, surrounded by all his pots and potions. I missed the wicked old goat. And I was sorry I hadn't had the chance to learn more from him. I still keep his little gold spectacles folded up in a drawer.

Steve stopped work at my shout of hello, looking up from what he was doing, which seemed to be trying to press the glazing bar of a cabinet door with a hot iron. 'I'm softening up the old putty,' he explained, putting the iron down, 'it'll make it easier to remove the glass later. It'll all have to come out.'

'Don't let me stop you.' I was quite happy to wait, to watch him work.

'No, no,' he pushed back the sleeves of an old jumper further up his forearms. 'Let's look at what you've brought me.' He began to examine the writing table. 'It's a bit wobbly,' he said, leaning his weight on it. He pulled out the drawer, squinting along one of its edges. 'This has warped.'

I told him I'd found a letter in the secret drawer and he grinned. 'It's surprising what you find in old furniture.

I found a pair of false teeth down the side of a sofa once. I've never found any treasure, though.' He passed a hand over the table's surface, rubbing a finger over the blisters in the veneer and tapping with his knuckles. 'This veneer has lifted. I can't just patch it. I'll have to replace this entire half.' He looked behind him at a wall of shelves, where veneers from different woods were laid flat, their colours ranging from palest yellow through deeper and darker browns and reds to black, some cut as thin as paper. He pulled out one or two and placed them on the table's walnut surface, comparing colour and pattern. 'I should be able to match it easily enough,' he went on, 'with a bit of jiggery-pokery.'

He listed all the ills my poor table was suffering from. His quote made me gulp a bit. But the only way to recoup my money was to get the table refurbished, put it in an auction and hope for the best, so I was forced to grin and bear it. I felt strangely sad about leaving it with him, parting with the one remaining connection to Vivian; but it had to be done.

On my way there I had called at Cold East Farm to see if there was any news. The police had completed their meticulous examination of Vivian's grave, packed up and gone away, and it seemed that despite the best efforts of Inspector Pitt and his rural theft team, Neil and Carol's sheep had disappeared into the Devon mist. There was no trace of them or the vehicle they were taken away in. But work on the ramparts had started; an impressive earth bulwark against intruders that was growing bigger every day.

It was on my way back from Widecombe, trundling along in White Van, enjoying the return of the sunshine and not thinking about anything in particular, that I noticed the parked silver Peugeot. I slowed the car and hesitated for as long as it took a pheasant to pop out and cross the road ahead. Then I pulled in across the end of the lane, effectively blocking the car's exit, and climbed out of the van.

Was this the same silver Peugeot I had seen before? It was the same model. I had a squint at the inside. It was a lot cleaner than the interior of White Van, the only item of interest a soft black camera bag, open and empty, on the front passenger seat. I headed up the lane, branching off beyond the end of Fred's garden.

It was breezy on top of the hill, the wind straight off the moor rushing through the old fir trees, knocking their branches together with a dull clapping sound. Otherwise, all I could hear was the distant bleating of sheep from Cold East Farm.

I trod carefully, stopping now and then to scan the view around me. Leaves glimmered in the sun, ferns and grasses rustled, tiny movements flickered at the corner of my eye, but whichever way I turned I could see no one. Yet the driver of that Peugeot had to be out here somewhere.

I walked from beneath the shade of the trees, arriving on sunlit grass. A few yards ahead, on top of the sloping outcrop of granite, I noticed a tripod and an expensive-looking camera with a very long lens. No one leaves a camera like that unattended, even in the middle of nowhere. Its owner was standing behind me. I could sense him. I turned and stared straight into his blue-green eyes.

'Why are you spying on me?' he asked softly.

Close up, he was not a disappointment in the looks department. I jerked my head towards the camera. 'I'm not the one doing the spying.'

'I'm just admiring the view.' There was a lilt to his voice, the slightest uplift on his final word: Australian, perhaps.

'Again?' I asked. 'You were here before. I saw you at Fred's cottage.'

'I saw you too.' There was the merest glimmer of a smile. 'You were watching me from behind the bushes. You thought I couldn't see you. I ask again, why are you spying on me?'

'Just curious.' I lifted my chin, determined to meet his eye, not to waver beneath that burning turquoise gaze, not to look away first.

'Curious about what?'

'About why you were in my shop asking about a wardrobe.'

He grinned suddenly and held out a tanned hand. 'Jason Beck,' he said. 'Why don't we continue this conversation somewhere more comfortable?'

'Journalist?' I repeated uncertainly. 'You're a journalist?'

We were sitting outside The Rugglestone Inn in

Widecombe-in-the-Moor, lucky to get a table to ourselves. On any sunny afternoon this famous old pub is busy with visitors. I cradled my glass of cider, enjoying the warmth of the sun on my shoulders. Jason had donned a pair of dark glasses, which made him look cool and mysterious and gave me relief from the intensity of his eyes. 'You're not from the *Dartmoor Gazette*.' I stated it as fact.

He grinned. 'No, I work freelance, mostly for feature magazines in Australia.' He dug in the pocket of his jacket and flipped a business card on to the table in front of me. I picked it up and read his name: Jason Beck. He'd lived in Australia for years, he told me. For a long time, before he took up journalism, he'd enjoyed a happy existence as a beach bum. That explained the tan as well as the accent: sun, sea and surf, it suited him. As we sat with our drinks, two young women in summer dresses walked by. They were looking at Jason, smiling and whispering. There was something infuriatingly attractive about him, not just his good looks, but a magnetism that hung in the air about him.

'Afternoon, ladies.' He winked at them and they walked away giggling, turning back to look at him.

'Are you married?' I asked.

He returned his attention to my face and smirked. 'Why do you wanna know?'

I nodded at his bronzed hand, the left one. There was a paler band around the base of his third finger, as if he'd once worn a wedding ring.

'Divorced,' he said airily. 'Marriage is a mug's game.'

'Children?'

'Two.' He shrugged. 'They live with their mother. Don't see much of them these days.'

I tried to conceal my irritation at his careless demeanour. 'Why were you taking photographs of Cold East Farm?'

He shrugged. 'I came here to write a story. When I'd finished, I decided I'd take a trip around, hook up with a few folks I haven't seen in a century. I read an article about livestock theft down here in Devon. It seemed there are a lot of parallels with what goes on back home. I thought I might work it into a feature – one of the magazines might be interested.'

'You must have sheep rustling in Australia.'

'We have a lot of sheep to rustle. But what interests me over here are the lengths farmers are going to in order to defend their land.'

'Like building medieval fortifications,' I suggested.

He laughed. 'I've seen a lot of that in Devon.'

'It's not funny. Farmers are desperate.'

'I was hoping to interview the people at Cold East Farm. I still am – but then the body of that woman was discovered, the whole place was crawling with police, local reporters buzzing around like flies . . .' He shrugged. 'I thought I'd let them all do their stuff and clear off.'

'But aren't you interested in that story?' *In Vivian's story*, I nearly said, but stopped myself. 'In the dead woman's story?'

'The discovery of an old murder over here probably

won't have much interest for the readers back home.' He was silent a moment. I couldn't read his expression, his eyes hidden behind those dark glasses. 'I usually find that you get more from people,' he said eventually, 'if you give them a little time . . .'

'Let the flies settle?' I suggested.

'That's right.'

'But aren't you reporters always racing each other to get a story first?'

He shrugged. 'In feature magazines it's a little different.'

'I was there the night that Neil and Carol's sheep were stolen.' I told him. 'I was at the farm.'

He leant across the table. 'You want to give me an exclusive?' he asked mockingly.

'I'd rather you got it from them.' I took a sip of cider, the cold glass beaded with condensation. 'And at Fred's cottage, were you chasing a story there too?'

'I'd heard rumours about what had gone on. I was just nosing around.'

'And what led you to my shop?'

'If you want to find out about something, the best place to go is the local newspaper office.' He laughed as I hung my head and groaned. 'No, really!' he protested. 'The guy in the wardrobe, he's the interesting part of the whole thing.'

I frowned. 'But the police didn't release details about the wardrobe to the press.'

'Ashburton's a great place for gossip. You don't have

to hang around for very long to pick up bits of interesting information' – he grinned – 'especially about you.'

'Don't believe everything you hear.'

'No?' He raised his eyebrows. 'Pity.'

I sighed, pushing my hair back, and he frowned suddenly, reaching out towards my head.

'This looks new. You hurt yourself?'

'Oh, nothing serious,' I drew my head back. 'Someone tried to kill me.'

He whistled softly. 'What happened?'

'It's old news now.' I swept a tangle of hair back over the scar. I didn't want to talk about me. 'Did you find out anything about the man in the wardrobe?'

He shook his head. 'Did you?'

'His name was Peter Gillow. He was a retired teacher here on holiday. The police think he died of a heart attack. That's all I know.' I wasn't going to share what Henry had told me. I glanced at my watch. I wanted to look in at *Old Nick's* before it closed. 'Look, I need to get going. If you want to talk to Neil and Carol about the theft of their sheep—'

'Do you think they'd be willing?'

'I don't see why not. But I would phone them first. I'll give you their number.' I looked it up for him and he put it on his phone. Then I rose to go.

He stood up, picking up his business card from the table and holding it out. 'Take it, my number is on it. In case you think of anything else. Or in case you want another drink sometime,' he added, smiling widely.

I studied him a moment. 'When do you fly back?' I asked.

'Oh, not for a while.'

'I'll think about it,' I promised.

I gave myself a stern talking to on the way back to the van. *Precisely what*, I asked, *is it that you think you are going to think about? Jason Beck is a very handsome man, and he's in a glamorous job. You are not immune to the dangerous sexuality pumping out of his every pore, but he lives in Australia. He is about to go back there and all that's on his mind is fitting in a quick fuck before he goes. And whilst that might not be an altogether unpleasant experience, you would never see him again, so why even consider it? Isn't Daniel's absence bad enough?* The thought of Daniel made me feel guilty. I hated myself.

By the time I had reached Ashburton, I was ready to toss Jason Beck and his business card straight into the bin. But I didn't get around to it; I forgot all about him, because when I arrived at the shop, who should be sitting there waiting for me, but Henry Gillow.

Horrified astonishment got the better of good manners. 'What the hell are you doing here?' I demanded, before the bell on the shop door had even finished jangling.

'Ah . . . er . . . M-Miss Browne,' he stammered, getting up from a chair. He clutched a mug in one hand. Elizabeth had been entertaining him with tea, it seemed.

'Mr Gillow has been waiting here for you for some

time,' she said, barely able to conceal her amusement.

I shut my mouth because I realised it was hanging open. I glared at Henry. 'What,' I began again, 'are you doing here, Henry?'

'Well, I thought, after our telephone conversation the other day—'

'Excuse me, Mr Gillow,' Elizabeth interrupted. 'Perhaps, as you're here now, Juno,' she asked, her eyebrows faintly lifted in enquiry, 'I can go home?'

'Yes,' I agreed hastily. 'That's a very good idea.' The last thing I wanted was anyone else listening to what Henry had to say. 'Thank you, Elizabeth. You go home.'

She picked up her bag, bid Henry a polite goodbye and slid by me, giving my arm a gentle pat as she went. 'Holmes,' she added softly.

I didn't like the sound of that. I frowned at Henry. 'Holmes?'

'What a very charming lady,' he said as she went out. 'I did say to her, that if I could persuade you to change your mind, to take an interest in Peter's case, I might act as Watson to your Holmes.'

I let out a long groan, my shoulders slumped and my bag fell to the floor. 'Henry,' I sighed, sitting down heavily in the chair that Elizabeth had just vacated. 'I am interested in what happened to Peter, of course I am. But I really don't know what you think I can do that the police are not already doing.'

'You've solved other cases.'

'More by luck than judgement, believe me. Please,

Henry,' I begged, as he continued to stare at me pleadingly, 'go home. You may just have to accept that we will never know what happened to your brother.'

He looked down into his mug of tea. 'We buried him yesterday,' he murmured.

I felt bad then. 'I'm sorry.'

He was quiet for a moment. 'I just can't accept that, you see, not knowing.' He took a handkerchief from his pocket and blew his nose noisily. 'I think it would drive me mad.'

'I can understand you feeling that way, but the truth is . . . as I said to you on the phone . . . we've nothing to go on. Perhaps if you talked to the police again—'

He shook his head. 'I have. They say they're doing all they can, whatever that means.'

'I'm sure they are.'

He got control of himself, stowing his handkerchief in his pocket. 'I'm staying at the guest house, where Peter stayed.'

'Is that wise?' I asked. 'I really think it would be better if you went home.'

'I may never go home,' he said defiantly. 'Marjorie and I . . . well, we quarrelled. She refused to come to Peter's funeral.'

So Marjorie the Uncompassionate was acting true to form. 'I'm sorry.'

'Some of his old school colleagues attended, of course, and a few members of the archaeological society, but it wasn't quite the turnout I had hoped.'

'I'm very sorry, Henry,' I began, 'but—'

'I was so hoping we could crack this case together,' he said, gazing at me earnestly from his pale blue eyes. 'I thought perhaps, in the morning, we could begin by—'

'In the morning?' I repeated. 'Henry, let me tell you what I'm going to be doing in the morning. I'll get up at six, round up five dogs from their various homes and take them for a long walk. After I've brought them back again, I'll go and do two hours of someone's ironing. Then I'll go around to the homes of two other clients and deal with their laundry, shopping, cleaning or whatever else they need. If I'm lucky, sometime, I'll fit in lunch. Then I'll come here and make sure everything is all right, because this is my shop and my responsibility. If I'm not on the rota for a shift here in the afternoon and I have no other clients to see, I'll try and give some help to two friends struggling to fill a theatrical costume order. If I get any free time at all during this week, I'll be out hunting for stock, not chasing criminals. Now, if you don't mind, Henry, I want to cash up before I go home, and I would like to run a mop over this shop floor before I leave.'

'You devote yourself to all these things, Juno, and you're wasted. With your brain—'

'I haven't got a brain!' I snapped. 'What I mean is,' I sighed, struggling to compose myself, 'I'm not the sleuth you think I am. Please, Henry,' I begged him, 'just go home. Go back to Marjorie and *Ye Olde Sweet Shoppe*. Please.'

It was quite a long time before I managed to dislodge a disconsolate Henry and do the things I had to do before

I could lock up. It seemed *Old Nick's* had enjoyed a reasonable day's takings, with Pat, Sophie and Fizz all making sales. Even I had sold a vase. This was all likely due to the excellent Elizabeth being on duty; she's very persuasive with customers. I phoned her. Several ladies had been in to sign up for Fizz's silk painting workshop, she told me, and this accounted for the unexpected flurry in sales.

'How did you get on with Watson?' she asked, voice dripping with amusement.

'I sent him home, I hope.' I told her what had passed between us.

'Oh, dear,' she sighed, 'poor little man.'

'Do you think I was too hard on him?'

'No, I'm sure you've done the right thing. He's seriously deluded. And if he's going to pester anyone, it should be the police, not you.'

'Thanks. I appreciate that.' But I still felt wretched with guilt when I put down the phone.

I picked it up again to phone Carol. I thought I'd better warn her that Jason Beck might be in contact, if he hadn't been already.

'Not so far,' she told me. 'But we've had the *Dartmoor Gazette* pestering us. We were only too happy to give them interviews at first, what with the sheep being stolen and then the discovery of that poor woman's body, but they keep snooping about. Last night we caught someone standing out in the middle of the field in the dark, shining a torch into the grave.'

'Did you call the police?'

She laughed. 'Neil chased him off. But it's a bit ghoulish; there's nothing to see, not now.'

'Well, in that case, if Jason Beck does get in touch, will Neil mind talking to him?'

'Probably not,' she laughed again. 'He'll be only too happy to show off his ramparts.'

Later, after I'd scoffed my way through a portion of roasted vegetable quiche left outside my door as an offering by Kate, I dug out Mr Beck's business card, opened the laptop and looked up his website. It occurred to me that if you wanted to snoop around farms, assessing the value of livestock and checking on their security arrangements, because you were, for example, a member of a gang involved in rustling said livestock, then posing as a reporter investigating similar crimes was a good way to gain access to the information you wanted. I wanted to check that Jason Beck was who he said he was. After all, anyone can get a business card printed.

I found the website easily enough. There was a picture of Jason Beck, photo-journalist, tanned and turquoise-eyed, posing with his long-lens camera against a background of spectacular beach. There were several articles written by him, published in various glossy and prestigious magazines, and references to a lot more. He was obviously genuine. There was no mention of his family or home life. He no longer wore his wedding ring. I wondered if he had a new partner back home. Then I wondered why I was wondering, and snapped the laptop shut.

CHAPTER EIGHTEEN

The next day more or less followed the outline I had given Henry. I walked the Tribe, cleaned house for the Brownlow family, tackled a pile of ironing for Simon the fussy accountant, shopped for Maisie and Tom and made it back to *Old Nick's* in the early afternoon. An envelope was waiting there, addressed to me. Sophie said she had found it shoved under the shop door that morning. It was from Henry:

Dear Juno,

After giving it much thought, I have decided that you are right. It is foolish of me to try to pursue Peter's murderer when there are no leads to follow. I hope you will forgive me if I have made a nuisance of myself. I am going home to Basingstoke today.

Yours,
With every good wish,
Henry Gillow

'Thank God for that,' I muttered, although I felt sorry for the poor little man, going back to *Ye Olde Sweet Shoppe* and Marjorie.

As I had a couple of hours free later on, I drove up to Druid Lodge to see how *The Mikado* costumes were coming along. When I got there, Yum-Yum had just arrived for a costume fitting.

Her real name was Phoebe. She was short, plump and pretty with a rose-petal complexion and long dark hair. She squealed with delight at the sight of her pink kimono and couldn't wait to try it on. It was kept in place by a wide sash of deep, dull purple satin that stretched from under her armpits to her waist. It was elaborately pleated and folded at the back to mimic a geisha's traditional obi and to provide an interesting back view.

'You've flattened out my boobs,' she cried when she saw her reflection in the mirror.

'Well, they needed flattening,' Ricky informed her rudely and she cracked up with laughter. 'God, Phoebe, you've got a filthier laugh than Juno and that's saying something.' He picked up strands of her long dark hair and began piling it on top of her head. 'You won't need a wig. We can put your hair up and dress it with a few flowers.'

'What about knitting needles?' she asked. 'Japanese ladies have knitting needles sticking out of their hair.'

'She's right,' Morris agreed, 'although they're not knitting needles, exactly.'

He pointed to the pictures that had been pinned up

around the walls of the workroom. There were several geishas, and they each had hair decorations that looked like knitting needles but with long strings of decoration hanging from them.

'I can make those,' I said. 'We could use long hatpins and hang beaded earrings from them. They'd look just the same. I could ask Pat to make them. She's the one that makes the earrings these days.'

'Do you think she would?' Morris asked.

'Oh, sure! You two are in her good books these days.'

'Makes a bloody change,' Ricky muttered.

'You know you are.' Since the two of them had put on a concert to raise money for the animal sanctuary they could do no wrong in Pat's eyes.

'What colours are Pitti-Sing and Peep-Bo wearing?' Phoebe asked innocently.

'Your sisters are in lemon yellow and pale green,' Morris told her.

She smiled. 'Good, just as long as their kimonos aren't as pretty as mine.'

Costume fitting over, Ricky and Morris persuaded Phoebe to sing. We all trooped down to the music room where Ricky took a seat at the grand piano. Phoebe, who had never been to Druid Lodge before, had no idea that Ricky and Morris were also performers, and exclaimed with delight at the theatrical photos on the walls. They told her about their alter egos, Sauce and Slander, and she said she'd only sing if they performed one of their comic songs. I find there is nothing like a little mutual congratulation to get theatricals going. They'd be at it for hours. I went off to make the tea while they performed for each other's benefit. But I must admit, Phoebe did have a lovely voice.

'How old's your lover?' Ricky demanded. 'Who's playing Nanki-Poo?'

'Oh, he must be every day of fifty,' she giggled, 'but he's a lovely man and he's got a super voice. And anyway, under all that Japanese make-up,' she added, dimpling, 'no one will be able to tell how old he is.'

That evening I got a call from Vicky Smithson, tipping me off about someone who wanted to get rid of some Beswick pottery figures. His late wife used to collect them and he didn't want the bother of selling them himself. She thought I might be interested as they're very collectible and she knew I was looking for replacement stock, and thought they might be around my price. It was kind of her to think of me. The truth was I couldn't afford much just now, but on the other hand, I couldn't afford to have empty shelves and cabinets either.

It turned out that the seller lived in Christow, and as I never mind an excuse to drive up the beautiful Teign Valley, I took his number and phoned him to make an appointment. I'd checked the shop rota and, if I talked nicely to Pat, I could wangle a couple of free hours the following afternoon.

I spent the rest of that evening looking up Beswick figures online to see what they were currently fetching.

It all depended of course, on whether I could buy them at the right price. So, late the following afternoon I set out for the village of Christow, following the winding road through the lush fields of the Teign Valley, and had it almost to myself – except for someone on an old Lambretta scooter who was following at a sedate pace and appeared in my rear-view mirror now and then.

I was familiar with only two places in Christow, the medieval church and the even older Artichoke Inn, but I found the house I was looking for, not far from either of them, and was greeted warmly by an elderly Mr Clifford.

His wife's collection of Beswick pottery was extensive. There were hundreds of animal figures, most not more than four inches high and I certainly couldn't afford to buy them all.

A few were original Beatrix Potter characters brought out in the 1940s, which were now worth hundreds of pounds each. Most of them were farm animals which wouldn't fetch anything like as much, but which were of more interest to me. Dear Mr Clifford told me he was in no hurry to sell, and if I wanted to take some now and come back for more at a later date, I was welcome to do so. I made a careful selection of sheep and pigs as well as some sheepdogs, a lovely ram, a cockerel and a few Highland cows. We struck a bargain, enjoyed a glass of sherry and a chat, and I promised to call round again. Well pleased, I stowed my box of goodies, each one individually wrapped in newspaper, in the back of White Van. I decided I'd put the figures in the shop and advertise them online to double my chance of selling, then began to thread my way contentedly through the streets of Christow towards home.

I'd barely got going when the Lambretta appeared in my rear-view mirror. I knew it had to be the same one that had been behind me before, the rider's face concealed by a helmet and scarf. On the journey out I'd assumed that he and I were simply travelling to the same place: the idea that someone might be following me on an old cream and red scooter with a shopping basket on the front, hadn't occurred to me. It occurred to me now as I made several false turns around the village, bringing myself round in a circle. The Lambretta stuck like glue. I went through the whole procedure a second time and then I pulled in by the churchyard, got out, leant against the bonnet of the van, folded my arms and waited. Moments later the scooter appeared, the driver slowing to an uncertain stop, his engine pootling. For a few moments he sat there as if he wasn't sure what to do.

'Henry,' I said, keeping my voice as steady as I could, 'you told me you'd gone home.'

He raised the visor on his helmet, lowered his scarf and beamed at me. 'That's what I wanted you to think,' he said smugly, as if he'd pulled off an incredibly clever con trick.

I was tempted to dash my brains out on a nearby gravestone but decided to resist. 'Take my advice, Henry, don't ever get a job as a private detective.' His face fell. 'Why are you following me?'

'Well, I thought—'

'You didn't travel down from Basingstoke on that thing, did you?'

'No, no, I came down on the train. I borrowed this from Joan's husband at the guest house.'

'Borrowed it?'

'Yes, Colin buys old bikes and does them up,' he said enthusiastically. 'I used to ride one of these before I got my first car.'

'Yes, well, whatever. I don't know what you think I'm doing here,' I went on, 'but I am not following clues to anyone's murder. I've been buying some ornaments for my shop. I'll show them to you if you like.'

'No, there's no need,' he assured me hastily. 'I believe you.'

'Thank you. You can also believe me when I say I am now going home. And that's what I want you to do. Go back to Basingstoke, Henry,' I went on, my voice growing louder. 'Leave me alone.' He started to blurt out something, but I ignored him, slamming my way back into the van and starting up the engine.

I pulled away while he desperately tried to kick-start his machine. I knew he'd follow me, so I decided not to take the same road back to Ashburton. I was determined to shake him off. I accelerated as much as I dared but couldn't really put my foot down on the narrow winding road so, for several minutes, Henry kept swinging into view in my mirror, doggedly following behind me.

We were entering forestry commission territory, the

view of open fields lost behind ranks of tall conifers. The dark, gloomy woods lined the road for miles, trees towering on either side with trunks as straight as pillars. I lost sight of Henry on a bend of the road and took a sharp turn down a gravel track that led off through the trees. I didn't know where it came out. It was probably just a track to allow access for logging and I'd almost certainly have to double back. But in the meantime, with any luck, Henry would go riding past, oblivious, not realising I was no longer just ahead of him until it was too late; by which time I would have sneaked back down the road and gone home the other way.

I slowed out of sight of the main road, thought about turning round, then decided to idle along a bit further, to see how far this track through the forest might take me. Then I spotted a car parked at the side of the track, tucked well in under the trees: a silver Peugeot. I pulled over to the side, turned off the engine and got out.

The trees rose up on either side of the track, their straight trunks branchless until high above my head where the dark canopy spread, allowing only glimpses of a melting golden sky. Beneath my feet the ground was milky brown and soft as a carpet, with years of fallen fir needles. It was silent, no evening birdsong. Moths would soon be hunting in the dusk, and later bats, but for now the forest was still: no one about.

I took a look at the Peugeot. It was the same model as Jason Beck's. I should have taken a note of his number plate when I had the chance. Great detective I was.

Henry would be disappointed in me. There was no sign of a camera case inside, just a chocolate bar wrapper on the front seat. Anyway, what would Jason Beck be doing here in this forest? And why could I not rid myself of the idea that he was up to something?

I began to take a walk along the gravel track. After a few moments someone shouted, and I stopped. I couldn't see anyone among the trees. The sound of voices came again, more than one. I realised no one was shouting at me, but people were shouting at each other. Men's voices. I could hear other sounds now, sounds that didn't belong in this conifer forest: the bleating of sheep. The track curved away from me and through the trees I glimpsed something large and red. I sneaked forward, crouching low, dodging from one tree to another until I got a clear view.

Two cattle trucks stood end to end in a clearing, their ramps facing each other, almost touching. A group of men were manhandling sheep, driving them down the ramp of one vehicle and up into the next. Another kept watch, armed with a shotgun. Was I looking at the same gang that had robbed Neil and Carol, the same gunman, his face hidden behind a mask?

What I should have done was to creep back through the trees to the van and call the police. Instead, I dropped to the ground and peered from behind the safety of a tree trunk, watched the poor bleating ewes being hustled from one truck to another. The man with the shotgun kept turning, scanning the clearing and the dark silent trees for the slightest sound or movement. He seemed nervous, jittery. If I made any noise, if I moved, I could get my head shot off.

Then I heard something that made me stifle a gasp, my hand flying to my mouth: the *put-put-put* of an old Lambretta. A moment later, Henry rode into view, drove straight into the clearing, his tyres screeching on the gravel as he found himself confronted by a masked man levelling a shotgun at him. He braked messily, both hands shooting above his head in surrender, his terrified scream muffled behind his visor. I watched in horror.

The gunman advanced, ordering him off the bike, making him kneel on the gravel, his arms behind his head. My heart was thumping. I had to force myself to take a breath. One of the sheep wranglers, a guy in a checked shirt, started remonstrating with the gunman, yelling at him not to shoot. Perhaps he hadn't signed up for murder.

I had to do something. I looked around and picked up a broken branch, a short piece from many strewn at my feet. I hefted it in my hand, assessing its weight and lobbed it through the trees, aiming for the far side of the clearing. It turned over in the air and landed short, crashing noisily against a tree trunk. The gunman swung round and fired, letting the tree have both barrels. Wood cracked and splintered; shards of bark went flying.

Then all hell broke loose. There was a sudden shout of 'Police! Put down your weapon!' Dark figures in helmets charged from between the trees on the far side of the clearing, rushing out through the undergrowth, their guns raised.

I gaped in astonishment. They'd been bloody well hidden. The gunman and the guy in the checked shirt began wrestling for the shotgun as the rest of the gang scattered and fled. A police car roared up the gravel track from nowhere, sirens screaming. A van screeched in from the opposite direction and cut the other gang members off. The gunman dropped his weapon, tried to make a break for it but was floored by the guy in the checked shirt. With mayhem going on around him, Henry crouched in the middle of the clearing, his nose almost touching the gravel, his arms clamped protectively around his head. The sheep decided they'd had enough, spilt out of the truck and began running around the clearing, bleating in panic.

Dodging my way between sheep and policemen wrestling villains to the ground I made it to Henry's side and tried to drag him to safety. I yelled his name, pulling on his arm, but he wouldn't budge. I couldn't even persuade him to look up. Car doors slammed as three plain-clothed officers got out. My heart sank when I saw who they were: Detective Constable Dean Collins, Detective Sergeant Cruella deVille, and worst of all, Detective Inspector Ford.

'Juno Browne!' he yelled at me furiously. 'What the bloody hell are you doing here?'

CHAPTER NINETEEN

It seemed that Henry and I had unwittingly ruined a covert police operation. A joint operation, in fact, involving Inspector Ford from South Devon Serious Crimes and Inspector Pitt from Rural Theft, that had been eighteen months in the planning. We had blown the cover of an undercover policeman, he of the checked shirt and, as it turned out, the silver Peugeot, who for six months had been risking his life infiltrating a gang of thieves linked to organised crime. It was he who had tipped-off the police. They had been lying in wait amongst those trees for a lot longer than was comfortable before Henry came bumbling on to the scene. Forced to spring their trap early in order to prevent an innocent civilian from being murdered, they had only succeeded in arresting a few low-level grunts. If they'd been able to pursue their original plan and follow the cattle trucks to their destination, where they knew a considerable sum of money was about to change hands, they could have caught the men they were really after; the villains higher up in the food chain. They also could have rescued the stolen livestock, which were now running free all over the forest.

Inspector Ford was ready to throw the book at me. The gang members safely handcuffed and taken away in a police van, he turned his attention to Henry and me, waiting nervously where we'd been ordered to wait, at the side of the track. It took a great deal of persuasion to convince him that we had stumbled on the sheep rustlers by accident, that I was not trying to interfere with police business and that I had not been following some bungling investigation of my own since the day the sheep were stolen from Cold East Farm.

'If I'd really been pursuing thieves,' I protested indignantly, 'do you think I'd have stopped off to buy antiques along the way?' I thrust the receipt Mr Clifford had written me under the inspector's nose. 'See, he's dated it today. And if you want to know what time I was at his house you can ring him up and ask him. There's his phone number.'

'She was there,' Henry added, in an attempt to be helpful. 'I was waiting outside for an hour and a half.' I threw a scorching look at him, but instead of dropping dead, he just hung his head, his cheeks reddening.

The inspector was unimpressed. 'This doesn't explain what the two of you were doing on this road. This is not the way back to Ashburton.'

I could have told the truth. I could have explained that I was trying to escape Henry who had been following me because the deluded idiot believes I am some kind of amateur super-sleuth, but I didn't want to look an even bigger idiot than the inspector already thought I was. If Henry started on about Holmes and Watson, I'd have to kill us both. I foraged for an answer. I was given a few more moments to think by a uniformed officer who wandered up to us, seemingly unaware that we were being interrogated. He must have thought we were having a cosy chat.

'Is that your Lambretta, sir?' he asked Henry.

'N-no, no,' Henry stammered, as if he wondered what else he'd done wrong, 'it belongs to the people who run the guest house. They let me borrow it.'

'It's in beautiful condition. I've been trying to find something like that for my mother-in-law—'

'Constable, do you mind!' the inspector bellowed at him.

'Oh, sorry, sir!' he said and hurried off, pulling a face at Dean Collins as he turned his back.

'Now, Miss Browne,' the inspector returned his thunderous face to me, 'you were saying?'

'Well, you see, Henry and I had arranged to meet each other at Christow. I knew he would be interested in St James Church. It's medieval, you see, and with Henry being a keen historian . . .'

The inspector's heavy sandy brows drew together in a frown. 'Like his brother?'

'Exactly. It has a Norman font—'

'And the granite tower,' Henry added helpfully, 'is a particularly fine example of . . .'

'A granite tower, sir?' Dean suggested helpfully.

225

'And then there's The Artichoke Inn,' I babbled on, 'it dates back to the twelfth century.'

'If you wanted to show Mr Gillow the delights of Christow, why were you travelling separately?' The inspector demanded. 'Surely it would have made more sense to use the same vehicle.'

'Well, as I've just told you, I had business beforehand. That's why we agreed to meet afterwards. And in any case,' I added, struck with sudden inspiration, 'Mr Gillow can't ride in my van. He's allergic to dog hair.' I turned to look at him. 'Isn't that right, Henry?'

'Oh, yes, right,' he agreed after a moment's hesitation.

Cruella, who was lurking behind the inspector along with Dean Collins, decided it was her turn to contribute to the conversation. 'That still doesn't explain what you're doing here, now, in this clearing, in this forest.'

I glared into her smirking violet eyes. 'It was the nightjar,' I explained after a moment.

The inspector frowned even more heavily. 'Nightjar?'

'Yes,' I plunged on, 'as you know, they're very shy birds, beautifully camouflaged, very difficult to see. This is one of the few places one can be pretty sure of hearing them, in this coniferous forest. In fact, they've been reported in this very patch of the woods. Henry is a keen ornithologist and—'

'Historian and ornithologist,' the inspector interrupted. 'Is there anything he isn't keen on?'

I saw Dean Collins lips press together hard, as if he was having difficulty controlling them.

'And in order to hear this rare, shy bird he drives his scooter right into the forest?' the inspector asked.

'Ah! Well—'I began but he silenced me by holding up his hand. 'No, spare me the rest. You needn't explain any further.' He shook his head. 'I don't believe a word of this nonsense.' He was silent for a few moments. 'Mr Gillow.' His voice made Henry straighten up as if he was standing in the dock and about to receive sentence. 'I don't expect to see you ever again. When are you returning to Basingstoke?'

'My train leaves from Exeter in the morning.'

'Make sure you're on it.'

'Yes, I—'

'You can go now.'

'But I—'

'Just go.'

Henry's face puckered, he sounded close to tears. 'I'm afraid I don't know the way back to my guest house from here.'

'Don't worry, a police car will be escorting your scooter,' he shot me a look, 'and also Miss Browne in her vehicle.'

'Inspector Ford—' I began.

'Juno, go home,' he told me sternly. 'Think yourself lucky you're not being charged.'

'What with?' I demanded.

'Oh, I'd think of something,' he swore devoutly. 'Go home,' he warned me as I was about to open my mouth, 'and don't say another word.'

I was mortified. I'd have cheerfully marched straight into Vixen Mire and sunk myself in the bog. I couldn't say goodbye to Henry because we had orders not to talk. The last I saw of him was when he raised his hand in sad farewell as he turned the Lambretta into the drive of the guest house. Poor Henry, his dreams of being a sleuth had ended in ignominy.

As for me, I was forced to follow Cruella in her wretched police car all the way into Ashburton, blue lights flashing. I thought that was really unnecessary. I don't think my cheeks stopped burning all the way. At least she didn't have the siren going. When we arrived at the house the flashing lights attracted the attention of Kate and Adam who came out to see what was going on. The police car drove away, thank God. Cruella didn't feel it necessary to escort me physically into the building.

'You OK, Juno?' Adam asked as I stomped up the front path.

By now I was crying tears of vexation. 'No! I'm bloody not!'

Kate looked worried. 'Come on in and have a drink.'

'No, thanks. I don't want to talk about it.' What I wanted to do was to scream and throw things. I ran up the stairs to my flat, unlocked the door and slammed it behind me. I gave vent to a string of the filthiest words I could think of. Then I repeated the best ones. Then I did something I had promised myself I would never do: I rang Daniel.

CHAPTER TWENTY

Next morning Dean Collins came to see me. I left Sophie in charge in the shop, took him up to the kitchen away from flapping ears and made us both a coffee.

'Are you all right, Juno?' he asked.

'Not really,' I admitted. 'I'm sorry that Henry and I buggered up your investigation.'

He shrugged. 'Our lords and masters are none too pleased, but these things happen. At least no one got hurt.' He grinned. 'It was bloody funny, though. What were you really doing there? And don't give me any old toss about nightjars.'

I told him the truth about Henry and how I'd been trying to shake him off.

'Well, you don't need to worry about him any longer. We made sure he was on that train this morning. He's out of your hair.'

'Poor Henry!' Despite the fact that he was an infernal

nuisance, I couldn't help feeling sorry for him. Now he'd have had no choice but to go back to *Ye Olde Sweet Shoppe* and Marjorie the Uncompassionate. I was surprised he hadn't phoned me. Perhaps he felt too embarrassed to call.

'Now, come on, Juno, tell me the rest,' Dean insisted. 'If you'd just been avoiding Henry Gillow, you'd no need to get out of the car. What were you really up to?'

'Remember I told you about the man with the silver Peugeot?'

He frowned. 'The man who came to your shop to ask about a wardrobe?' he said, after thoughtfully dunking a biscuit.

'That's the one.'

'You thought that was his car parked up the track?'

'I thought it could be.' I explained how I'd seen Jason again and talked with him, and then I showed Dean his business card.

'He was investigating livestock theft for this Australian magazine he works for. He wanted to interview Neil and Carol at Cold East Farm – at least that's what he said. So far I gather he hasn't talked to them.'

Dean shrugged and helped himself to another Hobnob. 'Perhaps he found a better story somewhere else. Livestock theft in Devon can't be of much interest to people in Australia, can it?'

'He seemed to think it would be.' I hesitated a moment. 'I wondered,' I began cautiously, 'if he might be involved in it himself.' I didn't add that, when the balaclavas came

230

off, I'd had a good look at all the rustlers' faces in case one of them had turquoise eyes.

Dean looked mystified. 'Why would an Australian journalist get involved in livestock rustling here in Devon?'

'For the same reason as anyone else,' I answered, 'money. And when you think about it, posing as a journalist is a great way to get access to information. People will talk to you, tell you things.'

Dean picked up the business card and looked at it more closely, flipping it over to read both sides. 'But you checked him out on the Internet. He's bona fide?'

'Oh, yes. He's genuine enough, it's just . . . I don't know, there's something about him. I can't believe he's all he's cracked up to be.'

Dean nodded wisely. 'That's because you've got a suspicious mind.'

I snatched away the packet of biscuits before he could grab another one.

He grinned. 'No, it's a good thing – well, it's good if you're a copper – to suspect people who seem too innocent or whose alibi is foolproof. Never believe in people who are too good to be true.' He took a sip of coffee. 'But don't worry, Juno,' he added, winking, 'no one's going to think that about you.'

Next day, Saturday, I was on duty at *Old Nick's* with Pat. I was working out how to put together Japanese hair decorations. Above our heads, a small herd of elephants was enjoying Fizz's silk painting workshop, six ladies sitting around the large worktable in her studio, stretching pieces of silk on frames and having a wonderful time. I'd sneaked up to listen shortly after they'd arrived, but when I heard Fizz ask them if they'd all remembered to bring their hairdryers, I decided I was better off not knowing what was going on.

Ricky and Morris came in, as they often did at weekends, to check on their vintage clothing stock, and I told them how Henry and I had inadvertently sabotaged an important police investigation. Morris stared at me in horror over his little round specs and kept repeating 'Oh, Juno!' while Ricky laughed so much he gave himself hiccups.

Meanwhile, Pat was becoming increasingly annoyed with what was going on upstairs. She was working on one of her country panoramas, intricate little pictures that she makes from felt and wool, of fields and trees and cottages, often with animals and dressed figures of shepherds or farmers made from peg dolls. The tourists love them. This one was of a cottage, with silver and grey shirt buttons overlapped to form the slates of the roof, cotton-wool smoke coming from the chimney and flowers embroidered on the walls.

'They could be good for business,' I told her, watching her work. 'There are six women up there who might come down here and spend money later.'

Pat was not to be placated. 'They all had coffee just now. They've used our mugs without so much as a by your leave and left 'em in the sink in the kitchen. I don't know who Fizz thinks is going to wash them up, but it ain't going to be me.'

'No,' I sighed, 'it'll be me,' and I went upstairs to do the deed. A great deal of laughter and chatter was coming from the studio. I don't know if much silk painting was being done but the ladies were certainly having fun.

And I was right, when they broke at lunchtime for their sandwiches, they came down into the shop for a look around. Three of them had visited before when they signed up for the workshop, and one mollified Pat by buying a second pair of her beaded earrings. Unfortunately, a little knot of them gathered watching her work, fascinated by the panorama she was making. Pat's not used to an audience while she works. Sophie has learnt to adjust to it and has developed the skill of talking to customers while she paints. Pat seemed determined to ignore them.

'Isn't that delightful?' one asked. 'Oh look, there are some more on the wall. Just look at the little sheep!'

'Can I buy the kit to make one of those?' another asked innocently.

'Kit?' Pat stopped working and glared crossly. 'I don't use a kit.'

'You mean they're all your own design?'

'Course! I make 'em up.'

'You are clever! You wouldn't like to show me how to make one?'

'No, I wouldn't.'

'No?' the lady echoed in surprise. She glanced at her companions. 'Why not?'

'I don't do workshops,' Pat informed her. 'I make these to raise money for the animal sanctuary. I don't want other people making a profit from 'em.'

'Oh, surely just one . . .'

I'd had enough drama recently, so I didn't hang around to listen to the ensuing argument. I went into the storeroom to amuse myself by rearranging Beswick figurines. But looking at the little pottery sheep just reminded me of the trouble I was in and I went off the idea.

The silk painters resumed their labours upstairs and when I wandered back into the shop Pat was alone. She'd stopped working on her panorama and was happily selecting beads for the hair decorations. 'Why don't you go home, Juno?' she suggested. 'You're only mooching about and there's no need for the two of us to be here.'

'I can't do that.' Saturday was the only day I gave myself full time to the shop instead of leaving it to her or Sophie.

'Why not? I can lock up. And I'll make sure that lot upstairs leave everything as it should be, don't you worry. You've been looking like a sick horse ever since you arrived.'

'Well, *thanks*.'

'Oh, go home, for pity's sake!'

'Are you sure?' I felt guilty, but not enough to refuse her offer.

'Course I am. Go home.'

'You're a star!' I grabbed my bag. On my way to the door, I dropped a kiss on the top of her head. She just grunted.

As I don't have clients or dogs to worry about on a Saturday, I usually walk to the shop, which means that I have to walk home again. The sky was grey and it was raining slightly. It was as I was sauntering rather gloomily homeward that I realised something was hurtling towards me at great speed, something small, silvery-brown in colour and in imminent danger of colliding with my knees. I crouched down and held out my arms. 'Lottie!' I yelled at the approaching missile and she gave joyous yelps of greeting as she launched herself into my arms. Lottie has always adored me.

'Oh, Lottie, I haven't seen you for ages.' The wriggling whippet was trying to lick my face and snuffling about in my hair. I cuddled and pet her warm body for a few moments and then looked up. For where there was Lottie, somewhere there must be Daniel.

He was a long way up the road, a tall figure striding towards me, untidy black hair blowing about his face, his raincoat flapping like the wings of a giant bird of prey. 'Miss Browne with an "e"!' he called out, waving his long arms.

I grabbed Lottie's trailing lead and hurried to meet him, resisting the urge to run.

We both stopped and stared for a moment, taking each other in.

'Mr Thorncroft,' I said, hoping my resemblance to a sick horse had disappeared. I wish I'd known he was coming: I'd have glammed up, got myself gorgeous.

'My dear Miss B, how lovely to see you.'

'Daniel, what are you doing here?'

He made a valiant effort not to yawn. 'I thought you needed cheering up, so I caught the sleeper down from Glasgow.'

'You needn't have done that.'

'No, I needn't.'

'But I'm glad you did,' I added hastily.

'Good,' his dark eyebrows drew together in a puzzled frown, 'yet I can't help but observe, Miss B, that I don't seem to rate the same rapturous greeting as my dog.'

Lottie was dancing up and down on her tippy toes like an excited ballerina, trying to bind the two of us together by circling us and wrapping her lead around our knees. We were in danger of toppling over. Daniel reached out to brush back a lock of my hair. 'How's your poor head?' he asked, inspecting my scar.

'Fine,' I smiled.

'And your ankle?'

'Getting better.'

His grey eyes stared thoughtfully into mine. I'd forgotten how dark they were, like storm clouds. 'I sense that cheering up is still in order.' He grabbed my arm, thrusting it through his. 'Turn around,' he ordered, 'the wine bar is this way.'

* * *

236

'My only remaining relative is my Uncle Brian,' I explained, a Chardonnay and a half later, 'although he's not really an uncle, he's my cousin. He's a diplomat, currently in South Korea. He comes back to England on leave occasionally but I don't see him much.' I pulled a face. Brian's hag-wife Marcia and I did not get on. 'He paid for my education when I lost my mother, sent me to boarding school.'

Daniel popped a large green olive into his mouth and chewed thoughtfully. Lottie was sitting under the table, her smooth muzzle resting on my knee. I fed her a sly crisp. 'Didn't you tell me once you had another cousin,' he asked, 'in Totnes?'

'Cordelia,' I nodded, 'I used to spend my holidays with her. She died too.' Any thought of her still catches at my heart. I could sense Daniel watching me closely and looked back at him. 'She had a little shop at the top of the town. She sold beads and jewellery. She was an astrologer.'

'An astrologer?' he repeated. 'Claire was into all that stuff. What do you think about it?'

'About you being a Scorpio, you mean?'

He raised his eyebrows in surprise. 'Touché! I'm impressed. So, you're an astrologer too?'

I shook my head. 'Not really.'

'What sign are you?'

'Capricorn.'

He poured me more wine. 'Scorpio and Capricorn, are they considered compatible?'

I pulled a face. 'Cordelia hated all that pop astrology stuff, the stuff you read in magazines. She didn't think people should be encouraged to believe that there were only certain signs that they could love and others they would never be able to get on with. She said you had to look at the whole of someone's birth chart, not just one bit of it.'

Daniel smiled. 'Have I touched a nerve? I assure you, Miss B, it was only a frivolous question.'

I smiled. 'I know.'

He took my hand across the table, threading his fingers through mine. I became aware we were being stared at. There was a man seated alone a few tables away, watching us. I looked into the turquoise eyes of Jason Beck.

'Would you excuse me for just a moment?' I asked Daniel, getting to my feet. 'There's someone over there I must say hello to.'

Jason grinned as I arrived at his table and nodded in Daniel's direction. 'Now I know why you never phoned me.'

'Were you expecting me to?' I sat facing him. 'I thought you'd gone back to Australia.'

'Not quite. I've been down to Newquay.'

'Surfing good?'

'Excellent.'

'No more chasing stories about livestock theft?'

'I hear there was a spot of bother around here a couple of days ago.'

I shrugged. 'I wouldn't know.'

He eyed me shrewdly for a moment, the hint of a smile on his lips. 'That's a pity, I thought you might.'

I changed the subject. 'Did you get around to talking to Neil and Carol at Cold East Farm?'

'Not yet,' he admitted. 'I'm going home in a few days. That's one thing I intend to do before I leave.'

'Well, good luck.' There didn't seem to be any more to say. I stood up and held out my hand.

'Goodbye, Juno.' He shook it without getting up. 'Nice knowing you.'

I returned to the table where Lottie greeted me as if I'd been gone for hours. Daniel was scowling as I sat down. 'Who's your friend?'

'He's not a friend. That's Jason Beck.'

'The journalist you told me about?'

He turned around to look at him and Jason raised his glass in an ironic toast.

I was surprised Daniel remembered the name. 'He's going back to Australia soon.'

'Good. He's too good-looking to be hanging around here.'

I laughed. 'Jealousy, Mr Thorncroft?'

He lowered his voice. 'Lottie does not approve.'

Jason chose that moment to get up and leave the wine bar, giving me a lazy wave as he reached the door. As he stepped into the street, he must have bumped into someone he knew because he exchanged a surprised hello, and a female voice said, 'Fancy meeting you!'

I couldn't see who it was and I didn't care. I didn't feel comfortable with him around. I was glad he'd gone. I turned my attention back to Daniel.

'To get back to your original question,' I began, lowering my voice, 'about Scorpio and Capricorn and whether they are compatible, the answer is . . .' I paused, pretending to consider '. . . quite good.'

He pulled an expression of mock dismay. 'Only quite good?'

'Well, no two people are completely compatible, are they?'

'Aren't they?'

'On the other hand,' I continued, lowering my voice, 'your Scorpio sun should make a deeply harmonious angle to my moon in Pisces.'

He smirked. 'Indeed?'

I took a sip of wine. 'That's the theory.'

He leant in closer to me. 'And how does one go about testing this theory?'

It was my turn to smile. 'There's only one way I can think of.'

Daniel's whisper was very close, almost in my ear. I lay with my eyes closed, basking in the happy afterglow of our astrological experiment. 'Has anyone ever told you, Miss B,' he asked softly, 'that your eyelashes are lighter on the ends, as if each one has been brushed with gold?'

'No,' I sighed happily, 'no one's ever told me that.'

'And did you know that amongst your delightful

freckles, you have some that make a pattern like the stars in the constellation of Orion?'

I started to laugh. 'No.'

'Ah, well, here's Betelgeuse up on your shoulder.' He kissed it lightly. 'And down here on your ribcage you have three little freckles in a straight line like the stars on Orion's belt. These are called Alnitak, Alnilan and Mintaka,' as he named each one, he kissed it, 'which means that somewhere lower down there must be Saiph.'

'Saiph?'

'The star at the tip of Orion's scabbard.' He slid down, his head disappearing under the duvet. 'Ah yes,' he murmured softly, 'here it is.'

Some time in the deep dark night I found myself floating blissfully on an ocean of sleep, where the waves meet the shore of wakefulness; warm, deeply content, drowsily conscious of Daniel breathing steadily, sleeping close by me, and a small animal body lying across my feet. Then Bill strolled in and all hell broke loose. I was jerked awake by a barking whippet running madly around the bedroom and a hissing, yowling fuzzball spitting outrage from the top of the wardrobe.

'What?' Daniel muttered sleepily, squinting as I switched on the bedside light. 'Shut up, Lottie!' he ordered, dragging himself up on one elbow. She stood at the foot of the wardrobe, looking up at Bill, her whole body quivering with excitement. Bill was still hissing, glaring from one emerald eye like an angry cyclops, his teeth bared in a ferocious snarl.

'Come here, Lottie!' Daniel insisted, clicking his fingers. 'Shut up! Come here and lie down!'

She did as she was told, leaping daintily up on to the bed and curling up next to his legs, but she still continued to quiver, her instinct to chase running through every muscle of her body.

'I didn't know you had a cat,' Daniel said.

'I don't. He belongs downstairs.'

'How did he get in here?'

'I wish I knew.'

'What's his name?'

'Bill.'

'He's only got one eye.'

'Yes, I know.'

He looked safe enough on top of the wardrobe. He'd probably settle down up there. 'He'll be all right,' I said, 'let's forget him,' and we snuggled down under the duvet again.

But my bed was Bill's territory and he wasn't about to be usurped by some canine upstart; as I reached out to turn out the lamp he leapt, claws extended like grappling hooks, landing on Lottie's back and smacked her on the snout with a mighty paw. She ran whimpering into the living room, a droplet of blood glistening on her nose.

Daniel eyed him with grudging respect as he sat on the duvet, smugly washing his paw. 'Round one to Bill, I think,' he said.

* * *

Next morning, we checked out our harmonious angles again, just to make sure, and after a lazy breakfast in bed drove up to Daniel's house on Halshanger Common. It was a dry day, but cloudy and chilly, still too early in summer for the wind coming off the moor to have lost its biting edge. The house stood in an isolated position overlooking the valley, its walls of solid, grey granite. It was urgently in need of a new roof, rows of missing slates covered temporarily by sheets of corrugated iron.

'Well, at least it's still standing,' Daniel observed as we got out of the van.

'Do you think it was thatched originally?' I asked. We stood by the gate looking towards the front door while Lottie raced around on the grass chasing invisible rabbits.

'Originally, perhaps, but I'm replacing the slates,' Daniel said. 'Thatch would add another ten thousand to the cost of the roof, and anyway, it's not a good idea.'

I was surprised. I'd have thought thatch would have appealed to him as a more environmentally friendly option. 'Why not?'

'We've destroyed too many reed beds in this country,' he explained. 'We don't grow enough these days for making thatch. The reed has to come from Poland or China. That makes it expensive. And it's not the strong material that it used to be.'

'Why not?' I asked again.

'Water pollution has weakened the reeds. A new thatch won't last as long these days as it once did.'

I wondered if Neil and Carol knew that. 'That's a shame. Thatch looks lovely.'

'Slate is more in keeping with the rest, anyway.' Daniel grinned, nodding towards the house. 'It's suitably austere.'

Austere just about summed it up, with its thick granite walls and dark, lifeless windows. Gloomy, forbidding and grim described it quite well too.

Inside it wasn't much better. Cold as a tomb and smelling of damp, it had been locked up and vacant for too long. By comparison, the weather outside seemed quite balmy. Any idea that I had nurtured that we might spend the night there in order to avoid another confrontation between Bill and Lottie evaporated when my breath came out of my mouth in a cloud. Lottie at least seemed happy to be home. Her nails clicked across the stone-flagged floor as she went straight to her old armchair, leapt into it, turned around a few times and settled down for a nap. Outdoors she races around like a maniac; indoors she is a complete couch potato.

Daniel rattled the acrow prop that held up the cracked oak beam running across the kitchen ceiling, sending down a fine drizzle of lime plaster. 'Ah, the dear old homestead!' He looked around him at the kitchen and rubbed his hands together. 'I'll get the fire going in the range, Miss B, we'll soon warm the place up a bit.' He flashed a grin at the doubtful look I cast him. 'Don't worry. I swept the flue last time I was here. Make yourself at home. Have a wander about if you like. I don't think I've ever given you the grand tour, have I?'

No, I told him, he hadn't, so whilst he fetched logs and kindling from the woodshed, I took the opportunity for a nose through the empty rooms, with a warning to be careful on the stairs.

Daniel's aunt had lived alone for years. Her furniture had been cleared out but there were odd traces of her presence here and there: an old rug in the kitchen, dusty curtains at a window. I trod the creaking stairs with caution and found a coat button lying on a windowsill, a speckled mirror in a bedroom, a plastic comb. I wondered what she would have thought of the place now, spiders spinning webs at the cracked windowpanes, the dusty floorboards, the smell of mould and mice. I looked down into what had once been her garden, a long rectangle dry-walled against the moorland winds, the grass grown high, the flower beds eaten up by greedy weeds. An ancient rose tree clinging to a wall was bent double, crippled by a storm, and threatening to bring the wall down with it. Even more than the empty rooms the garden spoke to me, cried out for someone to rescue it, to love it, to restore order.

I could hear Daniel moving around downstairs and went down to join him. 'What do you think of the place?' he asked, poking screwed up newspaper amongst the wood he'd put in the stove.

'I think it has potential,' I answered tactfully.

He reached for a box of matches on the mantelpiece, laughing as he struck a match. 'That's one way of putting

245

it.' He set the paper alight. 'If I didn't have to go back tomorrow, I'd get the builder over for a chat but . . .' he shrugged. 'It'll have to be next time.'

'Do you know when that will be?'

'I'm in Oslo next week for the conference, sometime after that. I'll have more time then.'

I'd heard that before. I said nothing, watched him fanning the feeble yellow flame.

'That's going to take ages,' I grumbled, 'and it's freezing in here.'

'What we need is hot coffee.' We'd brought a bag of provisions with us, and Daniel had invested in a new flat-bottomed kettle that would sit on the stove.

'That'll soon be boiling,' he promised cheerfully as he set it on the top, 'just give it three or four hours.'

We drew up two kitchen chairs close to the old iron range and sat with our coats on, waiting for the kettle to boil whilst Daniel outlined what he planned to do to the house, and in what order he wanted to do it, when, if ever, he finally settled in Devon. 'Of course, the work can be ongoing,' he told me, 'I don't need to be here. Once it's started, I just need to find a good project manager to keep an eye on it, make sure things are progressing.'

We got fed up waiting for the kettle, decided to huddle together for warmth and possibly indulge in some kind of indoor exercise to stop us from freezing to death. We moved on to an old sofa in the corner where Daniel slept on the rare occasions he visited the house, and bundled up together.

'God, your hands are cold!' Daniel complained as I slid them slyly under his jumper to warm them up. 'But not as cold as mine!' he muttered, attempting to do the same. He grabbed my wrists and pushed me back on the sofa, straddling me and we wrestled. Then I wrapped my legs around his waist.

'This is very forward of you, Miss B!'

'I just want to try out something.'

He raised an eyebrow. 'What?'

'Something that Elizabeth taught me.' I'd enjoyed my fun self-defence session, although Olly had been useless in the role of my adversary. Every time I'd touched him, he'd become helpless with giggles. Most of the time had been spent with Elizabeth teaching me how to fall without hurting myself, a useful skill to learn, she explained, especially if I was planning on getting up again. She had taught me one or two nifty moves, though.

'Curiouser and curiouser,' Daniel grinned. 'What have you girls been up to?'

'This,' I responded, pushing hard with my thighs, and tipped him neatly on to the floor.

My flat may be pretty basic but at least it has hot water, so we went back there later for a bath. Before that I drove Daniel up to Fred Crick's place. We walked around the blackened walls of the cottage but didn't trespass inside. The police tape that still garlanded the door didn't represent any physical barrier, but it was still a crime scene. After we'd wandered around the garden and looked into the shed where I had haggled with Fred over his furniture, we walked along the brow of the hill and climbed up the rock. From its flat top we looked down the hill at Cold East Farm spread out below us. I pointed out the trench where Vivian's body had been uncovered and the earthworks that Neil had built to protect his fields.

'And this is what your friend Jason was taking photographs of?' Daniel asked.

I nodded.

'There's nothing inherently suspicious in that if he's writing an article.'

'No,' I agreed with a sigh. 'But there's something about him that doesn't seem right, somehow.'

Daniel grinned. 'Isn't that what you used to think about me?'

'I still do,' I told him, sliding my arms around his waist.

He pointed, sweeping his arm around the valley. 'Do your friends own all of this land?'

'I don't really know,' I admitted. 'I'm not sure how much of this belongs to their farm.'

'I wonder if they've ever considered re-wilding any of it. I'd like to talk to them about it sometime.'

'We could wander down there now, if you like,' I suggested, 'see if Neil and Carol are at home.'

He dropped his face into my hair. 'Not today,' he muttered. 'Today you're mine, Miss B. I want you to myself.'

In the evening, we went out to dinner at a lovely pub. I made sure I'd glammed up this time. I didn't have time to go to Druid Lodge and raid Ricky and Morris's wardrobe, so I settled for my doublet in apricot silk, the one they had made me for my birthday, and a black skirt.

Lottie came with us; we couldn't leave her in the flat on her own with the danger of Bill wandering in, and in any case, she'd be miserable. Cats allowing, she's very well behaved when she's out, and she sat decorously under the table, either sleeping or resting her muzzle on my knee as I stroked her smooth head. Daniel and I lingered over a long dinner, drank too much wine and spent a ridiculous amount of time just gazing at each other and smiling. I tried not to think of the fact that by this time tomorrow Daniel would be on his way back to Scotland.

'I have a confession to make, Miss B,' he said, taking my hand and rubbing it gently. 'When I get back from Oslo, I won't be coming back here for a while.'

I frowned. 'I thought your wolf project was almost finished.'

'It is. It's certainly reached a point where it doesn't need me . . . and that's why I've taken on another project,' he added slowly, 'in Ireland.'

'Ireland?' I repeated, not sure I'd heard right.

'It's not for long,' he went on. 'I'll still be able to come to Devon from time to time . . .'

'Bloody Ireland?' I said crossly.

'It's looking at new methods of peat bog conservation,

and that's something that I'll be involved in here on Dartmoor, so it is relevant.'

For a moment I was speechless. But before I could think what to say, I heard a voice coming from the other side of the dining room. 'Hello,' it said, 'fancy meeting you!'

It was the same voice and the same words that had greeted Jason Beck yesterday when he left the wine bar. I turned to look at the woman who had spoken. I didn't recognise her at first, nicely dressed and made-up, with her hair styled. When I'd seen her before, she'd worn an overall with a duster stuffed in the pocket: it was Joan who ran the Hemsworthy Gate Guest House. Outside the wine bar she had greeted Jason Beck as if she knew him. I watched her return to her table, to a group of other women.

'I seem to have lost you, Miss B.'

'I'm sorry.' I returned my attention to Daniel but then made the usual excuse about wanting to powder my nose and headed with my handbag to the loo. In the ladies, I dug around for my phone and the several odd business cards I knew were in there among all the other rubbish. 'Gotcha!' I whispered as I pulled out the one I'd picked up at the guest house. I phoned, and after a minute or so, a man answered, probably Joan's husband, Colin the Lambretta restorer. 'May I speak to Jason Beck please?' I asked.

'I'm sorry, he's not here,' he responded. 'May I ask who's calling?'

'Just a friend,' I replied. 'But I've lost his mobile number.'

'You mean the Australian gentleman?'

'Yes, that's right. He's a reporter.'

'Oh, yes.' Colin's voice relaxed; he was on surer ground now. 'That's the fella.'

'He is staying with you, isn't he?'

'Well, he was,' he continued, 'but that was a while ago. He's not here now.'

'You don't remember exactly when he left?'

'I can look in the book.' After a few moments of muttering to himself he came back with the date.

'Thanks very much,' I said. 'Sorry to have bothered you. Goodbye.'

So, on the day that Peter Gillow died, Jason Beck checked out of the Hemsworthy Gate Guest House. I wonder why he hadn't mentioned that?

CHAPTER TWENTY-ONE

Monday morning, we rose early. Daniel and Lottie came with me to walk the Tribe. Lottie was timid at first but left the other dogs behind when it came to racing around in the fields. She was so much faster than any of them; otherwise she behaved like a lady.

'I like this little fellow,' Daniel bent to stroke EB, the miniature schnauzer who was snuffling around his feet. He was wearing his little jacket with 'emotional support dog' embroidered on it. His owner Val likes to show him off.

'Lottie would make a good emotional support dog,' he commented. 'She has empathy.'

'I think EB just likes being cuddled.'

'Ebee? Is that his name?'

'Those are his initials. EB . . . I'm not allowed to tell you what they stand for,' I added before Daniel could ask, 'I promised his mum. You have to guess.'

He bent down and swooped an unsuspecting EB up in his arms, taking his whiskered jaw in one hand and looking him in the eye. EB wasn't too sure about this at all.

'Eyebrows,' Daniel said after a moment.

'You're not supposed to guess it just like that!' I'd been tormenting Sophie for two years, making her try to guess and he had done it in seconds.

'It's obvious,' he said, studying EB's bushy, overarching brows, which were twitching uncertainly. 'Although I have to say I think it's cheating to call him EB when *eyebrows* is all one word.'

EB had started to squirm by now and Daniel placed him back down on the ground and he scampered off across the field to join the others. Daniel leant his forearms on the gate and stared out across the moor, where the furthest hills were lost in a misty haze. Then he said, 'I have another confession to make, Miss B.'

'Another?' I glanced at his hawk-like profile. 'Let me see, after you finish your project in Ireland, you're joining the Antarctic Survey?'

He smiled. 'Nothing like that.'

'What then?'

'I could have come down before, to see you, to spend time with you,' he admitted, still staring ahead. 'I've had several opportunities to get away, but each time I chickened out.'

'Because of Claire?' I asked.

He nodded.

253

I tried not to sound as crushed as I felt. 'Grief's a complicated thing,' I said after a moment. 'You can't rush it. It'll take the time it takes.'

He turned to look at me and smiled sadly. 'I don't want to hurt you, Miss B.'

'You won't,' I said, which was a lie. His words already had me aching inside. 'But just remember,' I added, watching the dogs racing around one another, 'that I have Lottie's approval.'

He raised my hand to his lips and kissed it. 'You're a goddess, Miss Browne with an "e".'

'Too right,' I told him.

I had time to drive Daniel to Newton Abbot Station so that he and Lottie could pick up the connection to Exeter and their train back to Scotland.

'I'll call you when I get back,' he promised, enveloping me in a giant hug.

'If you can,' I muttered into his overcoat. He took my face between his hands and kissed me. Then I hunkered down to hug Lottie. As Daniel led her on to the train, she turned back to gaze at me anxiously from sad, dark eyes, as if she'd suddenly realised I wasn't coming too. Then it was door slam, whistle blow, off. I waved. And they were gone.

I watched the train grow small and disappear. I felt a strange gnawing inside, as if a little piece of me had been hollowed out. But it was better Daniel stayed away if he couldn't reconcile his feelings for me with his memories of Claire, a good thing he had gone again so soon. *Absence makes the heart grow fonder*, that's what Maisie would say. But wasn't that the whole problem with Claire, that she was absent for ever? No point in brooding, I told myself sternly. Buck up. Now you can get on with things. Although what I was going to get on with, I wasn't quite sure.

As I was a bit early for my next job I decided I'd pop in and see Maisie. Her carer from the agency had called and so she had already bathed, dressed and eaten her breakfast. But she was still grumpy.

'I've had this thing from the church,' she told me in disgust, waving a piece of paper in my face. It was about the coffee morning that she regularly attended in the church hall, advertising a list of future events, including a Memory Cafe.

'What the hell's a memory cafe?' she demanded.

'Well, it says here that everyone is invited to take along an old photograph that brings back memories, something they can talk about with other people.'

'I don't need a memory cafe,' she grumbled, 'nothing wrong with my memory.'

'Don't be like that, Maisie, it'll be fun. You've got lots of old photos. Where are they?'

She shook her head, 'Can't remember.'

'Oh, come on! You've got some albums somewhere.'

'On top of the wardrobe,' she admitted grudgingly. 'I can't reach 'em.'

'Well, I can.'

She gave a grunt of laughter. 'I should think you could,' she muttered, 'big tall dollop like you!'

After a few moments of groping around in the dust on top of her wardrobe, I found three old albums and a shoebox of loose photos, mostly black and white. I blew off the fluff, with note to self to dust the top of the wardrobe next time I cleaned, and carted them into the living room. 'It'll take you days to sort this lot.' I laid them on the table next to her. 'You have a good look through them.'

She scowled. 'I won't know what to choose.'

'Just pick a few you like. I'll help you if you want me to, next time I come.'

'Oh, all right,' she agreed as if she was doing me a favour, and I left her, her shopping list in one hand and Jacko straining at the lead in the other.

She was in a better temper when I returned.

'Here's me, look,' she held up an old sepia print, 'when I was just a littl'un.'

I smiled at the disagreeable-looking infant pouting at me. She'd obviously been dressed up for the photograph in her little smocked dress with puffed sleeves, her ringlets poking from beneath a cotton bonnet. 'Lovely!' I cried dutifully, 'don't you look sweet?'

'I didn't like having my photo taken,' she told me sunnily, 'my mother said I wouldn't smile for the camera.'

I could see that. I promised her we'd have a good look through all of her photos together the next time I called.

I made it back to *Old Nick's* by lunchtime and got the full report from Pat about how the rest of Saturday had gone. We had been quite busy as it turned out, but nothing she couldn't handle on her own. The ladies of the silk painting workshop had departed around 4 p.m., much pleased with their first efforts at silk painting, which according to Pat, varied considerably in ability. They had cleared up after themselves, so she had nothing to grumble about. Fizz had been so delighted with the way it had gone she was planning another workshop shortly. Pat rolled her eyes towards heaven.

'If all of her students buy something in the shop,' I told her, 'she can hold as many workshops as she likes. I know you're not keen on Fizz, well . . . none of us are,' I admitted, lowering my voice, 'but she could be good for business.'

Pat grunted. 'We'll just have to put up with her, then.' She reached out for a piece of paper she had propped up on the shelf behind her. 'Some woman phoned to speak to you. That's her number. She owns an antique shop in Barnstaple. She said that woman came in and tried it on with her.'

I frowned. 'What woman?'

'Her with the gap between her teeth!' She gave an impatient little shake of her head. I was obviously being thick.

'Really?'

'She asked this woman who owns the shop to write a receipt for something, but she'd heard about what happened here from some dealer friend in Moretonhampstead. Anyway, she wanted to speak to you. I promised her you'd phone.'

I took the number and phoned straight away. I spoke to Mel, the owner of *Aladdin's Cave* in Barnstaple, who told me that our fraudulent little friend bought a silver cake slice, asked for a receipt and then called at the shop again a few days later when her niece was in charge. Luckily, the niece had been warned, and when the woman produced a receipt with several other items on it, she pulled out the carbon copy from the receipt book and showed her that these items weren't listed. Old Gappy protested and demanded her money back, but the girl told her she'd have to call again and speak to the owner. They didn't see her again.

'I thought you'd like to know that this time she didn't get away with it,' Mel told me, 'largely thanks to you.'

'That's good to know.'

'I'm spreading the word,' she went on, 'seeing that she's still trying her luck in this area.'

'Let's hope she gets caught before she robs someone else.'

We chatted for a bit and I promised to pop in on *Aladdin's Cave* whenever I was in Barnstaple.

Sophie had arrived while I was on the phone and I told her and Pat the whole story.

'The evil old cow must have been furious,' Sophie giggled, delighted. 'We must tell Fizz when she comes in. It might make her feel a bit better about things.'

'She's not the one who needs to feel better,' Pat told her sharply. 'It's Juno who needs to feel better.'

'I'd feel better if I got my stuff back, but I don't think Fizz is still wallowing in remorse. Where is she, anyway? Is she coming in today?'

'Oh no,' Pat assured me solemnly. 'She's going to take a couple of days off to rest because she finds giving a workshop so *draining*.'

'She's supposed to be looking after the shop this afternoon,' Sophie said crossly.

I grunted. 'Perhaps it's just as well she's not going to if she's *drained*.'

Sophie sighed. 'It doesn't matter. I'm going to be here anyway. I've got a painting to finish.'

'Good,' Pat said. 'I'm glad you'll be here, cos Juno's always out on a Monday afternoon and,' she went on, turning to me, 'I'm driving our Loopy in the trailer over to your friend at Cold East Farm.'

'So Carol's been in touch. That's good. It's a really lovely place over there. I'm sure it'll be a good home for Loopy.'

'It better be,' she told me firmly. 'I shan't let her go else.'

It was a pity I couldn't go with her, but I go to Woodland on Monday afternoons to help Mrs York with her housework. I promised myself a phone call to Carol later to see how it went.

'I don't care what you get up to in your bedroom,' Adam told me plainly as he answered the door to my knock when I got home, 'but we can do without the barking dog in the middle of the night, thanks.'

Kate was looking at me over his shoulder, a hand to her mouth to stop herself from giggling.

'I'm very sorry,' I told him, trying to sound sincere as he stood back to let me into their kitchen, 'but blame it on your cat. If you can't stop Bill from breaking and entering whenever he feels like it, then it's not my fault.'

Adam sighed. He'd been trying to find out how Bill got in and out of my flat for years. He'd blocked up all manner of holes, but nothing stopped him.

'Anyway, talking about my lover,' I carried on, 'he wanted me to convey to you his horror and revulsion – *his* words – at the idea that you're contemplating selling *Sunflowers*. He thinks it's a lousy idea.'

'It may not happen, anyway.' Kate fiddled despondently with the end of her dark plait. 'It all hinges on our getting a buyer.'

'Timing's crucial,' Adam agreed. 'I can't really start this job and leave Kate to run the cafe on her own, and we can't afford to close up if we haven't sold.'

'You've worked so hard on the place,' I said, drawing up a kitchen stool. 'Are you sure you want to sell it?'

There was a moment's hesitation that spoke volumes. 'And honestly, Adam,' I dived in during the silence, 'I can't see you as a chef in some posh spa. I know you're a brilliant cook,' I added hastily, 'but you're too . . .' I searched for a word, running my eyes over his bearded face and burly frame '. . . rustic.'

Kate erupted into giggles. 'She's right!' she told him, nodding. 'You are!'

'Oh, charming!' He huffed at both of us. 'Thanks.'

'It's true,' she said. 'And you know how impatient you get with difficult customers in the cafe. It'll be a hundred times worse in a spa.'

'The customers are there to be pampered,' I added.

Adam frowned and scratched behind his ear. 'I know all that,' he admitted, 'and I don't really fancy it that much, either, but it's well paid and we just don't have enough money coming in. Your rent's a help, Juno, but with the baby coming—'

'Can't you afford to employ someone,' I asked, 'to help run the cafe when the baby comes?'

He gave a snort of laughter. 'Hardly.' He glanced at Kate. 'We'd like to. We thought about opening a few evenings in the summer, a chance for more trade. We tried a couple of years ago if you remember, but it wasn't worth it.'

'Well, things have moved on a bit since then,' I said. 'The town's busier, more people are eating veggie. Perhaps it's worth another try.'

'Perhaps.' He didn't sound convinced. And who was I to offer business advice? I had trouble getting people to come in through the door of *Old Nick's*, let alone buy anything.

Ricky came up with a good idea when I went to Druid Lodge. He and Morris were working on the Mikado's elaborate black and gold kimono. Most of the chorus had been fitted by now and I was busy with hems and fastenings.

'They want to try out a few musical evenings,' he suggested, 'jazz nights, folk nights – that kind of thing. People love a bit of live music while they nosh.'

'There's not a lot of room in that cafe for musicians,' I said doubtfully.

'They'd only need a duo and there's room in there for that.'

'I don't think Adam and Kate could afford to pay them.'

Ricky rolled his eyes. 'You don't *pay* musicians! They'll work all night for a bottle of beer and fag money.'

'He means customers' tips,' Morris explained, just in case I didn't understand.

'Throw in a plate of free food,' Ricky added, 'and they're yours for life.'

'There is a big appetite for live music in Ashburton,' Morris added. 'Just look at what goes on at the arts centre!'

'I know some of the pubs have live music,' Ricky went on, 'but an intimate little cafe with some gentle jazz going on, that's different. We'd go, wouldn't we, *Maurice*?'

'Oh yes!' He nodded enthusiastically.

'So would I. It's a good idea. Perhaps they could get waiting staff to work the evening for food as well. Sophie does waitressing, I bet she would.' I would, if it came to it.

'It just needs a bit of advertising, that's all,' Ricky

pointed out, 'a few flyers around the town. But that wouldn't cost a lot.'

The doorbell rang and Morris looked at his watch. 'That'll be Digby,' he said and bustled off to answer the door. 'He's come to rehearse,' he added to me as he passed.

'Digby?' I repeated.

'Oh, haven't you heard?' Ricky asked. 'Poor old Gordon's had to drop out.'

I was mystified. 'Who's Gordon?'

'He was playing the Mikado, the title role.'

'What's happened to him?'

'Shingles.' Ricky shuddered. 'Anyway, good old Diggers is stepping into the breach. He's going to play it. Well,' he went on, 'it's not a huge role and there's only one big song, really. We said we'd help him run through it.'

I stared at the Mikado's elaborate costume. 'Will it fit him?'

He rolled his eyes. 'We'll find out, won't we?'

I carried on with my sewing job. There was a lot of chatter downstairs for a while, and then the sound of the piano began to drift up from the music room below and Digby started warbling.

Before I left, I stuck my head around the music room door to say goodbye to Ricky and Morris and hello to Digby. As I let myself out of the front door, I could hear the words of his song 'Let the Punishment Fit the Crime'. It sounded vaguely nasty to me.

I didn't mention Ricky's idea about *Sunflowers* that evening, I didn't get the chance. Adam and Kate had gone out, which was rare, leaving me with a slice of spinach pie from the cafe and Bill for company. He had forgiven me for having a dog in my flat, now that he was back in sole possession. 'You and Lottie are going to have to learn to get on,' I warned him, but he closed his eye and pretended he was deaf. I tried Daniel's number but there was no response. I wanted to tell him about Ricky's idea for the cafe and that Loopy the llama now had a new home. I had already phoned Carol and all was well. 'You've started something now,' she'd told me, laughing. 'Loopy is so gorgeous. Neil thinks she needs a friend, he wants to get another.'

I gave up on Daniel after three attempts. On an impulse I tried Jason Beck's number, but there was no reply from him either. He could even be back in Australia by now. I decided to give up on trying to make phone calls and read the rest of a novel I'd been enjoying. I had saved myself the final satisfying chunk for bedtime but decided on an early start.

I found myself at the end of the story all too soon. What I had assumed were the last few chapters were in fact the first chapters of the author's next book. I hate it when that happens. I know it's done for marketing reasons, but I always feel cheated. Thwarted of a good long read and unable to face studying any more hallmarks for the moment, I watched a film on TV. It was a cop thriller; everyone in it had very complicated relationships. In fact, they were all carrying so much emotional baggage it was a wonder they could walk. I got fed up with them and went to bed.

Early next morning, just as I was getting up to go and collect the Tribe, there was a gentle knock on my door. Adam was dressed, ready to leave for the cafe, but looked tired and heavy-eyed. 'I didn't want to wake you but I heard you moving about,' he told me softly. 'Someone was messing about with your van last night.'

'What?' I reduced my voice to a whisper. Kate was probably still asleep. 'What time was this?' I stepped back to let him inside.

He shrugged. 'About two this morning. Kate had a sudden craving for hot chocolate, so I got up to make her one. Whilst I was waiting for milk to boil, I wandered into the living room in the dark and I saw him outside, crouched down by your van.'

'Some bloody kid after my valve caps again,' I muttered fiercely. 'They're always pinching them.'

'As soon as I opened the window he ran off down the lane. I went out with a torch to make sure there was no damage. Everything seemed OK, but I thought you ought to know, just in case.'

'Thanks, Adam.'

'I wish I could've caught the little bastard,' he said, yawning, 'I'd have given him what for.'

'Perhaps it's just as well you didn't.'

He nodded, yawning again, and shuffled off down the stairs.

I took a good look at the van before I got in but as Adam had indicated, everything looked undisturbed, no slashed tyres, scratches or cracked wing mirrors, my cheap and nasty plastic dust caps still in place.

I gathered up the Tribe and walked them out of town along the lane between hedgerows turned lush and green, into fields where the grass was still damp and silvery with dew. The sun was up, the day fine and clear, the air fresh with a hint of cowpat. The dogs raced around, chasing the balls I threw, whilst above our heads a pair of swallows cut up the sky with scissored tails, hunting for flying insects. We tramped back through the woods, with much sniffing and snuffling in the undergrowth and splashing in streams, losing Schnitzel from sight completely in a white mass of wild garlic. I breathed in deep. I love the smells of emerging summer.

I was hungry as a hunter by the time I'd delivered the dogs back home. Veggie breakfast was what I needed, I decided, and headed for *Sunflowers*.

'Is everything OK with the van?' Adam asked as I wandered in.

'Fine.' I stood at the counter, staring at the chalkboard behind his head, trying to make up my mind between a full veggie or eggs Florentine. Finally, I decided on sweetcorn fritters with avocado, salsa and a poached egg. That would keep me going.

Adam was dealing with a customer collecting a breakfast takeaway, so after I placed my order I looked around, deciding where to sit. I spotted a man at the corner table wearing dark glasses and a baseball cap. As I stared, he pulled his cap down and shrunk lower in his seat; but he couldn't disguise his round, cherubic cheeks, which grew pinker as I watched.

'Henry!' I hissed, pulling out a chair and sitting at his table. 'You are not supposed to be here. Inspector Ford sent you home.'

'It's a free country,' he answered sulkily, removing his sunglasses. 'He can't stop me coming to Ashburton if I want.'

'I think you'll find he can,' I responded, although I didn't press the point. 'Are you staying at the guest house again?

'No. I'm . . . I'm somewhere else,' he said, with what was meant to be an air of mystery.

I eyed him suspiciously. 'You're not here to follow me about, are you? I'm not going to find myself looking at that bloody Lambretta in my rear-view mirror all the time?'

He looked down at his coffee cup and spooned sugar into it. 'I've changed my mode of transportation.'

'I'm warning you, Henry,' I threatened in a low voice, 'I won't put up with it.'

He gave an infuriating little smile and wouldn't answer.

'I mean it.'

He dug about in a rucksack that rested on the seat beside him and pulled out a crumpled paper bag, which he pushed across the table towards me. 'I bought you a quarter of pineapple rock and,' he added, diving in his bag again, 'some liquorice misshapes.'

I suppressed a sigh. 'Thank you, Henry, that was very kind of you, but if you're hoping to bribe me with sweets—'

'Not bribe, no!' He looked shocked.

'How long have you been here?' I asked. 'I don't mean sitting here at this table, I mean, how long have you been in Ashburton.'

'I arrived yesterday,' he admitted. 'I went to your shop, but you weren't there. There was a pretty dark-haired girl, wonderful artist . . .' He gave another smug little smile. 'But I knew I'd bump into you sooner or later.'

'Yes, and now you have.' I hesitated, considered for a moment sharing with him the fact that Jason Beck had been staying at the guest house when Peter died, but decided against it. I wanted him to go away, not launch himself into another disastrous investigation.

I looked at my watch. 'As soon as I've eaten my breakfast, I shall be off to work, so there really isn't much point in you hanging around.' I wished Adam would hurry up; if I'd spotted Henry before I wouldn't have ordered breakfast in the first place. But Adam was working single-handed until Kate arrived and she hadn't shown up yet; she probably still had her head down the loo.

'You know, I'm not surprised the police have given up on finding Peter's murderer,' Henry said, 'but I'm disappointed in you, Juno.' His little mouth worked emotionally. 'I thought you cared.'

'I do care,' I retorted, stung. 'But we've already talked about this, Henry. We have no suspects except for whoever killed Fred Crick, and we don't have anything to go on there either. If Fred was killed by thieves, then the police are far more likely to find them than we are. And quite frankly,' I carried on as Henry opened his mouth to speak, 'after what happened in that forest, I am not willing to be responsible for botching another of their investigations.'

'I am determined to find my brother's killer,' he told me with great dignity, 'and if I must do so alone, then so be it. Perhaps if I do, then Marjorie—'

'Marjorie?' I interrupted, leaning forward intently. 'What's this got to do with her?' I frowned at him a moment. 'Are you really after your brother's killer or do you just want to prove something to your wife?'

He had flushed to the roots of his hair. He stood up and wouldn't look at me as he tossed down a ten pence piece on the table as a tip. 'Enjoy your breakfast,' he muttered and stomped out, leaving his coffee undrunk.

'What was all that about?' Adam queried as he placed my plate of sweetcorn fritters in front of me.

'Don't ask!' I told him, picking up my cutlery. With Henry's departure the cafe had quietened down. 'Got a minute?' I asked him. 'Sit down. I've got something for you to think about.'

CHAPTER TWENTY-TWO

For the rest of the morning I couldn't get Henry off my mind and I hoed the weeds in the vicar's garden with an ungodly vigour. He had accused me of not caring about his brother's death and that had rankled me. I did care. The problem was that the key to his murder lay with Fred Crick; find his murderer and I'd almost certainly find Peter's. But the police didn't have a clue and neither did I. I wondered if Ron had managed to talk to Fred's old drinking chum, Sam Weston, and popped down to *Keepsakes* at lunchtime to find out.

Sheila was busy rearranging things in the window when I arrived. Ron was at the back of the shop, she told me, having a sandwich. I found him sitting in an old armchair, surrounded by clocks balanced on piles of dusty leather-covered books.

'I did catch up with Sam,' he told me, 'and I've been meaning to phone you, but I keep forgetting.'

From that I gathered Sam didn't have anything significant to say, but Ron went on, 'He said he saw Fred on the Saturday evening, the night before he got killed, in the Victoria.'

'He saw him on the Saturday – are you sure?'

'That's what he told me.'

'Has he told the police this?' I asked. 'He may have been the last person to see Fred alive.'

Ron sniffed. 'Well, if he was, he wasn't the only one. Sam said there was quite a crowd in there that night. Lots of people would have seen him.'

'I see. And did he say if Fred was all right, if anything was troubling him?'

I had to wait while Ron chewed his sandwich. 'He didn't say,' he answered at last, 'but I didn't ask him that. What I did ask him,' he went on with slow deliberation as he wiped his fingers on a paper napkin, 'was if he knew if Fred had ever been in trouble with the law. That was what you wanted to know, wasn't it?'

I nodded. 'And what did Sam say?'

'Not to his knowledge, other than getting thrown out of pubs and fighting, and as far as Sam is concerned that doesn't count.'

'That's disappointing. I had hoped Fred might turn out to have had criminal connections.'

'Well, if he did, I don't think Sam knows about them.'

Sheila came back to join us just then, puffing a little after extricating herself from the goods in the shop window. 'You could ask Sam yourself,' she suggested.

'I've just seen him pass by on the other side of the road.'

Ron looked at his watch and gave a grunt of amusement. 'He'll be on his way to the Silent Whistle. It's time for his lunchtime pint.'

'I'll go and catch him, then.' I thanked Ron, said hurried goodbyes and nipped down St Lawrence Lane to the pub on the corner. In my haste I hadn't thought to ask Ron what Sam Weston looked like. But as there was only one man of around Fred's age in the pub, sitting at a table by himself, I bought myself a ginger beer at the bar and took a chance.

'Do you mind if I sit here?' I asked. He was a pleasant-looking man with a thick head of silver hair and a healthy tan. He looked wholesome, the exact opposite of Fred Crick.

He raised his eyebrows and glanced briefly around the unoccupied seats and tables.

'Well, it's a long time since a beautiful young woman has asked to sit next to me in an empty pub, so the answer's yes.'

I slid into the seat next to him and held out my hand. 'Juno Browne.'

He smiled, nodding sagely as he shook it. 'I know who you are.'

I pulled a face. 'Really?'

'"Famous local heroine",' he quoted with a chuckle. 'I've seen your picture in the paper. I'm Sam Weston.'

'Yes, I know,' I told him. 'How do you do?'

'Very well, maid, thank you,' he answered. Then he

frowned. 'But I haven't had my picture in the paper, so I'm wondering how you know me.'

'I've just been talking to Ron and Sheila. Sheila said she'd seen you go by and I wanted a word with you, if you don't mind.'

He gave a grunt of amusement. 'You want to talk about Fred Crick.'

'Ron says you knew him well.'

'I knew him for years. I wouldn't say I knew him well.' He shook his head sadly. 'You wonder whether you ever knew someone at all when you find out he murdered his wife.'

'Did you know Vivian?'

'Oh yes. Some people thought she was a bit simple but that's unkind. She was *trusting*, shall we say.' He sucked in his breath. 'She was too good for the likes of Fred Crick, poor maid. But she was a pretty girl and Fred was mad to have her.'

'She must have liked him. She married him.'

'My Frances always said Viv must've been desperate. And then when their baby came so soon . . . premature, that's what they said. Well, Frances went to see it in hospital. I remember she came home and said to me, "That baby's never premature."'

'So, you don't think the baby was Fred's son?'

'I'm not saying that,' Sam said, lifting his pint. 'All I'm saying is, Viv was pregnant before she got married. Whether 'twas Fred's or not, I couldn't say.'

'He ran away, didn't he, the son?'

'Tony? Yes, he did.' He contemplated the glass of ale on the table. 'Nice lad,' he said after a moment, 'a bit quiet.'

'When Vivian disappeared,' I began, a little cautiously, 'didn't anyone think it was strange? Suspicious?'

'Well, 'twas easy enough to believe she'd have left Fred but . . .' he shook his head and laughed softly. 'Poor old Frances.'

'Your wife?' I asked.

He nodded. 'She had her suspicions, all right. She accused Fred, came straight out with it one night in The Victoria Inn, told him she knew he'd done away with her.'

'That was brave. What happened?'

'He pulled out this letter, all folded up in his pocket it was, and he flung it on the table. "Read that," he said to her, "and then tell me she didn't run off with a fancy man." Well, she could see it was in Viv's handwriting, so she read it. And it was written to some chap, telling him how she was saving up the money to run away and join him. Well, Frances is sitting there reading it, her face getting redder and redder, and old Fred's laughing fit to bust. He said he'd caught Viv putting it in an envelope. He said if he'd come home five minutes later, she'd have written the address on it and he'd have known who she was writing to. He claimed she'd tried to throw it on the fire.'

'There was no name on the letter itself?' I asked. 'The name Jay doesn't ring a bell?'

Sam shook his head. 'Not to me. I'd have to ask my Frances. Anyway, poor maid, all she could do after reading this letter was apologise. But she never spoke to Fred Crick again. And when they dug up Viv's body, she said to me, "There you are, Sam Weston, what did I tell you?"'

He drained his pint. I offered to buy him another, but he shook his head.

'Ron mentioned that you'd seen Fred on the night before he was killed,' I said.

'He mentioned that, did he?' Sam scratched his cheek thoughtfully. 'Yes, I saw him.'

'And he seemed OK to you?' I asked. 'Not worried in any way?'

'No, he was his usual horrible self. Bit quiet, perhaps, but he was a moody bugger, so I didn't take any notice of that. Mind you, he must have been getting worried, seeing as how close that digger was getting to where he'd buried his missus.' He stared at me silently for a moment. 'But what's on your mind, maid? Why do you ask?'

'The police think Fred's murder was a case of robbery gone wrong. But not long after he was killed, there was trouble at his old farm. The couple who live there now had sheep stolen by an armed gang.'

'And you think Fred might have had some hand in it?' he asked.

'Perhaps that's what got him killed.'

Sam was quiet, thoughtfully studying the beer mat on the table in front of him.

'I know a lot of this livestock theft goes on,' he said soberly, 'but I never knew Fred mixed up in anything like that.'

'Has it ever happened to you?' I asked.

Sam pulled a face. 'Me? No. Mind, I retired from farming a few years back, handed the farm over to my son, John.' He smiled. 'Frances wanted a little bungalow. But no, I never had any trouble like that, and nor has John, to my knowledge. I guess we've just been lucky.'

He stood up, obviously ready to depart. 'It's been nice talking to you, maid, but it's time I went home for my lunch. It's always ready on the table, one o'clock prompt.'

'Are you sure I can't get you that other pint?'

'Oh, no, thank you, maid. John's popping in for a bite today as well, so I'd better not be late. I should get in trouble with my Frances.' He smiled as he shrugged on his coat. 'I'll tell her and John I've been having a drink with the famous Juno Browne.'

Next morning Elizabeth came in through the shop door a few minutes after I'd arrived.

She smiled. 'I didn't know you were going to be here this morning.'

'I'm not really,' I admitted, glancing at my watch. 'I just popped in on my way past.'

After my chat with Sam Weston the previous afternoon I'd been busy and I hadn't made it to the shop before closing time. I'd just come in to see if the place was still standing and to check up on sales.

'Well, you may not want to linger,' she warned me, 'Fizz is due in this morning and she wants a word with you.'

Immediately I felt a sense of foreboding. 'What about?'

'I think she wants more space.'

'More?' I suppose I shouldn't have been surprised. She was obviously finding it difficult to contain her silk merchandise within the confines of the space she'd rented. Her scarves and cushions regularly encroached on to Pat's space, an invasion that was ruthlessly repulsed; and I noticed that one or two of her silk paintings had sneaked onto the wall among Sophie's watercolours. In addition, examples of her partner Don's woodturning had begun to appear. I didn't mind her scattering his pieces amongst her own stuff, but a large beech platter had appeared, hanging on a wall that didn't belong to her. I dimly remembered her asking if she might bring some of his stuff in, but I didn't expect her to start hanging it up wherever she liked. 'Well, she can't have it. She's got more space than anyone else, as it is. She's got her studio to display her stuff in. She can't take the whole place over.' I might need her rent but there was such a thing as balance. 'Has she complained?' I asked.

'No, but Don came in . . .'

I hadn't yet had the pleasure of meeting Fizz's partner. 'What's he like?'

'He's not the sort to hang back,' she responded after

a moment's deliberation, 'full of ideas about things he thought we should be doing differently. "Forthcoming" is probably the right word.'

That didn't sound good. 'Did he come forth with anything in particular?' I asked.

'He felt that Fizz's work should have pride of place in the window,' she answered calmly. 'And he asked who all those old paperbacks belonged to. He said they were a waste of space.'

I twisted around to look at the bookshelves behind me. I'd been building up a stock of second-hand paperbacks, hoping they might draw in the locals. 'Did you tell him they were mine?'

'Yes, and he backed off.'

Bloody cheek, the man coming in and coming forth in my shop.

'But I think Fizz now has her eye on your shelves.'

'Well, she's not having them.' It was true I had not got much in the way of a second-hand book department as yet, but I liked the idea, and I was determined to stick with it.

'I've been thinking about your book department,' Elizabeth went on. 'Why don't you make it a book exchange?'

I frowned. 'Like a library?'

'We stamp all the books with the shop's name. If someone brings back a book with "Old Nick's" stamped in it, they can purchase their next book at half price,' she explained.

'Doesn't that halve my profits?'

'It might double your turnover, and it could bring people into the shop more regularly. And look at it this way, at the moment you're only selling each book once; this way you're getting the chance to sell it every time someone returns it.'

'That's true.' I sighed. 'Why don't I think of these things?'

'Because you're not here enough,' she responded honestly. 'You're busy trying to juggle two businesses. You don't give yourself time to think. But if you decide to run a book exchange,' she added, 'you will need to stock far more books.'

'I will,' I decided. 'It's a good idea.'

'I'll stamp up the existing stock,' she volunteered. 'And leave buying more books to you.'

'Excellent. At least we'll be getting some use out of that stupid rubber stamp.'

At that moment a large white vehicle drew to a stop outside the shop, blocking out the daylight and obstructing the lane outside.

'That's Fizz's camper van,' Elizabeth shot me an amused glance, 'and Don is driving. This means they're probably here to load up stock for a craft fair.'

I groaned. 'I can't get involved with them now. I've got to get going. I'm due up at the Brownlows' house in ten minutes for an extra clean. Their daughter had friends overnight for a sleep-over and the place looks like a bomb's dropped, according to her mother.'

'In that case, you'd better escape out of the side door,' Elizabeth recommended, 'while you have the chance.'

CHAPTER TWENTY-THREE

I love people who buy new books, read them once and then donate them to charity shops. Charity shops are the best places in the world to pick up popular second-hand paperback books at affordable prices. If you want them in bulk, that is. And as I reckoned there were more charity shops per square foot in Newton Abbot than anywhere else in Devon, that's where I went. I could also have a sneaky look at the bric-a-brac of course, in the hope of picking up some fabulously rare and expensive antique that had so far gone unnoticed. The problem is that the charity shops are too savvy these days. They have eagle-eyed experts of their own who divert the really good stuff into auctions before it ever gets on the shelves with the unwanted fondue sets and jigsaw puzzles. I did pick up an art deco dressing-table set in pink glass, though, with only one of its lids missing.

When it came to the books, I was being selective.

I didn't want yellowed or dog-eared pages or books smelling of cigarettes, but titles by popular authors, in pristine condition, so it was a question of buying what I could find at each shop and then moving on to the next. I managed to pick up some romance, science fiction and one or two dark and moody thrillers. You can tell whether a thriller is going to be dark and moody by the photo of the author and whether or not it's in colour. Dark and moody thriller writers like to be photographed in shadowy black and white.

If I couldn't buy enough books in Newton Abbot, I decided, I'd drive the few extra miles to Teignmouth, a seaside town with a pleasing number of charity shops contained within easy walking distance. I got there in the afternoon, a reasonably-sized book haul from Newton Abbot bouncing around in boxes in the back of White Van.

I took the road that winds along the bank of the Teign, occasional breaks in the hedge giving me glimpses of the view down the slow, grey water to the mouth of the estuary and the open sea. On the opposite bank, softly moulded hills come green to the water's edge until the river passes under Shaldon Bridge, and the red cliff of the Ness, crowned with trees, stands as a sentinel where the river meets the sea. Boats moored in the estuary bobbed on the incoming tide.

I parked near the fishy-smelling quay, just around the corner from Teignmouth's artists' quarter, a little cross-section of cobbled streets, shops, artists' studios and cafes, and a tiny theatre set in a building that was once an ice factory. As I locked the van, I did what I'd done at Newton Abbot and cast an eye around for Henry, just in case he'd been following me. There were no suspicious vehicles drawing into the car park behind me, and so far, despite paranoid glances into my rear-view mirror at any vehicle that seemed to be sticking with me, I'd not spotted any sign of him on the road. I sincerely hoped by now he'd buggered off back to Basingstoke.

I realised I'd been a bit hard on him. Life with Marjorie the Uncompassionate couldn't be much fun. His ego was probably crushed; I couldn't really blame him for having fantasies about finding his brother's killer. It must be hard losing a twin in the first place. Whatever their differences, they must have been close; you can't share a womb with someone and not feel a tug on the umbilical cord.

I took a wander down to the seafront for a blast of salty air and stood on the prom. There was a stiff easterly blowing off the sea, churning up frothy white spray on the incoming tide. I was glad I'd worn a windproof jacket. To my right, just across the water, the sugar almond houses of Shaldon village clustered at the foot of the Ness. Below me the beach was being swallowed by the tide, incoming waves splashing against the foot of the sea wall. Further along, beyond the pier, there was still enough beach for kids to dig with buckets and spades and dogs to run heedless with joy along the wet sand. I resisted the temptation to take a longer walk along the sea wall which follows the railway line all the way to Dawlish – I was on a mission after all – and headed back into the town, drawn to the paved Triangle, Teignmouth's geometric approximation of a town square, by strains of music.

Two buskers, one on fiddle and one on clarinet, were entertaining passers-by and bench-sitters with some lively klezmer music; an accordion and guitar on the pavement beside them waiting their turn to be played. Despite the number of people who had stopped to listen there was only a smattering of coins in the open violin case at their feet. I think it's mean to stop and listen to the music and then not pay for the privilege. I wandered over to add my contribution, and as they had stopped to draw breath between numbers, asked them for a card or contact number. I ended up investing in a copy of their latest CD, which was not what I had planned but gave me something to take back for Kate and Adam to listen to. They were now actively seeking musicians to play at their first evening opening of *Sunflowers*.

Good deed done, I decided that before I went hunting for more books, I'd treat myself to a cup of tea. I wandered through the artists' quarter and into *Polly's*, a pretty little cafe that I had not visited before. It was a traditional tea room, its pink walls hung with local art, flowery curtains at the windows, lace cloths on the tables, and pretty cups and saucers decorating the shelves. I sat facing the window and after dithering over the display of cakes under glass domes on the sideboard, decided on an apricot tart to eat with my tea. It was quiet in the cafe and I didn't have to wait long before a tray with a teapot, strainer, hot-water jug, dinky milk jug and sugar bowl, delightfully mismatched teacup and saucer, and plate with the apricot tart arrived. The young waitress in a frilly apron deposited it all with a smile and off she went, leaving me to wait for the tea to brew. I recognised the design on the bone china teacup as *Albert Rose*. I was just picking up the saucer to flip it over and read the name on the reverse when a woman came in.

For a moment we made eye contact. It was one of those moments when you see a face you recognise, but can't immediately think who it belongs to, or where you've seen it before. She was a short, dumpy little woman with grey curls under a green felt hat. We did what all women do in that split second of confusion; to avoid potential embarrassment, we smiled at each other. She smiled at my red curls, and I smiled at the space between her front teeth. Her face barely had time to register shock and dismay before she turned tail and scurried off through the door.

'Just a minute!' I roared after her and leapt to my feet. Unfortunately, I hadn't noticed that the Velcro fastening on the cuff of my windproof jacket had hitched itself in the lacy tablecloth. As I jumped up ready to give chase, I swept everything off the table like an inept magician trying to pull a trick. Teapot and dinky milk jug went flying, splattering wetness across the nearest pink wall, china teacup, plate and saucer crashed to the floor and the sugar basin upended, dumping an avalanche of glistening crystals across the carpet.

'Sorry!' I yelled to the horrified waitress as I headed for the door, the tablecloth still clinging to my cuff. 'I'll be back!' I could see the fat backside of my quarry bustling off down the street, her little legs going as fast as they could. She'd gained a momentary advantage when I'd upset the tea things, but I was gaining on her fast, the lace cloth flapping like a sail. There was no way she could escape me with those short legs. I could hear her huffing and puffing as I caught up with her in the Triangle. When I was two steps behind, I grabbed the trailing end of the tablecloth, flipped it over her head like a net and wrangled her to the ground. She fell with a squawk of alarm, me landing on top of her as she kicked and cried out for help. Her handbag burst open and all kinds of sparkly swag scattered across the paving stones. I hissed in her ear. 'Gotcha!'

I was not assaulting a pensioner with a tablecloth, I explained to the two police officers a few minutes later, I was making a citizen's arrest. They'd been summoned by anxious onlookers. Various people had intervened to save the poor old dear from a vicious attack by what appeared to be a demented Viking woman, including the two buskers. No one had seemed to notice that during our bout of fisticuffs she gave as good as she got. My nose was throbbing. I pointed to the valuables that had tumbled out of her handbag and scooped up a handful of jewellery. 'She's a thief!' I told the police. 'Why do you think she's carrying all this lot in her bag?'

The officer looked to her for an explanation, his brows raised questioningly. 'I've bought and paid for it all,' she gasped between sobs. I had to admire her performance. She could cry real tears. 'If you look in my bag, you'll find the receipt.'

Sure enough, the receipt was there, from *Bijouterie*, an antique shop just around the corner. I almost snatched it from the policeman's hand. 'Go there right now,' I told him, 'and I can guarantee you two things. First of all, the owner won't be on the premises, and secondly when whoever *is* serving looks at the copy in their receipt book, they'll only find the first item listed. The rest have been forged at a later date,' I pointed, 'by her!' I tried to explain what had happened at *Old Nick's* while Gappy kept sobbing into a dainty handkerchief, unaware that her hat and grey wig were slightly askew. She told the police her name was Mrs Rowena Palfrey.

'This is all nonsense! Vicious lies,' she protested. 'I've never seen this person before.'

'Well, as the shop is just around the corner, it won't take long for us to check this story out, will it?' The policeman smiled at Mrs Palfrey. 'Shall we?'

She turned a bit white around the mouth but had no choice but to grit her teeth and go with him. 'I'm suing you for assault,' she hissed at me, eyeing me with venom as she turned to go.

I turned to the other officer. 'I need to go back to the

cafe,' I told him,' I've left my bag there and I'm afraid there's some damage I'll have to pay for.'

'We'll pick it up on the way.'

'On the way?' I asked.

'To the station. You're under arrest, dearie,' he told me amicably, 'for assault.'

I didn't think I'd heard right. 'I beg your pardon?'

'Don't worry. We're just going to have a nice sit down in the police station until my colleague has checked this receipt with Mrs Palfrey.'

At the cafe they were still clearing up the mess. I was allowed to linger long enough to make a fulsome apology and for the owner to reckon up the cost of the damage. It was a good thing I hadn't spent all my book money. She also told me I was banned.

I didn't have to wait at the police station long. I gave the officer the names of the other antiques dealers who'd been victims of Mrs Palfrey and her accomplice, and also told him to check with either Sergeant DeVille or Constable Collins, who'd verify my story. By the time he'd phoned the station at Ashburton, his colleague had already returned from *Bijouterie*.

My prediction as to what he'd find there had been spot on. The owner had been sent for, recognised Mrs Palfrey, and confirmed that the only item she had purchased a few days before had been the first one on the list. The rest was a forgery. Mrs Palfrey was still sobbing and protesting her innocence, saying it was all a misunderstanding, threatening to faint and demanding a doctor as well as a solicitor. I was allowed to go, released without charge.

Unfortunately, she and I had to pass each other in the corridor. If looks could kill I'd have been dead. 'Bitch!' she spat at me and aimed a vicious kick at my ankle.

'Hey, that's assault, that is,' the officer warned her. 'Behave yourself.'

'She assaulted me first,' she retorted. 'I'm going to sue you!' she snarled.

'Not really in your interest, madam,' the officer told her, 'not at the moment. Now come into this interview room and if you're a good girl you can have a cup of tea.' He winked at me as he closed the door. Rubbing my ankle, I hobbled back to the van.

A call from Dean Collins that evening was inevitable. 'What have you been up to now?' he asked. It's funny how on the phone you can hear someone grinning from ear to ear. He seemed particularly amused by my failed conjuring trick with the tablecloth. Mrs Palfrey had refused to confess to fraud even after the police had called at her address and found thousands of pounds worth of jewellery and small antiques stowed in shoeboxes in her wardrobe. They also arrested her accomplice, son Gerald, who had arrived a little late for the rendezvous with his mother at Polly's cafe, heard about the fracas in the Triangle and slipped slyly home. He was not made of such strong stuff as his mama and asked for thirty-four other cases to be taken into consideration. The pair of them had been having a high old time for years, apparently. I couldn't believe this was the first time they'd been caught.

'I wonder if any of the stuff they found was mine?'

'It's going to take quite a while to sort it all out,' Dean warned me. 'According to Gerald, what was found was just a small fraction of what they've got away with over the years. Most of it's been sold on.'

I pondered my losses and sighed. 'Well, it would be nice to get my stuff back, but I expect it's too much to hope for. I'll settle for putting a stop to Mrs Rowena Palfrey's career.'

'That's not her real name,' Dean chuckled. 'She's Joan Higginbottom.'

I smiled. If I had a name ending in 'bottom' I'd change it too, especially if I had an arse the size of hers.

CHAPTER TWENTY-FOUR

The following evening, I picked up my writing table. Steve had phoned to tell me it was ready. I seemed to have spent the entire day recounting the capture of Mrs Joan Higginbottom aka Mrs Rowena Palfrey and, as it later turned out, aka Celestine Parkinson and Angela Whittington, to every person of my acquaintance. I'd gone into the shop early to take in the books I'd bought. Elizabeth had done a sterling job in stamping all the existing stock and arranging it on the shelves in strict alphabetical order of author's name. There was a note from her asking if I'd prefer them organised according to genre – romance, thriller etc. I thought about that but decided to keep it simple.

As each came in, I had to repeat the story to Sophie and Pat as well as phoning Ann at Okehampton and Mel at Barnstaple, and of course Ricky and Morris. I'd tried phoning Daniel the night before but couldn't get through. At least Steve the restorer was someone I didn't need to tell.

'I've got a bit of paper here for you,' he'd told me on the phone. I thought he meant his bill, but he didn't. 'It's just one piece of paper,' he went on, 'but as you told me you'd found a letter in the secret drawer, I kept it for you. I thought you'd like to see it. It had slipped down behind the back. I wouldn't have found it if I hadn't had to take the frame apart to re-glue some wobbly joints.'

I felt far more excited about finding another piece of Vivian's letter than seeing the table restored to its former glory. I drove over as soon as I'd closed up the shop.

I have to admit the table did look magnificent. The fogged and buckled surface now was smooth and gleaming, impossible to resist running a hand across, the colour a rich glowing walnut. I opened the little drawer with its pendant brass handles, and it slid in and out smoothly. 'You've done a beautiful job,' I told Steve as I handed over the balance of the cash. He wrote me a receipt.

'And the other piece of paper?' I asked.

'Oh yes, almost forgot.' He pulled it from his shirt pocket. 'There you are.'

It was a single folded sheet. I resisted the temptation to open it there and then, but I could see at a glance it wasn't from the same letter I had found. At least it was written on different paper – blue, not white – and it was lined. I popped it into my bag whilst Steve wrapped the table in an old blanket I had brought with me and we loaded it into the van.

I drove it straight back to the shop, carried it carefully through to the storeroom and stood it in the middle of the floor. Then I stepped back to admire it. At last, a proper antique. The trouble was it made the rest of the furniture for sale look shabbier than ever. 'I'll have to do something about you next,' I said to the chaise longue as I perched my bum on it, 'as soon as I've saved up.'

Then I unfolded the sheet of paper. It was in Vivian's handwriting. On the top line just one word was written, followed by a full stop, as if it was the last word of a paragraph: '*desperate*'. Poor Vivian.

I will send this to the last address I have for you, she carried on, *but with little hope that you will ever read it. You haven't got a message to me for such a long time. I don't even know where you are. I pray every day that you are safe and I will hear something from you soon. I have managed to scrape a little money together, but you know how careful I have to be. I think he would kill me if he found out. Please, my darling, I beg you, don't abandon your—*

That was it, that was all there was. Another letter that Vivian couldn't post, stuffed hastily into the secret drawer in her desk as she heard Fred's footsteps climbing the stairs, another letter she intended to finish one day but never lived to send. That word, 'desperate', tore at my heart. Poor Vivian, she'd endured a loveless and abusive marriage, been murdered by a cruel man and buried in the cold earth. Jay had not returned. Unless, I thought, staring numbly at the page in my hands, he had come back, and he had been the one who had killed her.

I decided not to share this latest letter with Connie. It shed no more light on what had happened to Vivian and it would only upset her. It had upset me. I barely slept, mourning a woman I never knew, and who it was too late to save. I decided the idea that Jay might have killed Vivian was stupid. If he wanted to be rid of her, he'd already achieved that by abandoning her and not letting her know where he was. Job done. There was no need for him to return. No, it was Fred Crick who'd murdered her. In a jealous rage when he'd found out that she was planning to leave him, to escape to her lover, or in a fit of anger when he'd discovered the money she'd been trying to scrape together. It was the discovery of these secrets that had killed her.

The next morning I sat with Maisie, looking through old black and white photos of the war and pictures of her husband Bob in his army uniform. She told me all about their romance. If nothing else, going through these photographs for the Memory Cafe had got Maisie reminiscing.

I was busy all day and realised I probably wasn't going to make it back to *Old Nick's* before closing time. I let myself into Chloe Berkeley-Smythe's cottage late in the afternoon to clear the mail that accumulates in her porch. If I don't do it regularly whenever she's away on a cruise it would be impossible to get in through the front door by the time she makes dry land. As well as the latest reports on how her investments are accruing, I pick up wedges of chunky glossies from her doormat, mostly shopping catalogues for expensive clothes or the latest cruise brochures. I'd just placed the newest batch of correspondence in their respective piles on her coffee table and was about to reset the burglar alarm, when the phone rang in my pocket.

'Juno?' Sophie sounded breathless and tearful. 'Juno, where are you?'

'Soph? Are you all right? What's up?'

'Something . . . terrible . . . has happened,' she wheezed. 'The police are here.'

'Sophie, breathe slowly.' Her asthma could be triggered by any stress and she sounded perilously near the edge of an attack. 'Have you got your inhaler with you?'

'Yes . . . I'm all right,' she assured me, but her breathing sounded tortured. 'The police . . . want to see you . . . can you come . . . to the shop . . . right away?'

'I'm on my way,' I told her. 'Don't try to speak.'

'I'm all right,' she gasped. 'It's Fizz.'

I hurtled through the door of *Old Nick's* to find Sophie huddled at her worktable, her jacket around her shoulders, clutching her inhaler. Her face was white, and her dark eyes were huge with tears. A policewoman was sitting with her and there was a cup of tea placed on the table by her elbow.

'Sophie!' I knelt by the table and took her hand. Her

fingers were like ice and they clutched desperately at mine. 'What's happened?'

'She's had a nasty shock,' the policewoman explained. She stood up, vacating her chair.

'You sit there, Miss Browne. I'll go up and tell the sergeant you've arrived.'

I could hear heavy footsteps above our heads in Fizz's studio and the thumping base from her radio. 'What's going on?'

'Mrs Drummond has been taken to hospital,' the policewoman told me, her voice hushed with sympathy.

'What's happened?'

'I'm afraid she's been attacked.'

I looked from her to Sophie and back again. 'Will she be all right?'

'We don't know as yet,' she told me firmly as she turned to go. 'Please wait here.'

I slid into the chair next to Sophie. I could feel her shaking. I told her to drink some tea.

She seemed to be breathing more easily than when she'd spoken on the phone. A few moments later the thumping rhythm of the radio stopped abruptly. 'Are you all right, Soph? Can you tell me what happened?'

She nodded, drawing breath. 'I only left her . . . for about twenty minutes,' she began slowly, drawing deep breaths. 'Mum wanted me to pick up some shopping . . . Fizz was in her studio. I went up to ask if she could look after the shop while . . . while I was gone . . .' She began crying. 'I'm sorry, Juno.'

'It's all right, Soph. Slow down, take your time.'

'She'd started working on this piece of silk,' she went on, wiping away tears with the heels of her hands. 'She had it stretched on the frame. She was wetting it with this big sponge . . . She said she'd have to get some paint on the silk while it was still wet . . . she'd come down in a minute. I asked her to . . . um . . . turn her radio down so she'd hear the bell. She did.'

She sniffed and took another sip of tea. 'When I came back the radio was blaring really loud and she wasn't down here. The place was empty. I was really cross. I thought . . . I thought she'd turned the volume back up after I'd gone and hadn't bothered to come down. I called out to her . . . but she didn't answer. I went up to the studio . . .' She began to sob. 'I must have walked past him . . . He must have been hiding in the bathroom on the landing.'

'Who?' I put an arm around her shoulders. 'Who d'you mean, Soph?' I groped in my pocket for a tissue and gave it to her. She blew her nose and looked up at me, her eyelashes drowned into wet spikes.

'I didn't see him,' she sniffed wretchedly. 'I looked in the studio . . .' her voice shook. 'I thought it was blood. I thought that she was dead . . . then I heard him run down the stairs, through the shop . . . Fizz was slumped over the frame and the silk was all red . . . I thought she'd been stabbed . . . there was blood on the back of her head . . . she started making this moaning noise. And then I called the ambulance . . . and the police.'

'You heard someone run down the stairs,' I asked, 'someone you didn't see?'

Sophie nodded, sobbing. I gave her a hug. After a minute or so she got control of herself. She was still upset but her breathing was steadier and her colour warmer. 'I'll be back in just a moment,' I promised her. I had to take a look upstairs.

'Don't touch anything, Miss Browne!' Cruella's voice cut into me as I arrived in the studio doorway. She and two uniformed officers were bending over Fizz's worktable, examining the framed silk.

It looked like the scene of a massacre. A pot of red silk paint had been tipped over and spread in a pale bloody wash across the wet silk. Where the silk was dry it had formed a dark pool, a rounded shape with a hard line at its edge. No wonder poor Sophie thought Fizz had been stabbed.

Cruella straightened up. 'You were told to wait downstairs.'

I ignored that. 'Is Fizz badly hurt?'

'We don't know yet. She was struck over the head.' The tiniest of smiles tugged at her little mouth. 'You know what that's like.'

The scar on my scalp began to itch in sympathy. But I'd seen what I wanted to see.

'I'm going back down to Sophie.'

'Try not to touch the bannisters or the bathroom door on your way down. It seems Mrs Drummond's assailant may have hidden in the bathroom.'

Shit, I cursed silently as I walked down the stairs, my arms stiffly at my sides. That means the damn fingerprint men would be here again.

Sophie was still sitting quietly, sipping at her tea.

'Was Fizz still unconscious when they took her to hospital?' I asked.

'She was mumbling a bit, but she wasn't talking properly.'

'Do they know what she was hit with?'

Sophie shook her head. 'I don't know.'

A moment later Cruella and her crew came down into the shop.

'No one is to go into the studio or the bathroom,' she announced. 'In fact, don't go upstairs at all. Not until forensics have been. I'm sorry if that's inconvenient,' she added with a tight smirk that said she wasn't sorry at all. She drew up a chair and sat down. 'Now,' she began pulling out her notebook. 'Do either of you know why anyone would have attacked Mrs Drummond? I think we can rule out robbery. From what Miss Child here says,' she indicated Sophie with her pencil,' the shop was unattended and anyone could have walked out with the takings. There was no need for a thief to go upstairs.' She paused, searching our faces with her violet stare.

We looked at each other and shrugged. We'd both felt like killing Fizz more than once, but we weren't about to say so.

'No,' I said after a moment. 'I don't know of any reason.'

'You see, this looks like a targeted attack. It was deliberate. It's likely that it was only your return,' she said to Sophie, 'that prevented it being a murder. Assuming Mrs Drummond survives,' she added grimly. 'Her assailant hid when he heard you calling out.'

Sophie sniffed. 'I wish I'd never gone out in the first place,' she said dolefully.

Cruella ignored this. 'You said earlier that the radio was turned low when you left but turned up loud when you returned, is that correct?'

'Yes.'

'It's possible that her assailant turned it up to cover the sounds of any struggle, which again suggests the attack was premeditated and deliberate.'

We were both silent for a moment, taking this in.

'Do you know what he attacked her with?' I asked.

Cruella shook her head. 'There is no sign of anything up in the studio that could have been used as a weapon. Presumably her attacker took it away.' She leant forward suddenly, frowning at my feet. 'What's that under your shoe?' she asked, pointing.

I wriggled my foot out of my trainer without unlacing it and picked it up. There was a rubber band hanging from the sole, attached to a piece of metal with three sharp hooks that had dug themselves into the thick rubber sole. I levered it out. 'It's a stenter pin,' I told her. 'Fizz uses them for stretching silk.'

She reached out a hand for it and I dropped it into her palm. 'Careful,' I warned her. 'It's sharp.'

One of her uniformed companions spoke up. 'There were several on the floor in the studio, Sarge, I nearly trod on one myself.'

She nodded, still staring at the pin. 'There was a little box of them on the edge of the table. It had tipped . . .'

The policewoman came back into the shop then. I hadn't noticed her slip out.

'I've made contact with the husband, Sergeant. He's going straight to the hospital.'

'Go and meet him there,' she ordered. 'I'll be there myself soon. Let's see if he can account for his movements for the last few hours.'

Sophie took in a shocked breath that made Cruella glance at her. 'If this was a deliberate attack, then we're looking for motive.' Again, came the little smile. 'Husbands and wives are often good for quite a few.' She sat thoughtfully for a moment, waggling her pencil between her fingers. 'Mrs Drummond was already on a stretcher when I arrived,' she said eventually. She directed her gaze at Sophie. 'Is she tall?'

'Quite tall.' Sophie gave a weak smile, 'but everyone's tall to me.'

Cruella's raised her dark brows. 'As tall as Miss Browne here?'

'Oh no, she's not as tall as Juno.'

'But tall,' she insisted. 'How would you describe her hair?'

Sophie glanced at me, puzzled by the question. 'Auburn.'

'Auburn?' Cruella repeated. 'Red, then?'

'Yes,' Sophie answered doubtfully, 'but not a golden red like Juno's. Darker. Auburn,' she repeated.

'The point I'm making,' Cruella explained, 'is that if I were to describe Mrs Drummond as a tall woman with red hair – it would be an accurate description. Yes?'

Sophie shrugged. 'Well, yes.'

'What exactly are you getting at?' I had a sickening suspicion I knew where this was heading.

Cruella fixed her ice-violet stare full on me. 'This appears to have been a targeted attack on an innocent woman,' she said deliberately. 'We don't know the motive. But I'm wondering if someone had been sent to attack a woman working in this shop, and picked the *wrong* tall, red-haired woman.'

Sophie eyes stretched wide in horror. 'You think he meant to attack Juno?'

I was silent, staring back at Cruella. I felt sick.

'I think she might be a more obvious target,' she added, 'given the kind of things she gets up to.'

'I haven't been up to anything.' I struggled to keep my voice calm, but I doubt if my eyes concealed my loathing.

'Not poking your nose into any criminal investigations recently?' She flipped her little notebook shut and stood up. 'I'm going to the hospital to talk to Mr Drummond. In the meantime, Miss Browne, I suggest you have a long, hard think about anyone who might hold a grudge against you. There might be quite a list.'

She walked to the door and then turned. 'And if you have been indulging in any of your sleuthing activities lately, we can only hope that your amateur meddling has not cost Mrs Drummond her life.'

The shop door shut behind her; the bell jangled. I felt as if I'd been turned to stone.

Sophie sprang to her feet. 'You should report her,' she cried angrily. 'You should tell Inspector Ford. She can't talk to you like that, making allegations—'

'No, it's all right, Soph,' I muttered. Rage was churning in my stomach but the thing that was really choking me up was that Cruella could be right.

'No, it's not. She can't say that the attack on Fizz had anything to do with you—'

At that moment one of the uniforms came back in through the shop, carrying a reel of blue and white tape.

'Sorry, ladies,' he said, looking sheepish. 'I'm going to have to tape off the bottom of the stairs.'

'There's no need,' Sophie told him indignantly. 'We won't go up there.'

'Well, this will just be a reminder,' he answered.

We sat in silence while he did his job. 'I guess you'll be shutting up shop shortly,' he said to me, glancing at his watch. 'We'll try and get forensics over tomorrow.'

'Thank you,' I muttered.

'Oh no!' Sophie cried, realisation dawning. 'That means until the forensics people have been and gone, we won't be able to make tea and coffee or use the loo.'

''Fraid not.' I sighed. 'Anyway, don't you worry about it, I'll come in tomorrow and open up as soon as I've walked the dogs. I might be a bit late, but it won't matter.'

'No. I'll come in,' Sophie insisted. 'I'm fine, Juno, really.'

'Are you sure?' She was still very pale. 'You might not feel so good in the morning.'

'I'll be OK. Anyway, Pat will be here too.' She gave a weak giggle. 'We can take it in turns to go out for coffee and a loo break.'

'I'll come in anyway. Oh, God!' I hung my head, thrusting my hands into my hair. 'If the forensics people don't make it tomorrow, this could go on for days.'

'They will, won't they? After all, they want to catch this man.'

I began to unknot the laces of my trainer so I could put it back on. Sophie raised an eyebrow at my socked foot. 'Are you sure mauve's your colour?' she asked. She was trying to cheer me up.

I managed a smile. 'Well, my socks are too far from my hair for them to clash.' Then I sighed. 'I'll ring the hospital later. I just hope Fizz is going to be OK.'

CHAPTER TWENTY-FIVE

It was Dean Collins who released me from my misery. I'd rung the hospital several times but as I wasn't a family member they wouldn't tell me anything. He phoned at around midnight.

'I know it's late, but I thought you'd want to hear.'

'Well?' I asked.

'Good news. They're keeping her in overnight but it's just concussion. She's had a couple of stitches in her scalp and they've run a few tests. But the X-rays are clear.'

'Oh, thank God!'

'She's been lucky. Whoever hit her didn't do a very good job.'

'If Sophie hadn't come back when she did—' I began.

He grunted. 'It could have been a different story.'

'Has Fizz said anything about what happened?'

'She says all she can remember is hearing the music on the radio suddenly very loud. She turned to see who'd upped the volume and *bang!* Something hit her and all the lights went out. It was probably her turning round that saved her. The attacker only struck her a glancing blow.'

'So, she didn't get a look at him?'

'Not a peep. Her husband's in the clear, though. He was in a meeting at work with half a dozen colleagues at the time the attack took place.'

'Cruella thinks the attack was meant for me.'

'A little bird at the station told me what Cruella said. She's out of order, Juno.' He paused a moment. 'You haven't been up to any of your old tricks, have you? Not since the last time I saw you?'

'No,' I answered truthfully. 'I really haven't.'

'You haven't been poking your nose in anywhere?'

I gritted my teeth. 'No!'

'Well, then. Forget her. This wasn't your fault.'

'Thanks, Dean, I appreciate that.'

'There are a lot of nutters about who'll attack any woman quite randomly, given the opportunity.'

'Yes,' I agreed.

'So, it wasn't your fault, right?'

'No.'

'The only person to blame,' he went on emphatically, 'is the bastard who coshed her.'

He was trying a little too hard to reassure me, which meant he believed what Cruella had said as well.

The forensics team arrived early next morning. I'd phoned Pat the night before to tell her what had happened to Fizz and warn her there might be white-suited aliens about.

She had already opened the shop by the time I arrived, and Sophie turned up a few minutes later. She said she felt fine and that she had a painting to finish. I stamped up the latest books I'd bought and arranged them on the shelves.

Pat was knitting. 'Have you told Elizabeth what's happened?'

Yes, I said, I'd phoned her. Elizabeth didn't waste any time trying to reassure me that the attack wasn't meant for me. Instead she suggested another self-defence lesson.

Our conversation kept returning to Fizz. 'I'll go to the hospital this afternoon,' I said, 'and see how she is.'

The man who more or less erupted through the shop door at that moment must have heard what I said. He wore a suit jacket and white shirt with jeans and trainers; his grey hair shaved to a close, silvery bristle. I disliked him on sight, felt as if a shark had just swum into our little fishpond. He strode into the shop, stopped about a foot in front of me and thrust his finger in my face. 'You stay away from my wife!' His voice was low and shaking, like a man struggling to hold on to his anger. 'I'll get a court injunction against you if you come anywhere near her.' His teeth were very white, his lips drawn back in a snarl. He smelt of expensive aftershave.

I stepped back instinctively but I was trapped by the bookshelves behind me. I took a deep breath. 'You must be Don,' I said, as calmly as I could. 'I'm Juno.'

'I know who you are,' he spat.

Pat was staring open-mouthed. 'Here, hang on!' she protested. 'You can't come in here shouting the odds—'

'Don,' Sophie began, hurrying around from behind her worktable. 'It's not Juno's fault.'

He ignored them both, blue eyes still locked hatefully on mine. 'She's not coming back here again.'

'How is Fizz?' I asked.

That made him pause. 'She's going to be OK,' he breathed. 'No thanks to you! I'm removing all of her stuff from this place,' he went on, 'and I don't care what the tenancy arrangement is, you're not getting another penny out of us in rent.'

'She's paid up till the end of the month,' I informed him steadily. I mustn't make the mistake of getting angry too.

'Good.' He made to push past me towards the door at the back of the shop.

'You can't go up there,' I warned him. 'The forensics team are in the studio, brushing for fingerprints.'

He sagged a little then, some of the anger escaping from him like steam from a pressure cooker. 'Oh.'

'Look,' I began, 'I'm terribly sorry about what happened to Fizz.'

My apology seemed to make him worse. He flared up again, taking another step towards me. If he didn't back off physically, I was going to have to make him. Again, the finger jabbed towards my face. 'You are a danger to yourself and everyone around you.'

'You need to calm down, mate.' We all looked towards the door. None of us had heard Jason Beck come in. He was standing in the doorway. 'And stop wagging your finger in the lady's face.'

Don Drummond spun around to stare at him. 'Who are you?' he demanded.

'I'm the guy who's going to throw you out of here if you don't give her some space,' he responded affably. 'Now, I can see you're upset, but I suggest you go away and come back when you're in a more reasonable frame of mind.' He stood aside and held the shop door open.

After a moment's fuming hesitation, Don let out a frustrated sigh and strode towards the door. 'I'll be back,' he warned, turning to glower at me. 'I haven't finished with you yet.'

Jason let the door swing closed after him. 'What the hell was all that about?' he asked, chuckling. 'You OK, Juno?'

'Yes, thanks,' I breathed.

'All right, sweetheart?' he asked Sophie, who was gazing at him as if he was some sort of god, and winked. He turned to Pat. 'I don't believe we've had the pleasure,' he said, holding out his hand.

'No, we haven't.' Pat looked like a rabbit caught in the glare of headlights, completely overawed by his eyes. 'How do you do?'

'So, who was that guy?'

Sophie immediately launched into the story of what had happened to Fizz yesterday, her dark eyes and sweeping black lashes working overtime. He listened attentively, but when she got as far as the police arriving, he held up a hand and stopped her. 'Look, don't think I'm being rude but I'm a bit short for time and I really need a chat with Juno. Do you mind if I whisk her off for a coffee?'

Poor Sophie blushed, obviously feeling foolish. 'Sorry.'

'D'you mind?' he said to me.

'I won't be long, girls,' I promised and followed him out.

We went to *Sunflowers* and took a seat in the corner. Kate hadn't met Jason before either and rolled her eyes meaningfully at me when she came to take our order.

'I thought you'd gone back to Australia.'

'Is that why you've tried to phone me three times?' he asked, with a smirk.

'I wondered why you didn't mention that you were staying at the same guest house as Peter Gillow, that's all.'

Jason frowned. 'Who?'

'Peter Gillow,' I repeated, 'the dead man in my wardrobe?'

'Oh, him! I'd forgotten his name.' He shrugged. 'I didn't realise we were staying in the same place. I don't think I ever laid eyes on the bloke.'

'You checked out on the day he disappeared.'

'Did I?' He frowned. 'I'm sorry, I don't see the relevance. I never met the man.'

I tried to read his eyes, to tell if there was a lie hidden

behind his casual dismissal; but if Jason Beck was a liar, he was a good one. 'No,' I sighed, 'it's probably just coincidence.'

'Probably?' His shoulders shook with laughter. 'I'm flattered you've been checking up on me, Juno.' He leant forward across the table. 'Tell me,' he asked, serious now, 'that fella this morning, why was he so angry?'

'Because he believes his wife was hit over the head in mistake for me. He believes I was the real target.'

Jason looked mystified. 'Where did he get that idea?'

There was only one person who could have put it into his head as far as I was concerned. 'Cruella deVille,' I told him.

'Who?'

'Local lady detective sergeant who seems to hate my guts for some reason,' I answered. 'The feeling is entirely mutual.'

'Could she be right?' he asked.

'I don't know,' I admitted. 'I can't think of anyone with a grudge against me who's not safely locked up in prison. But if Cruella *is* right, then whoever attacked Fizz didn't know me or he wouldn't have attacked the wrong woman. He was relying on a description – a tall woman with red hair. So . . .'

'He'd been sent by someone else,' Jason completed for me. He gave a long, low whistle. 'Do you think he was sent to kill you? You must really have got under someone's skin.'

'But that's just the point. I haven't. I haven't been

snooping around. I haven't even been asking questions. After what happened in the forest at Christow . . .' I tailed off, but it was too late.

Jason's smile gleamed. 'So, you *were* there.'

There didn't seem any point in trying to deny it. I told him the whole sorry, humiliating business. 'Since then, I've been trying not to interfere.'

Jason eyed me doubtfully. 'You're sure?'

'Yes,' I protested indignantly. 'The only person I've talked to is Sam Weston, an old drinking friend of Fred's, and he doesn't strike me as the kind of person who'd put a contract out on me.'

'Weston?' he asked quickly. 'Do you mean John Weston?'

'No. I talked to Sam. I believe John's his son, but I've never met him.' Jason was looking thoughtful. 'Why do you ask?'

He shrugged his shoulders. 'Someone must have mentioned his name to me at some point. He's a local farmer, isn't he?' He glanced at his watch. 'Look, I'm going to have to go.' He signalled to Kate for the bill.

'So, are you off home soon?' I asked. 'Back to Australia?'

'Very soon.'

I smiled. 'So this is the second time we're saying goodbye.'

'Looks like it. And we never really got to know each other.' He grinned again. 'Not that I'd have been in with a chance.'

I must have looked surprised. 'You think not?'

'I saw the way you were looking at that dark-haired

fella in the wine bar. And you're not the kind of girl to mess around. I can tell.'

I found myself blushing like an idiot. 'Well, thanks for rescuing me this morning.'

He shrugged. 'You'd have rescued yourself.' As we stood up, he gave me a kiss on the cheek. 'Bye, Juno.' He smiled. 'Take care.'

It was Sophie who went to the hospital to visit Fizz later that day. I was determined to go but she and Pat talked me out of it. Don might be there, and we didn't want another scene like this morning, not in the hospital, now did we? No, we didn't, I agreed. Although it was the thought of upsetting Fizz that concerned me; I wasn't frightened of Don Drummond. But I had come to a decision. What he had said about my being a danger to others had hit hard.

I was definitely reining in my activities. No more sleuthing.

'So, how is she?' Pat and I asked together when Sophie returned at the end of the afternoon.

'Well, she still seems a bit groggy. She said she couldn't bear the thought of going up in the studio again, or of being here in the shop alone . . . which is understandable.'

'Yes, I suppose it is,' I agreed, although Pat tutted as if she had no patience with such namby-pamby nervousness.

'At the same time,' Sophie went on, a puzzled wrinkle between her brows, 'I got the feeling that she doesn't really want to leave. But Don was there, insisting.'

'Isn't it up to her?' I asked.

Sophie sighed. 'I don't think so. Fizz may be the talent but it's Don who's in control. He never wanted her to come here in the first place, he told me. He wanted her to have her own shop.' She flicked me a hesitant glance. 'He said this was a crummy little back-alley dive that could never be successful.'

'Cheek!' Pat cried indignantly.

I said nothing, I know exactly what he means.

'He's coming in tomorrow to get her stuff.'

I groaned.

'I told him that we'd pack it up for her . . .' Sophie looked from me to Pat uncertainly. 'Well, I thought it was better than having him here doing it,' she went on. 'All he has to do then is collect it.'

'You're right, Soph,' I admitted.

'I don't mind boxing her stuff up,' Pat sniffed, 'but I ain't lugging that bloody table downstairs again.'

'No. Too right,' I agreed. 'He can do that himself.'

In fact, Pat couldn't come in next day because she was needed at the animal sanctuary, so Elizabeth came to help. It took all day, with Sophie and I taking the big silk panels down from the walls of her studio and carefully shrouding each one in bubble-wrap, disassembling the silk painting frames so that their pieces could be tied together for easy transportation, boxing up her paints and brushes as well as all the brushes, sponges, nibs, liners, paints and instruction books she had for sale. We carted dozens of rolls of silk down the stairs, her ironing board and her bloody microwave. Meanwhile in the shop,

313

Elizabeth bagged lampshades and cushions and neatly wrapped each of the scarves in tissue paper. They would be departing more carefully protected than when they had arrived, bundled up in Fizz's laundry bags; but we were determined Don would have no cause for complaint.

When he called at the end of the day his temper seemed to have died down. He was sullen and uncommunicative, the air of a man who knows he should apologise but isn't going to; but everything was ready for him. 'There's only the table left upstairs,' I told him. 'Here you are.' I slammed the screwdriver down on the counter in front of him. 'You'll need that.'

Out shopping the next morning, my attention was snagged by an advertising board on the pavement outside a shop. It was for the *Dartmoor Gazette*. 'Sheep Rustling – Gang Members Arrested'. I groaned audibly. What had happened at Christow was meant to be a covert operation, so who had tipped off the newspaper? I swore suddenly. Jason Beck. The treacherous bastard had leaked what I told him to the *Dartmoor Gazette*. I popped into the nearest shop and bought a copy of the wretched rag, fully expecting to see my name plastered all over the front page. But to my surprise there was no mention of the debacle in the forest involving me and Henry. The article referred to a different operation altogether: the arrest of local farmer John Weston, who was believed to be the brains behind a gang involved in a spate of local livestock thefts. It seems police had arrested him following a tip-off from 'an international investigative reporter'.

Jason, it had to be. He had mentioned John Weston's name when I told him I had talked to Sam. I tried him on his mobile but there was no response, so I marched down to *Old Nick's* and called Dean Collins.

'It's him, isn't it?' I demanded almost as soon as I picked up the phone. 'The journalist who gave the police the tip-off? It's Jason Beck, it's got to be.'

Dean sounded cagey. 'I can't tell you that.'

I was fretting with impatience. 'Oh, come on!'

'Just calm down, Juno!' he recommended. 'Why are you so cross, anyway?'

I floundered for a moment. I didn't know why I felt so angry, but Jason Beck made me feel like an idiot.

'Listen, we already knew John Weston was behind the livestock thefts because of the information the undercover guy had been able to give us. But we needed evidence and none of the charmers we arrested in Christow forest were prepared to talk. Then Beck told us something, something that you hadn't mentioned.'

'What?' I demanded, stung.

'Because you didn't know it was significant.'

'What?' I almost screamed.

'That you had talked to Sam Weston.'

It took a moment for the penny to drop. 'And Sam said he was going to tell John that he'd talked to me,' I remembered. 'And soon after that Fizz was attacked.' I let out my breath in a horrified gasp. 'Weston wanted me shut up.'

'Well, someone did. John Weston sent one of his farmhands to do it, a local lad who's been in trouble with the law before. Forensics got a match on the prints we found on the volume control on Fizz's radio and in the bathroom where he hid.' Dean chuckled. 'When we arrested him – you'll like this bit – he had one of those stenter pins in the sole of his shoe. Anyway, he confessed to the attack on Fizz and gave us valuable information on the livestock thefts. We were planning a raid on the Weston place, but when Beck told us that you'd been talking to Weston's father, we decided to make a move, in case John had any ideas about making another attempt on your life.'

'Was Sam involved?' I asked.

Dean hesitated a moment. 'I'm afraid so.'

I felt sick. 'He seemed such a nice man.'

'But John Weston's denying any part in Crick's murder. He swears Fred wasn't involved in any of this.'

It seemed I'd got it wrong again.

'Juno, all these details will come out eventually. But for now, you keep anything that's not in the paper under your hat, understand? Weston is just a link in the chain.'

'You mean, you haven't caught the real villains yet?'

He laughed bitterly. 'It's like a bloody great spider's web. It'll take us years to track this lot down. Anyway, you keep safe, all right? Keep your head down.'

I promised I would. I put the phone down, feeling defeated. The livestock thieves may have been arrested, but I was still no closer to knowing who'd murdered Fred Crick or who'd killed Peter Gillow.

CHAPTER TWENTY-SIX

''Ave a look at this,' Maisie said, almost as soon as I was through the cottage door. I took off my jacket, trying simultaneously to deflect a yapping attack from Jacko. A sly nudge from the toe of my boot soon settled him down. I drew up a chair and took the old photograph Maisie was waving at me.

'That's Our Janet,' she said proudly. The photo was taken in black and white and must have been fifty years old. Our Janet looked about fourteen. She was standing in Maisie's garden in a dress with a big crinoline skirt and puffy sleeves, her hair scraped back into a ponytail, a coronet of flowers on her head, smiling self-consciously.

'She looks lovely,' I said dutifully. 'Was she a bridesmaid?'

'No. She was a carnival princess.' Maisie handed me another photo. 'Here she is on the carnival float. There was two princesses and the carnival queen.' She pointed with a knotty finger. 'That's her in the middle, on the throne. Her dress was pink. Our Janet's and the other girl's was blue.'

The carnival queen's dress was certainly bigger and puffier than the others and she wore a tiara instead of flowers. It was easy to see why she had been chosen: she was dark-haired and very pretty, and quite cast Our Janet and the other princess into the shade.

'You know who that is,' Maisie told me, pointing. It wasn't a question, a statement of fact.

'The carnival queen?' I peered at the photo more closely, but I didn't recognise her. 'I don't think I do.'

Maisie tutted and nudged me. 'That's Vivian Crick! Course, she was a bit older than Our Janet,' she added.

In the photograph she looked about eighteen. 'That's her?' I stared, trying to reconcile this happy, vivacious-looking young girl with the sad, longing letters that she wrote years later.

'She was a pretty girl,' Maisie admitted. 'Why the hell she ever settled for Fred Crick, I'll never know. He was too old for her. Everyone thought so at the time. But he was determined to have her, just wore her down, I think.'

'How long after this did they get married?' I asked.

She frowned. 'Don't know. Not long, cos she was going with this other fella for a while and everyone thought they'd make a go of it. Then he went off – she never saw him again. There's lots said Fred got Viv on the rebound.'

'Do you remember who he was, this fella?'

'Hang on. There's more pictures here.' Maisie handed me a group photograph, taken in colour this time. The surface of the print was glossy, but the colours old and yellowed, as if it had been taken with a low-quality film. 'There's me in the yellow dress,' she pointed out, 'and my old Bob, God rest him. And that's Lambert and Connie – they hadn't been married long.'

'There's Our Janet,' I pointed out. It wasn't that easy to see who was who. The entire crowd had been facing into the sun and everyone was squinting.

'And there's Viv, look!' Maisie went on. 'And that was her young man. Well, he's got his arm around her, but he was one for the ladies. He was such a good-looking bloke, all the girls were after him. Even Our Janet was soppy about him for a bit, but o'course, he always went for the pretty ones.'

I stared at the young man with his arm around Vivian. Even in this poor shot I could see he was good-looking.

'And he disappeared?'

'Well, he wasn't from round here. He was a bit well-to-do, you know, bit of a charmer. Now I think about it, he was lodging up Nelly Mole's place. She used to take in students back then, from the agricultural college – you know, not far from here, place has closed down now . . .'

'Seale-Hayne?'

'That's it. He must have been one of them.'

'So perhaps he just finished his course and returned home?'

Maisie nodded and chuckled. 'Well, if he did, he left

broken hearts behind him.'

'You don't remember his name?' I asked. 'It wasn't Jay, by any chance?'

'Jay?' she repeated, scowling. 'What sort of name's that?' She shook her head. 'No, I don't think so. Connie might remember.'

I frowned. I didn't really want to ask a blind woman about people in a photograph. And surely, if the boyfriend's name had been Jay, she would have recalled that when I'd read her Vivian's first letter? She would have known it was him she was writing to. And I wasn't sure Connie hadn't been holding out on me, she hadn't mentioned Viv's boyfriend.

Maisie took the picture back from me and proceeded to take me through the rest of her photos, pointing out all of her old friends and relatives. Her stories were fascinating, but there were no more pictures of the handsome charmer, or of Vivian Crick.

In the end it was Our Janet I phoned, not Connie. I was quick to reassure her that Maisie was OK. It's Janet who pays me to keep an eye on her mother and I don't usually phone unless there's a problem. I told her about the memory cafe and the photographs.

'Carnival princess!' she laughed. 'God, that's going back a bit!'

'Vivian was carnival queen, do you remember?'

'Yes. Mum told me about her body being found. It was terrible. I never liked Fred Crick. I don't think anyone did.'

'This was before she married Fred. There was a young man in one of the photographs, standing next to her. He had his arm around her. He was very good-looking. Maisie seemed to think all you girls had a crush on him.'

Janet laughed. 'I remember the photo being taken. Yes, we all thought he was lovely – not that he'd ever have looked at me,' she added. 'But he and Vivian went out for a while. I think she had hopes, you know. But once he'd finished at the college he went back to where he'd come from. As far as I know, he never came back.'

'You don't remember his name?'

'Oh, I do.'

She told me. I was silent for a moment, just taking it in.

'You can't see from that photograph,' she chattered on, 'but he had lovely eyes, a really unusual colour.'

I felt a shiver of suspicion, like someone brushing the back of my neck with a feather. 'What colour were they?'

'They were a really intense bluey-green.'

'Turquoise?' I suggested.

'Yes, that's it,' Janet agreed, laughing. 'They were turquoise.'

When I put the phone down on Janet, I dug out Jason Beck's business card. I should have paid more attention to it. There had been a clue there all the time. I dialled his number, although I wasn't sure if he was still in the country. He could be back in Australia by now.

But after a few moments he answered.

'I fly back the day after tomorrow,' he said when I

asked the question. 'I'm driving up to London in the morning but tonight I'm still in Devon.'

'In that case, you'd better meet me this evening,' I told him, 'at Fred's place.'

There was hesitation in his voice. 'Why should I do that?' he asked.

'Because,' I answered, still staring at the business card, 'I know who you are.'

I made damn sure I got there before he did. I parked the van on the road so that his car couldn't block me in. Then I climbed the stairway of rocks to the top and waited. I wasn't sure that he would come. I waited on the flat top of the rock, looking down over Cold East Farm. The sun had melted into a golden sky threaded by low bars of dark cloud near the horizon and the sweeping valley and fields below were already lost in darkness. It was quiet all around, except for the occasional soft tapping of branches in the nearby copse when the wind stirred. I turned my back on the valley to look down the ladder of rock. I didn't want Jason Beck creeping up behind me.

He was there already, climbing towards me, his steps slow and measured. Wary.

'You look remarkably like your father,' I told him.

He hesitated, frowning.

'I don't mean Fred Crick, the father you hated and killed.' I went on. 'I mean your real father, the one you were named after – Tony.'

He tried a smile. 'I don't know what you're talking about.'

'Or do you prefer Anthony?' I asked. 'That was really your father's name. You call yourself Jason on your business card, but if you look at the small print, at your email address, it's Anthony J. Beck. J . . .' I repeated slowly. 'Jay.' I held out the piece of blue, lined paper. 'This is for you.'

He didn't reach out to take it, didn't move.

'It's a letter from your mother,' I went on, 'well, part of it. It was hidden in the secret drawer in her writing desk. I found another but I can't show you that one, the police have got it.'

He didn't respond, just bore into me with that scorching turquoise gaze.

'Shall I read it to you? There's only one word on the top line – "desperate"—'

Suddenly he snatched it, reaching out, tearing the letter from my fingers, leaving me clutching a tiny corner of blue paper. Then he turned his back and read in silence. He stood motionless but I could see the tension in his shoulders, in the taut muscles of his neck.

'It is for you, isn't it?' I said. 'The son who ran off because his father used to beat him? He took to beating your mother after you had gone.' He turned once more to look at me. 'Broke her wrist—'

'Shut up!' His chest heaved as he drew in a deep breath, fought to control his feelings. 'Mum wanted me to go. She was afraid if I stuck around, Fred and I might end up killing each other.' He gave a short bitter laugh, 'Funny, really.'

'You were only a boy,' I said, more gently.

'I was fifteen.'

'Where did you go?'

'London.' He shrugged. 'I lived rough for a bit, joined the army as soon as I was old enough, changed my name. We travelled a lot, got moved from place to place. At first, I kept in touch with Mum, but it was difficult. I couldn't phone. I could never be sure if Fred was around, if he'd answer. He'd take it out on her if he knew I'd called . . . in the end she begged me to stop phoning, asked me to write instead. She could hide my letters. But sometimes our unit would be moved on fast and it wasn't possible.'

'Where were you?' I asked.

'Different places.' He gave a grim smile. 'The only thing they had in common was flies, blood and sand. Believe me, Juno, you do not want to know.'

I knew he was fudging the truth, but decided not to dwell on it. 'Then you became a journalist.'

'I finally got posted to Australia. When I came out of the army, I knew that's where I wanted to stay. I decided to settle down, I got married . . .'

And you didn't think of rescuing your poor mother, I accused him silently, *trapped in a loveless marriage with a man you knew was a monster?* Maybe my thoughts were written on my face because suddenly his voice grew louder, more defensive.

'Look, I used to write, OK? I knew she couldn't always answer, she was too frightened of that bastard finding out, but I sent her money. She could have got out.'

I have managed to scrape the money together . . . Viv's words lay in his hands, in the letter he was clutching. Either he was lying or Viv didn't get to keep what he sent.

'I had a wife to think about. We both had our careers,' he shrugged. 'She didn't want . . .' he hesitated. 'We just didn't think Mum would fit in with the kind of lives we were leading.'

I could just imagine how inconvenient his needy, middle-aged mum would have been if she'd turned up, wrecking their lifestyle. 'So, twenty years after you left, you decide to come back here and pay your old mum a visit.'

'I don't know where you think this is leading,' he said resentfully. 'None of it's any business of yours. What's Vivian to you?'

Up until that moment I hadn't really thought about it. But I had found her letters, letters that no one else had read. Her longing, her hopes, her tragically misplaced faith in her son, had touched me.

He scowled. 'I don't have to justify my actions to you, Juno Browne.'

'No,' I agreed, 'just to the police.'

His shoulders slumped as if he was giving in to the inevitable, to the need to explain. 'I came back to England on a story, I told you that. I thought I'd come down here and see how Mum . . . well, see how things were. When I drove to the farm it was clear it didn't belong to Fred any more so I didn't go to the door. I drove straight past his cottage. I asked around a bit in the village, found out where he was and then went back to see him.'

He gave a bitter laugh. 'It was barely noon and the old bastard was drunk. He wouldn't have let me in if he'd been sober, but booze always made him reckless. No sign of Mum, of course. He told me she'd run off and left him, he hadn't seen her for years.' He smiled. 'Well, that was easy enough to believe. Perhaps it was what I wanted to believe,' he admitted. He hesitated, chewing his lip. 'He claimed he didn't know where she'd gone, didn't care, good riddance. I asked him what had happened to all the money I'd been sending her over the last few years. He just laughed and laughed. We got into a fight . . . You can guess the rest.'

I didn't respond. He shrugged and went on. 'He swung at me with a shovel, big, heavy thing. It could have taken my head off. I tore it off him—' He stopped suddenly, spreading his hands in a helpless gesture. 'Look, I didn't mean to kill him, OK? It was self-defence, but as soon as I had that shovel in my hands it was like . . . vengeance, for me and for Mum. I kept hitting him and I didn't want to stop. And later, when they found her body. . . that lying bastard had buried her in the earth, like an animal, all those years ago.'

'It was you that Carol saw standing by her grave that night.'

He nodded slowly. 'I knew then I had done the right thing . . .' He looked at me, considering, his strange eyes narrowed. The wind blew, ruffling his hair and mine, and the branches of the trees stirred gently, tapping a distant warning. 'So, Juno, what are you going to do, turn me in?' He took a step towards me. Instinctively I stepped back. 'It was an eye for an eye,' he said simply, as if that made it reasonable, justifiable. 'Can't we leave it at that?'

'What about Peter Gillow?'

'Oh Jesus,' Jason muttered. 'It was a farce. I was standing there in that kitchen with Fred at my feet . . . I wasn't even sure then that I'd killed him . . . but the bloody shovel was still in my hands . . . and I looked up and the back door was wide open . . . and there was this guy, this litte guy I'd seen at the guest house that morning, with an empty water bottle in his hand . . .' He was talking faster now, no longer possessed of the cool irony with which he'd described killing Fred. 'I think he'd come to the door to ask if he could fill it up . . . and he was just standing there, staring at me, wide-eyed . . . horrified. And before I could think what to say, how to explain, he ran. I chased him into the garden, into that shed. I didn't know what I was going to do but he must've thought I was going to kill him. And then he just dropped like a stone, right in front of me.' He clicked his fingers. 'Dead. He must have had a weak heart.'

'Didn't you try to revive him?'

'There was no time. There was a lorry stopping outside in the road, backing up to park. I had seconds to think what to do. I could see you and your friends opening up the tailgate, letting down the ramp. I had to get him out of sight. And there was the wardrobe right there, standing with its door open wide. I just bundled him in. Then the bloody door wouldn't shut. There was a bit of rope on the floor, so I tied it up. I barely made it back inside the house before you came in through the gate. I could hear you calling Fred's name. I was in the kitchen, sweating, my heart pounding like a jackhammer. The back door was still open. I just got to it, shut it and slid the bolt across before you all traipsed around the back and tried the handle.'

I remembered what Vicky had said, that she felt we were being watched. 'You were there the whole time.'

'I was terrified you'd look through the window, see Fred's body on the floor.' His shoulders shook with silent laughter. 'I couldn't believe it when I saw your mate wheel that bloody wardrobe off down the path. It was like some bizarre nightmare.'

It must have been. 'And when we'd gone, what did you do then?'

'I knew by then that Fred was dead. I arranged things, sat him in his chair, cleaned myself up – and then I searched the place, ransacked it, looking for—'

'Your money?' I asked.

'No, I didn't care about the money,' he shouted. 'The old swine had probably drunk it years ago. I was looking for some sign of Mum, of what had happened to her. I was searching for some vestige of her existence; anything I could take that was hers.' He smiled grimly. 'There wasn't even a photograph. So I set fire to the place.'

'And no one would have known you'd ever been

there,' I said, 'except that you couldn't resist returning to the scene of the crime.'

'Oh yeah, you saw me in the garden.' He grinned. 'I knew you couldn't be police or you'd have challenged me. I thought you were just a nosy local, come to gawp at the murder scene. Perhaps I should have shut you up there and then.' He gave a strange smile. 'But I'm not really the murdering type.'

'Then talk to the police. Tell them what happened.'

He shook his head. 'I'm going away, Juno. I'm going home. I'm sorry about what happened to that chap Gillow, really I am, but I'm not responsible for his death. I'm not going to prison for him, any more than for Fred Crick.' He turned to walk away. 'Goodbye, Juno.'

I grabbed his arm and pulled him round to face me. I didn't know what I was thinking, only that I wanted to stop him. He shrugged me off. 'Don't try it, Juno,' he warned. His voice was dangerously soft. 'I don't want to have to hurt you.'

'You can't just leave. It's not that simple.'

'What do you want? Justice? For Fred?' He sneered. 'I think he's had his justice.'

Suddenly he rushed at me, pushing me back towards the edge of the rock. From the corner of my vision, I saw his arm swung up and wide, fist clenched. I just had time to raise my forearm to ward off the blow. I stepped in towards him, and with my other hand struck his chin, not a punch, but a hard push, the heel of my hand under his jaw. It forced him back, staggering. He backed off, surprised, laughing and feeling his jaw. 'Good girl, Juno.' His voice was full of mockery, 'very good.' He stared for a moment his eyes as hard as glass. 'But let's not play around, eh?'

He came at me again. I wasn't quick enough. He grabbed my wrist and twisted it around. I swung my other arm at him, clapping him on the side of the head, my palm cupped, forcing the air back into his ear. If I'd hit him hard enough, I could have burst his eardrum. As it was, he only staggered, shaking his head as if his ear was ringing. I should have rushed him then, pushed forward in that moment and thrust him off the rock. But I hesitated. I didn't want to kill him.

Suddenly he was behind me, arms around my waist, dragging me towards the edge. My feet slithered on stone fragments that scattered the rock's surface. I leant forward, raking my nails across the back of his hand, kicking down hard with both feet, landing a blow on his shin that made him swear, but he didn't let go. His hold around me tightened. I twisted, stabbing backward with pointed elbows, trying to land a blow on his face or neck. For a moment his grip weakened, allowing me to turn and face him; but by then he had grabbed me again, pinioning my arms by my sides, seizing a handful of my hair. I couldn't move. He must have been able to feel my heart hammering against his chest. For a moment we stared at one another, our faces close. I looked into those turquoise eyes, hard as glass. Suddenly he kissed me, a brutal kiss that crushed my lips and sent a burning through my veins like a lit fuse. Then he drew back to look at me. 'You're fantastic,' he murmured, smiling. 'In another life, Juno Browne—'

And then the bastard flung me off the rock. I didn't realise what was happening until I was falling through the air, a moment before I crash-landed painfully on a mat of springy bushes. I rolled off on to the stony soil beneath and lay there, stunned. I was too frightened to move, too frightened to find out if I was broken. I lay still, trying to draw in some breath. I felt as if a steamroller had driven over me.

I had to get up. At any moment Jason could appear to finish the job. I dragged myself into a sitting position, clutching at the branch of a bush to haul myself up. I heaved myself to my feet and stood, my whole body shaking. I could taste blood where the thorn bushes had scratched my face. I staggered a couple of steps; my ankle protested but I seemed to be more or less intact. I could walk, at least.

I limped my way painfully around the rock. There was no sign of Jason. He was probably speeding away in his car by now. Perhaps his only purpose in throwing me off the rock had been to escape me. He knew I'd only fall a few feet. But he couldn't have known that I wouldn't bash my skull on granite on the way down, or break my neck when I hit the ground. He couldn't have known he wasn't killing me.

After what seemed like for ever, I reached the road. I stopped. Jason's car was parked on the verge. He was still sitting in it. I dodged back out of sight. Was he waiting for me, waiting to check if I'd survived before he drove away, or was he sitting there ready to kill me if I had? But if he'd meant to do that, he'd have done it at the rock, wouldn't he? Check I was alive, make sure I was dead?

I watched for several minutes. He didn't move. He was still as a statue. Gradually, I eased out from behind the trees and crept toward his car. As I came up on the driver's side, I saw his reflection in the wing mirror. I felt a sickening lurch and clutched at the vehicle for support. Then I inched closer, to his window, which was open.

I had nothing to fear from Jason Beck. He was dead, staring ahead of him with one turquoise eye. Something was jutting from his other eyeball, something that must have had a sharp point, savagely driven in, something that sat in his eye socket in a well of blood. It was a pencil, pink, with an eraser at the end, and the word 'Shoppe' stamped on it in gold.

CHAPTER TWENTY-SEVEN

I had underestimated Henry. He'd put a tracker on my van. When Adam thought he saw a kid stealing my valve caps, it was Henry attaching a bug beneath the wheel arch. He'd bought it from the Internet. It's easy to buy all that nerdy, creepy stuff online these days. He only had to look on his phone to see where I was. This allowed him to follow me about while maintaining a discreet distance. He knew everywhere I had driven in the last few days. He'd also purchased some kind of gizmo that allowed him to hear things from a hundred yards away. He'd heard my conversation with Jason Beck as he hid in the ruins of Fred's cottage. When Jason returned to his car, he waited until he was in the driver's seat, walked calmly up to him and driven that pencil into his eyeball. An eye for an eye, as Jason had said.

At first, I wondered how he'd accomplished his revenge so easily. But then I realised that while I had told

Jason that Peter had a brother, I hadn't mentioned he was an identical twin. Seeing Henry for the first time Jason must have been as shocked as I was. And it must have been in that moment of surprise, of disbelief, that Henry had literally rammed his advantage home. Then he drove to the police station in Ashburton, turned himself in and confessed to murder.

I'd underestimated him on all counts: determination, efficiency, cruelty and honesty. He hadn't tried to find me, the police told me later, because hearing my scream as I was thrown off the rock he was convinced that Jason had killed me. And besides, he didn't want to let his brother's killer get away. Add ruthlessness to that list of his virtues. You could argue, of course, that Jason wasn't really Peter's killer; that the punishment didn't fit the crime. But he hadn't checked whether Peter was actually dead, or made any attempt to revive him before he bundled him into that wardrobe; just as he hadn't bothered to discover whether I was still breathing when he'd thrown me off that rock, or for twenty years, if his mother was alive. As for poor Henry, at least he would be free of Marjorie the Uncompassionate.

It was Detective Sergeant Cruella deVille who came to mop up, who answered the call from my mobile as I sat shivering at the side of the road. The inspector, apparently, was on another job. The call from me had come more or less simultaneously with Henry's arrival at the station announcing that I was dead, which created a

334

little confusion, to say the least. But Cruella was coolly efficient, examining the body and directing her underlings to cordon off the crime scene around Jason's car whilst she sat on the roadside and interviewed me.

'Well, you're not dead at least,' she said, in a voice that contained just the slightest edge of disappointment. She took a brief statement and then called one of the uniforms to drive me down to Accident and Emergency.

'I don't need to go to hospital,' I told her.

She looked me up and down. 'I'll be the judge of that.'

To be honest, when I added up all the scrapes and grazes that go with falling off a rock and the scratches from landing among gorse bushes, I suppose I did look a mess. 'In any case,' she added, 'you're probably in shock. You've already confirmed what Mr Gillow has told us. We can take a full statement from you tomorrow.'

So I behaved and let myself be driven to Ashburton Hospital to get checked for damage and cleaned up. It was nothing I couldn't have managed myself with a bottle of TCP and some tweezers, but the sympathy was nice. Then I needed a lift home. I thought of ringing Ricky and Morris but resisted. I rang Adam, who came to fetch me, along with a shocked and anxious Kate, who insisted on giving me tea and more sympathy before they allowed me to do what I really wanted to do, which was to crawl into bed.

Just as I about to clean my teeth there was a ring on my doorbell. I winced my way downstairs to find Dean Collins standing on the doorstep. 'Juno, thank God!' he breathed. 'At the station—'

'I'm all right,' I assured him, 'I am genuinely not dead. But please,' I added, backing off hastily as he made a move towards me, 'do not try to hug me.' I didn't think my fragile bones were up to his bearlike embrace.

He grinned and nodded. 'Cruella called me up to Fred's place. I've driven your van back.' He held up my keys and dangled them in front of me. 'But don't leave these in the ignition next time, eh?'

'I wanted to be ready for a quick getaway.'

'You wouldn't have got away at all if Beck had nicked your keys.'

I took them from him. 'Thank you, Officer,' I said as I closed the door. 'I'll try and remember that.'

A few nights later, over a couple of gins, I discussed my performance on the rock with Elizabeth.

'You survived,' she pointed out mildly, 'that's all that matters.'

'Yes, but he threw me off the rock,' I said, 'I might not have done.'

'Do you know what I think put you at a disadvantage?' she asked. 'Apart from his having trained in combat, of course?'

I shook my head.

'You knew him and you liked him. You saw him as a person, rather than a living threat, and that slowed you down, made you think too much. If you'd been attacked by some nameless thug you'd never laid eyes on before, you would have reacted differently.'

I considered some of the nameless thugs who'd attacked me in the past and decided Elizabeth was right. And I confess I'd been hoping that Vivian Crick's precious son might not turn out to be a killer after all, that he might be worthy of her.

'And I wonder, considering that you knew he might be dangerous,' she went on, raising her brows in enquiry, 'why you chose to meet him alone and in such an isolated place?'

I'd already received this rebuke, delivered with varying degrees of wrath from Pat: 'Don't you never learn?', Ricky and Morris: 'You've only just recovered from the last person who tried to kill you', and Detective Inspector Ford: 'You should have called the police as soon as you realised who Beck was.' Ha-ha-ha on that last one. I've decided that when it comes to telling Daniel about it, I might have to be a little economical with the truth.

'I know it was stupid,' I admitted. 'But I felt that if he was going to open up to me anywhere, it would be there.'

She eyed me doubtfully. 'I would have thought after the previous incident—'

'All right!' I held my hands up in surrender. 'Next time I confront a killer I'll try and arrange it in the town hall car park on a busy afternoon.'

There were five tables booked for *Sunflowers'* first evening opening, four for couples and one large table booked for Ricky and Morris, Olly and Elizabeth, and for Sophie and me when we weren't helping with waitressing. Morris had offered us little frilly aprons and lacy headdresses so that we could feel like real waitresses, but we'd declined. Adam and Kate wanted to create a relaxed atmosphere and we thought our own clothes would be more suitable. The music was supplied by a jazz guitarist and saxophonist who Adam had met through the Arts Centre. My klezmer-playing buskers from Teignmouth were booked for next time. The cafe looked lovely, with candles in bottles on the tables and tiny vases of wildflowers. As *Sunflowers* didn't have a liquor licence, people brought their own wine. The food was excellent, with roasted vegetable ratatouille bake and sweet potato African curry being the most popular dishes on the menu.

The twilight deepened outside, the wine flowed and as the candles burnt down, the light more golden, the atmosphere inside the cafe became warmer, the music more mellow and laid-back. By the time Sophie and I got around to taking orders for passion fruit panna cotta, lemon posset or raspberry crème brûlée, it had become more like a party, with Ricky, Morris and several other diners singing along to the jazz standards.

One customer arrived late. He hadn't booked; he'd just come on the off chance. I certainly had no idea he'd be turning up, him or his whippet. I had to hastily relinquish plates I'd been carrying to two musicians to avoid a catastrophe, as Lottie launched at me in greeting and began running rapturous circles around my toes. She was followed into the cafe by Mr Daniel Thorncroft. A loud cheer went up as he wrapped his arms around me. I took no notice, returned his kiss and snuggled into his warm neck. 'This is a nice surprise,' I murmured into his ear.

'I found a brief window of opportunity, Miss B,' he murmured back, 'so I escaped through it.'

Then I turned to look at the lot at my table. 'Did you know he was coming?' They shook their heads, all innocent; but I wouldn't trust any one of them when it comes to matchmaking.

Unfortunately, any plan I had to give Daniel a slightly edited version of the truth about my recent activities was scuppered by the others, who all started to tell him what I'd been up to the moment he sat down at the table. I couldn't stop them. I was forced to give my attention to a couple on another table who wanted to pay their bill. He sat demolishing a large plate of African curry, occasionally flicking glances in my direction, his expression growing more and more serious as he listened to what they had to say. This, I knew, was going to lead to an interesting conversation when we were on our own. In the meantime, Sophie took over my waitressing duties so that I could sit with him and enjoy the merrymaking while it lasted.

'How could you do that?' he asked as we wandered home, Lottie trotting lightly at our heels. It was late and the streets of Ashburton were dark and quiet. I'd tried to stay and help Adam and Kate with the clearing up, to put off the inevitable inquisition, but they wouldn't let me. I should make the most of Daniel while he was here, Kate said. 'How could you take a risk like that?'

'Look, I've already had the lecture several times over—' I began.

'Because people care for you,' he said, clearly angry. 'Christ, Juno! I feel as if I shouldn't ever go away again, as if I can't turn my back on you.'

'I'm not your responsibility,' I snapped. But my words sounded childish, even in my own ears.

He stopped and turned to me, his hands on my shoulders. 'I don't want you to get hurt again.'

'I know. And I'm sorry. I know what I did was stupid, but—'

'I don't want to lose you.' He stared at me intently, and when I looked away, lifted my chin gently. 'Look at me,' he insisted, his face shadowy in the light of a street lamp, his eyes shining black. 'I couldn't bear it, Juno, not again . . .'

I laid a finger softly against his lips. 'I'm sorry,' I said again, and kissed him. He held me tightly and thrust his hand into my curls, cradling the back of my head, a loving gesture that always makes me weak at the knees.

'I know you can't avoid getting into trouble,' he murmured as we kissed again. 'Just don't go looking for it.'

'I promise,' I lied. No use to explain that as far as I was concerned, it was always the trouble that came looking for me.

It was rather crowded in bed that night. Daniel, who's tall and long-limbed, took up a lot of room. Then there was Lottie, who'd wriggled her body in between our feet and Bill, up on my pillow, nesting in my hair and issuing warning hisses in Lottie's direction if she so much as twitched. I've slept better, I confess. In the morning, I woke pinned to the bed by an arm that weighed as much as a tree trunk flung across my chest and someone snoring loudly in my ear. This is romantic, I thought.

At breakfast I had a serious chat with Daniel about buying the caravan he'd mentioned. He promised to get right on it.

CHAPTER TWENTY-EIGHT

The remains of Vivian Crick were buried in Ashburton churchyard at a special service. Not many people attended, although the headstone had been bought and paid for by the people of the town. *Vivian Crick, sadly missed, fondly remembered.* Her date of birth was on it, but no date of death; that could not be established. I was at the graveside, along with Neil and Carol, Ricky and Morris, Elizabeth and Maisie. Connie came with one of her carers and Our Janet sent flowers. Viv was never to be reunited with her son. Even in death they would not lie together. Jason's body was being returned to his ex-wife and children in Australia. But at least after twenty years lying in the cold clay of a muddy field, she had a more fitting resting place. Neil and Carol had filled in the trench where her body had lain and moved the foundations for the laundry block further up the paddock. It wasn't right that the place where her body had been so ignominiously buried should be built upon, they had decided. They had planted a sapling there; a young rowan tree.

I put her writing table into auction. I couldn't attend myself, but it attracted some lively bidding and went for a very satisfying price. I covered the cost of restoration and actually made a profit. I was very pleased, until I walked into the hall at Druid Lodge and saw it standing in the hallway.

'You bought it!' I accused Ricky furiously.

'And why not?' he demanded.

'Because you've only bought it to help me out,' I retorted. 'It's a sneaky way of giving me money.'

'But don't you think it looks perfect, Juno?' Morris asked, blinking anxiously. 'It just fits in that little alcove.'

'Well, yes,' I admitted.

'And that's why we bought it,' Ricky insisted. 'Because we were looking for something to put in that spot and knew it would look perfect.'

'Well, why didn't you ask to buy it when it was in the shop,' I asked, 'instead of bidding for it in the auction?'

'Because you would have refused to sell it to us, that's why, you silly cow.'

'You've probably paid a lot more for it this way.'

Ricky nodded gravely. 'We know.'

'But, Juno,' Morris said, taking my hand and patting it, 'we'll always treasure it. Don't you think it's nicer for Viv's writing table to have been bought by someone who knows her story, rather than to someone for whom it's just a piece of furniture?'

I had to smile then. 'Yes,' I agreed, squeezing his arm. 'Yes I do. Thank you.' I turned to Ricky. 'Both of you.'

Becky had finally changed the look of her mobile dog-grooming service. I walked past the van as I was shopping on West Street. I practically doubled up on the pavement with laughter. There was no sign of Pretty Paws, and the lurid pink was gone. Instead, each side of the van bore a cartoon of a shame-faced, mud-covered hound with a trail of muddy paw prints and the legend 'LaundroMutt' proudly displayed over the top. It looked fantastic. I stuffed another note under Becky's windscreen wipers to tell her so.

I was telling Sophie about it later in *Old Nick's* when the shop bell jangled and a woman came in.

'Fizz!' we both cried, more or less at once. 'How are you?' I asked, getting to my feet and pulling up a chair. 'Sit down.'

Sophie asked her if she wanted a coffee, but she shook her head.

'I'm not stopping, thanks.' She stood where she was, looking awkward.

'How's your head?' I asked.

'Fine.' She put a hand a little self-consciously to her hair. 'A bonk on the brain probably did me good. I just came in to say thank you, really, for packing up all my stuff so beautifully . . . and I hope Don wasn't too . . . I mean . . .'

'He was just worried about you,' Sophie said generously.

'He was fine,' I lied.

Fizz nodded, accepting what we said although it was clear she didn't believe us. 'And I wanted to say goodbye. I know I'm a frightful pain and I always try to take over any available space, but I did enjoy being here with you girls.'

Sophie flicked me a guilty glance. 'Well, you don't have to go,' she said.

Fizz laughed. 'I'll be much better off in my own shop. I can spread myself as much as I like. In fact, Don and I have just signed the lease on a new shop. It's lovely, used to be a gallery. *Swann's* it was called.'

My turn to flick a glance at Soph. That was Meredith's old place. Meredith was Daniel's previous girlfriend, the one we don't talk about. 'We know it.'

'And there's a big flat upstairs I can use for classes and workshops,' she went on, some of her old fizzy enthusiasm returning.

'Your stuff will look gorgeous in there,' I told her.

'And, um, I just wanted to give you a little present . . . each of you . . . for being so nice to me.'

She drew four flat packages from her bag and laid them on the counter. I could tell they were scarves: one each for me, Sophie, Elizabeth and Pat. 'I hope you like the colours I've chosen for each of you,' she went on. 'But if you don't, feel free to swap.'

'Thank you. Thank you so much,' Sophie cried. Fizz stopped her before she could tear into the wrapping paper. 'Please, open them after I've gone.'

'That's very kind of you,' I said, 'but you really shouldn't. And this isn't really goodbye, you know. You'll only be around the corner.'

'You can pop in for a coffee any time,' Sophie added.

'And I've brought this.' She held up a bulging carrier bag. 'It's just scraps really, offcuts from silk paintings. I've got thousands of them and I'm always meaning to get around to doing something with them and I never do. I thought Pat might like them. She could use them in her panoramas. You can even make beads and necklaces from them. I've popped a little instruction book inside.'

Sophie took the bag from her and pulled out a few of the scraps. 'These are gorgeous, all these different colours and patterns.'

Fizz nodded. 'Well, as I say, they're just odd bits. They're no use to me. If she can't use them, just throw them away.'

'If she can't use them, I will,' Sophie told her, pulling more and more scraps out of the bag.

'You've started something now,' I told Fizz. 'I think there might be a fight.'

She laughed. 'I must go. Don's waiting at the new shop.'

We promised we would attend the grand opening of the new *Fizzy Izzy's* and she submitted, rather shyly, to goodbye kisses from us both.

After she'd gone, Sophie and I looked at each other in silence.

'I feel dreadful now,' she confessed. 'I don't think I was nice to her at all.'

'You feel dreadful? I almost got the poor woman killed.'

'I think she might be lonely, you know.'

'Oh, stop it!'

'I think we'll miss her,' she sighed.

'No, we won't. Although,' I added after a moment's thought, 'I will miss her rent.'

For a moment we hesitated and then raced each other to the packages on the counter, tearing the paper open. My scarf was a shimmering bronzy gold, Sophie's a soft, deep rose.

'I wonder what colours Elizabeth and Pat have got,' she said innocently.

I frowned at her. 'No, Sophie.'

'We could wrap them up again afterwards.'

'No!' I told her. 'Behave. Anyway,' I lifted up the long gauzy scarf and gazed through the shimmering silk, 'I'm not swapping this for anything.'

'Nor me,' Sophie declared.

Elizabeth's scarf was jade and Pat's was blue. And they were really difficult to wrap up again afterwards.

'You're looking a bit down in the mouth, Princess,' Ricky observed. I'd gone up Druid Lodge for tea. 'What's up?' he asked, grinning. 'You missing the sex?'

'Take no notice of him, Juno,' Morris gasped, and flipped him around the head with a tea towel. 'You behave yourself.'

'Oh, shut up, *Maurice*! You said yourself it was nice she was getting some for a change.'

'I did not!' he protested, although his telltale blush gave him away.

Daniel has gone, of course. I have lost him to the Irish peat bogs. He promised he'll only be involved in the restoration project for a few weeks and then he and Lottie will return. But I didn't believe him any more than he believed me when I promised I'd keep out of trouble.

'What you up to tonight, then?' Ricky asked.

'Nothing much.' I had nothing planned except an evening's moping.

'Come with us!' Morris tapped my arm. 'We're off to *The Mikado*. Opening night tonight!' he added beaming.

'Well, it's not really my sort of thing.'

'Oh, come on,' Ricky urged. 'It'll be a laugh! Dear little Phoebe will be warbling away, and Digby. Come on, we've got to give Diggers our support.'

'Well, yes . . .'

'Oh, do come, Juno!' Morris pleaded, gazing at me over his little gold specs.

Ricky nudged my arm. 'I hear the costumes are amazing!'

I had to admit it would be interesting to see how they looked onstage under all the lights. And I'd like to see how those hair decorations had turned out. 'Oh, come for God's sake!' he cried, losing all patience.

I caved. 'All right, all right! I will.'

'That's the ticket, do yourself a favour,' Ricky grinned stubbing out his cigarette. 'Live dangerously for once.'

I didn't tell anyone. I could just imagine the reaction if I had. But I had to visit Henry. I felt responsible. Perhaps if I'd treated him differently things would not have turned out as they had, with him in a secure facility undergoing psychiatric tests. He had pleaded guilty to murder but claimed diminished responsibility.

He was remarkably philosophical about the prospect of a long incarceration.

'You meet some fascinating people in here, you know,' he told me earnestly. 'I'm thinking of taking a course in criminology.' He told me he had heard the sounds of Jason and me fighting from his lurking place in the ruins of Fred's cottage. 'I came rushing out to rescue you, but alas, I was too late. I saw him throw you bodily from the rock. I heard you scream and then,' he paused dramatically, 'and then a red mist descended. From then on, I didn't really know what I was doing.'

I don't actually remember screaming. I don't think I did. But it would sound better in court if I had.

I asked, tentatively, if Marjorie had been to see him. He shook his head. 'I wouldn't really want her to come to a place like this, she wouldn't feel comfortable. Eunice will help her look after the shop. To be honest,' he added a little sorrowfully, 'I don't miss her.'

'Is there anything you do miss?' I asked. 'Anything I could bring you?'

'It's a funny thing,' he said, after a moment's thought, 'but the only thing I really miss is the smell of the shop, that smell of the sweets when you open a jar . . . I miss that.'

I'd visit him again, I decided. And next time I would take him some mint humbugs, lemon drops and a quarter of pineapple rock.

ACKNOWLEDGEMENTS

I would like to thank the usual suspects: Kelly Smith, Susie Dunlop and the team at Allison and Busby, my wonderful agent Teresa Chris for her unfailing encouragement, my book buddy Di, and most of all Martin, always there for me, whatever madness I'm into.

STEPHANIE AUSTIN graduated from Bristol University with a degree in English and Education and has enjoyed a varied career as an artist, astrologer, and trader in antiques and crafts. More respectable professions include teaching and working for Devon Schools Library Service. When not writing, she is involved in local amateur theatre as an actor and director. She lives on the English Riviera in Devon where she attempts to be a competent gardener and cook.

Stephanieaustin.co.uk